THE BOY NEXT DOOR

JENNIFER SUCEVIC

The Boy Next Door

Cover Design by Mary Ruth Baloy at MR Creations

Editing by Kate Newman at Once Upon a Typo

Proofreading by Sid Damiano at SD Editorial Services

Home | Jennifer Sucevic or www.jennifersucevic.com

ALSO BY JENNIFER SUCEVIC

Chapter One

COLTON

Summer before freshman year of college...

My lips quirk at the corners as I glance around. It's fucking madness, and I wouldn't have it any other way. This is *exactly* how you kick off summer vacation. Leave it to Beck Hollingsworth to throw the mother of all graduation parties. The three key ingredients necessary for a kickass party are present—scantily clad chicks, plenty of free-flowing booze, and last but not least, parents conspicuously absent from the festivities. Never let it be said that Beck doesn't know how to do it up right. After all, this isn't his first rodeo. This guy has thrown some over-the-top, police-called-to-break-it-up, someone-almost-drowns-in-the-pool parties over the years.

There's a girl tucked under each arm as they stare adoringly up at me. Albeit drunkenly. A few more crowd around, circling like sharks, waiting for an opportunity to home in on the action. Delicate hands stroke over my bare chest. Another female presses her breasts against my back as her nimble fingers slide their way across my waist and wrap around my ribs.

One thing is for sure, I'm going to miss these girls when I leave for college next month. This is a carefully curated group I've trained since freshman year. I have rules when it comes to the opposite sex.

And the first one is that I don't do relationships. If that's what you're looking for, find your pleasure elsewhere. If you think you can parlay a one-night stand into a bona fide relationship, you've got the wrong guy. I have zero interest in getting serious or forming attachments.

Rule number two—what happens at a party stays at a party. Don't bring that shit to school Monday morning. As long as everyone walks away feeling good at the end of the night, it's a win-win situation. I'm careful to cull out the ones who are secretly looking for more of a connection.

Needy and clingy chicks need not apply.

Rule number three—

"Colton," a female voice purrs in my ear, "let's go upstairs."

My gaze flickers to Ella Sullivan. She's become a fan favorite over the years. Pretty face. Banging body. And has demonstrated an impressive stamina when it comes to blow jobs.

She's got that elusive trifecta going on.

"Yeah, Colton," Marissa Dix adds, trying to get in on the action as she presses her sweet titties against me, "let's get out of here. It's way too crowded."

Did someone order a threesome for the evening?

Yes, please.

What I've discovered is the more, the merrier. Added bonus, it's difficult to say that you were under the impression we were exclusive when you sat there and watched me bone your friend Saturday night.

I'm about to let these girls have their wicked way with me when I catch a flash of long blond hair from the corner of my eye. Before I can stop myself, my head snaps in that direction. It's like an automatic reflex.

Every muscle goes whipcord tight.

Alyssa Williams.

What the hell is she doing here?

I'd hoped she would remain conspicuously absent from tonight's gathering. If there's one chick I avoid at all costs, it's the blonde firecracker. My gaze slides to the girl she's dragging through the crowd like a ragdoll. By the stubborn set of Mia's jaw, my guess is that her bestie wasn't given much of a choice when it came to making an appearance. The dark-haired chick looks like she's being held at gunpoint. Now *that* brings a smile to my face. Mia is Beck's next-door neighbor. She hates the dude with the passion of a thousand burning suns.

Possibly more.

Interestingly enough, Mia avoids Beck in much the same way I steer clear of Alyssa, which hasn't been easy since my dick has decidedly different ideas on the matter. Even now, it's stirring in my board-shorts with piqued interest, attempting to rise to the occasion. Unfortunately for me, Alyssa doesn't understand the word *no*. Even though I shoot her down on a regular basis, she continues to come at me hard every chance she gets.

And that, my friends, only makes me want her more. She's a girl who knows what she wants and goes after it with single-minded determination. And what she wants is me.

Damn, if that's not hot.

I'd like to say that it'll be easier once I leave for college, but that won't be the case given that Alyssa will also be attending Wesley University this fall. At least there are ten thousand students on campus. With any luck, dodging her will be a hell of a lot easier than it has been in high school. Everywhere I go, there she is.

As ridiculous as it sounds, air gets wedged in my lungs as Alyssa's blue gaze steadily combs over the sea of drunken classmates before locking on mine. I steel myself for that little zip of electricity to sizzle its way through my blood. It takes everything I have inside to will down the growing erection.

Just the sight of her is enough to get me hard.

One of the girls wrapped around me like a python pretends to accidentally graze my wood with her fingers before making an appreciative noise deep in her throat and pressing closer.

If only she realized that my state of arousal has nothing to do with her.

Then again, she probably wouldn't give two shits.

"Colton, baby," Ella purrs before cupping the side of my face and turning my head until I have no choice but to stop staring at Alyssa. Once my gaze collides with hers, a seductive smile wreathes her face. "I thought we were heading inside."

A couple of seconds ago, that's exactly what the plan for the evening had been. As much as I wish it were otherwise, these girls pale in comparison to the blond, blue-eyed dancer.

"Not yet," I mutter before shifting my stance, only wanting to shake off these chicks as my gaze fastens on Alyssa. Once my sights are locked on her, everything inside me settles.

With a critical eye, I dissect her one feature at a time. What the hell is it about that girl that gets to me? I've spent more time attempting to figure out that conundrum than I'm comfortable admitting. Even privately, to myself.

She's gorgeous with a curtain of shiny blond hair that hangs down her back. Dark blue eyes that are, more times than not, lit up with mischief and laughter. I'll be honest, she's not my usual type. I like a big booty and nice round titties. Alyssa is long and lithe with a dancer's body. She's muscular and athletic with high, tight breasts.

That being said, beautiful girls are a dime a dozen around here. And if they aren't naturally alluring, they add extensions, fake lashes and have learned to apply influencer-level makeup to give the illusion. I could swing my dick around and hit five of them at this very moment.

Whatever this is with Alyssa, it's more than skin deep. I can't put my finger on what I find so appealing, but it's been simmering beneath the surface for as long as I can remember. We're talking way back in middle school when I first noticed the opposite sex. Luckily, that was right around the time they became aware of me.

Except for Alyssa. She was too busy dancing. It was probably better that way.

Some time during sophomore year, her sights locked on me, and she's been giving chase ever since. What I've discovered is that it's exhausting to keep someone at a distance that you really don't want to hold off. There have been times when I've been tempted to wave the white flag and give in. I have a feeling it would be nothing short of amazing. The attraction between us has always been combustible. It sputters and sparks to life whenever we're in the same room together.

The more I deny it, the more it ratchets up. Deep down, I know she's the one girl who has the ability to weasel her way into my heart, and that's the last thing I want.

A look of resolve settles over her features as she shoves her way through the sea of half-naked bodies gyrating to the music pumping on the patio. The closer she gets, the harder my heart jackhammers against my ribcage. As tempting as it is to run and hide in an effort to protect myself, I'm no longer sure that's a possibility. It feels like a losing battle. We are like two runaway trains barreling down the same track, destined for a head-on collision. There's no averting disaster.

Part of me wonders if I even want to.

I've spent so much time not only denying her but myself as well. It's all I can think about. All I want. The closer she gets, the more my self-control wavers. With her gaze pinned to mine, she pushes her way toward me.

"Hey!" one girl huffs as she's knocked aside.

Alyssa doesn't bother to glance in the brunette's direction. She's one hundred percent focused on me. Whatever happens tonight, I know I'll regret it in the morning, and yet, that's not enough to prevent it from occurring.

I step away from the other girls as Alyssa halts in front of me. She cocks her head as a defiant gleam sparks to life in her eyes. I can't help but answer the challenge and straighten to my full height, which is a good ten inches taller than she is, before looking down at her. She has to raise her chin to hold my stare.

When electricity crackles and snaps between us and the boisterous voices fade to the background, I know I'm in trouble. I've spent too many years denying myself the one thing I've always craved, and tonight, for better or worse, I'm giving in. There's no longer a choice in the matter.

Chapter Two

ALYSSA

Spring of freshman year of college...

"Do you have any idea how badly I need coffee?" At this time of the morning, I'm barely coherent. A girl walking in the opposite direction knocks into me as we make our way through the throng of student traffic moving across campus. I bare my teeth, ready to snap. "Watch where you're going!"

"Easy, tiger," Mia soothes, latching onto my arm and towing me forward. "Unfortunately for you, we don't have time for a pitstop."

"Ugh." I'm so blurry-eyed, I can barely see straight. I was up until the butt crack of dawn this morning working on a paper that is due for this class. If it had been any other instructor, I would have shown up during office hours and attempted to charm my way into a twenty-four-hour extension.

But with this guy?

No way. Professor Mendelson refuses to accept late work. Ever since I stepped foot on campus, I've heard horror stories about the man. And so far, I can say with absolute authority that they're true.

He's already brought a few students to tears in front of the entire class. So, I do my best to fly under the radar where he's concerned.

Plus, I've been spending a ton of extra time in the studio rehearsing a dance solo I choreographed for the annual showcase at the end of the semester. Between that and keeping up with my classes, I'm burning the candle at both ends.

"Hey, isn't that Colton?"

Those four words are all it takes for me to blink out of the thoughts I've become mired in. My head jerks up so quickly that I nearly give myself whiplash as the haze clouding my eyes evaporates. "Where?"

Colton Montgomery sightings have become increasingly rare on campus. There are times when I have the sneaking suspicion that he's deliberately avoiding me. Although, come on, that's just crazy, right?

"Well," Mia chuckles as we traipse along the cement pathway, "that certainly woke you up. Probably more than a straight shot of caffeine right to your veins."

The girl isn't wrong.

I kind of hate myself for the ridiculous infatuation I have with the blond football player. I've been crushing on him for three years. Deep down, I was secretly hoping there would be so many new guys at college that I would forget all about him.

That hasn't turned out to be the case.

Sure, I've met a ton of people since I've been at Wesley. In classes, at parties, and during football games. I even broke down and let a friend talk me into a blind date with her cousin. That, by the way, turned out to be a fiasco. Not one single guy has been able to obliterate Colton from my mind.

How do you move on from someone who wants nothing to do with you? If there were some voodoo magic to make this yearning disappear, I'd conjure it up in a heartbeat.

But there isn't. Which is exactly why I'm still lusting after the guy like a total loser.

What I need is a twelve-step program.

Like an addict, my gaze roves over the crowd before zeroing in on him like a heat-seeking missile. He's a little taller and broader than everyone around him. His hair is cut short on the sides and left long on top so that it falls over his forehead. It's a constant struggle to keep the golden strands out of his bright blue depths. I've been tempted on more than one occasion to reach out and do it for him.

That is if I could get close enough.

I narrow my eyes as hot licks of jealousy burst to life inside me. It's not even nine o'clock in the morning and he's already being mobbed by jersey chasers. The crowd that surrounds him has to be at least three-deep.

"I bet he's slept with every girl on campus," I grumble in irritation.

"Everyone but you," my bestie oh-so-helpfully points out.

I shoot her a glare.

As if the reminder is necessary?

The one and only time we hooked up had been at a Beck Hollingsworth party. I thought for sure we'd go all the way. We'd been in the pool. The making out had turned decidedly hot and heavy. I'd taken off my top and panties in an effort to hasten things along. Don't judge me—I'm a girl who goes after what she wants. Even though there had been more than a hundred people in attendance, the rowdy party had fallen away around us. Just when I thought we would seal the deal, Colton pulled the plug and left me high and dry.

Well, not so dry.

More like wet and frustrated.

I've heard many-a-story surrounding the sexual exploits of Colton Montgomery. Not a damn one of them ended with him walking away. It's funny—in a not so amusing kind of way—that the one guy who has a reputation for being a manwhore won't even look at me, much less have sex with me.

Go figure.

"And me, of course," she tacks on promptly.

My jealousy melts away as I flash her a grin before looping my arm through hers.

Mia Stanbury has zero interest in meathead jocks with a penchant for sleeping with every girl they come in contact with, which means she's definitely not into Colton or his best friend, Beck. Although, I'm pretty damn sure the dark-haired football player has a major thing for her. In fact, I have my suspicions that something might have happened between them, but Mia has never mentioned a word, no matter how much I've interrogated her. And you better believe that I asked all sorts of probing questions.

As we walk past Colton and his entourage, I can't resist throwing one last look in his direction. After all, who knows when I'll see him next. Electricity sizzles through my veins as our gazes collide. It takes everything I have to propel myself forward. Once I'm past him, the air rushes from my lungs.

That's the moment I realize that moving on from Colton won't be possible until another guy is able to rouse the same kind of feelings inside me.

And that, my friends, is all sorts of depressing.

Chapter Three

COLTON

Late spring of freshman year...

The soft strains of stringed instruments fill the theatre as I crack open one of the double doors and carefully slip inside the darkened space. A few people seated in the back turn and stare as I settle gingerly on a seat in the last row.

I've arrived in the middle of someone's performance. The ballerina leaps across the stage before halting. With her arms stretched out in front of her, she strikes a pose before gradually folding in half and sweeping her arms across the floor. The spotlight dims as the music fades into nothingness. There's a moment of hushed silence before applause breaks out in the packed auditorium.

Did I miss it?

Is the show over?

I'd planned on getting here earlier, but Coach kept us an extra thirty minutes. We might not be in season, but practice and lifting start up again in late winter and go through the summer. When you play Division I college sports, there's no downtime. It's more like a job. I wish I'd known that when I signed my NCAA paperwork senior year of high school. Some of these guys, like Beck, plan on turning pro after college. So, for them, they need to be constantly working out and improving their game.

After much thought, I decided not to continue playing football after graduation. The plan is to work for my father, which probably means attending business school. We'll see. That's yet to be determined. As much as I love the sport, I've gotten my brains beat to shit enough already. And my body? Some days, I feel like a seventy-year-old man rolling out of bed in the morning.

So, senior year will be it for me.

I plow a hand through my still-damp hair as the curtain drops into place. The showcase has been on my radar for months, just like it was last year. I can't believe I missed her performance. I'm halfway to my feet and ready to sprint unnoticed from the auditorium when the heavy screen rises, and the violin section of the orchestra takes up their instruments.

My heart stutters as my gaze fastens on to her. Carefully, I lower myself back onto the seat again. The last girl had been wearing the full ballerina getup. You know—pink leotard, tights, puffy tutu, hair slicked back into a bun, and a small silver crown decorating her head. Kind of overkill, if you ask me.

Alyssa, on the other hand, is outfitted in a tight, long-sleeved shirt that bares her midriff and black booty shorts that match the top. Her hair is swept back into a ponytail, and she's barefoot.

Her arms are stretched above her head, and her chin is tilted upward as if staring at something only she can see. Even from this distance, the expression on her face is one of serenity. Almost as if she's alone, unaware of the hundreds of spectators watching her every gesture.

It's only when the tempo of the violins change and other instruments join in, giving more depth to the music, does Alyssa break her pose. Her movements are graceful. Deep and sweeping. She soars across the space, using every square inch of the stage. My breath catches, becoming trapped in my chest as I lean forward. My gaze greedily follows every step. Every arc and bend. Every spin and dip. It doesn't take long before she becomes one with the music, conveying a story to the audience. Her expressions change and contort. She is pure poetry in motion as she lights up the stage.

Everything about her is captivating. It doesn't take long for the audience around me to fall away. And then it's like she's performing solely for my pleasure.

The first time I saw Alyssa dance was in high school. Jenna, my stepmother, dragged my father and me to a performance of The Nutcracker at Christmas. I hadn't been happy about it, but I love Jenna. As far as stepmothers go, she's a keeper. A hell of a lot better than my biological mother, who took off when I was five years old, and I haven't seen her since. Even though I try not to dwell on Candace, the fact that she couldn't be bothered to stick around to see how I turned out bothers me on a profound level.

How could it not?

Two years after that, Dad married Jenna, and she's been a permanent fixture in my life ever since. So, if she wanted me to experience a little culture? Fine, I would do it. Once the lights dimmed and the curtain was raised, I'd popped an earbud in and settled back in my seat, fully prepared to waste the next two hours of my life. Instead, Alyssa had danced her way across the stage. I'd pulled out the earbud and sat spellbound, unable to look away.

I'd let Jenna make the outing an annual tradition and didn't bitch one damn time about going. Maybe in real life, I couldn't stare at Alyssa the way I wanted to, but in a darkened theater, I could spend a couple of hours feeding the intense need I had for her. The craving that was deep inside. The one I continued to deny myself on a daily basis.

The best part, the most reassuring part, was that she would never be the wiser.

Chapter Four

COLTON

September of sophomore year...

"Dude, you know I hate this place." Beck glares at the wide-open space that surrounds him. "The silence creeps me out."

A librarian sitting behind a long stretch of counter in the middle of the second-floor scowls at us before raising a finger to her lips. "Shhh!"

Beck stiffens beside me as his mouth sinks at the corners. "That woman just shushed me."

I glance at the older lady, who is now full-on glaring at us. "Yup, that's her job."

"Why the hell did you bring me here?" His grumbled words are barely decipherable. "Is it payback for something I did to you? If so, I'm sorry. All right? Whatever it is, I apologize. And I'll never do it again." There's a beat of silence. "Can we leave now?"

I roll my eyes—what a damn baby. "Just give me a few minutes. I need to check out a couple of books for an econ project, then we can head out."

"Sounds seriously boring."

He's not wrong. Most of the time, economics is dry and tedious.

And micro-econ makes me want to hurtle myself off a cliff. It's a necessary evil for the finance degree I'm working toward.

As we wind our way through a few of the stacks, looking for the business section, Beck grinds to a halt. I stop and raise a brow. I swear to God, if he's about to bitch and complain again, I'm going to punch him in the face.

Then he can bitch and complain about *that*.

Instead, his gaze remains focused on something in the distance. He's like a bird dog who has spotted, well...a bird. Normally, Beck is a laidback kind of dude. Nothing riles him up, and he's not one to take life too seriously. I'm pretty sure his father, Archibald, attempted to beat the nonchalance right out of him, but it didn't work. Beck is who he is, and that's not going to change anytime soon.

"If you want to get out of here," I mutter impatiently, "then let's move."

"You know what? Go on without me. Baker is over there with Reinholtz and Collins. I'm gonna see what they're up to."

That's when my gaze lands on a table full of our teammates. My guess is that they're here, getting study hours in. By all the joking and laughing going on, it doesn't look like that's happening. And Baker...that guy needs all the study time he can get. "Whatever, dude. I'll swing by after I find what I need."

Beck saunters away with a wave of his hand. "Take your time."

Honestly, I'll probably get this wrapped up a lot faster without him in tow. Just like I suspected, it takes under five minutes to locate the books I'm hunting for. With a big breath, I blow off the dust covering them before pulling each one out and thumbing through the pages. One peek at the table of contents is enough to confirm this project will be every bit as excruciating as I originally suspected.

Fucking economics.

With the books in hand, I swing around, ready to find Beck. As I retrace my steps through the second floor of the library, I spot Alyssa sitting at a table buried in a corner of the business section. It's not exactly the most popular place for obvious reasons, but I guess if you're looking for a quiet area to work, this would be it. For a long moment, I take her in. Her long blond hair is piled on top of her head in a messy bun, and she's wearing a shirt that hangs off one shoulder. There are black glasses perched on her nose.

A zip of unwanted attraction ricochets through my heart. I don't think I've ever seen Alyssa wear glasses before. She looks all kinds of sexy in them. And studious.

Fooling around with her after high school graduation had been a mistake. One I regret. If I thought it would help evict her from my head, I was sadly mistaken—more like the opposite. One taste was never going to be enough.

Instead of giving in to my urges, I've steered clear of the west end of campus, where the fine arts building, and her dorm, are located. If I catch wind that she'll be at a party, I hit a different one. That's been my tactical plan ever since.

Has it helped to stomp out my feelings for her?

Not one damn bit. When we do happen to run into each other, the intensity is like a tidal wave crashing over me, threatening to suck me under. Instead of cautiously backing away, I take an unconscious step in her direction. Before I can think better of it, more distance gets eaten up between us. Even though my brain is shouting at me to turn around and walk away, instinct takes over, propelling me forward.

This is the one girl who continues to override my feelings of self-preservation. I've never understood how she's managed to circumvent the walls I've thrown up. Alyssa stirs emotions inside me that I'd rather not experience. There's something about her that draws me like a moth to a flickering flame. As much as I want to forget about her, I can't. She's always there in the back of my head. When I'm with other girls, it's Alyssa I envision. She's the only one capable of making me feel something which is precisely why I continue to deny myself.

It's all kinds of fucked up, and I know it.

When Alyssa flashes a smile across the table, my gaze shifts, and I realize she isn't alone. I straighten to my full height, only now noticing the guy parked across from her.

Jamison Daniels.

He's one of my teammates.

What the fuck is she doing with him?

His lips hitch at the corners as he reaches across the smooth surface that separates them and brushes his fingers across her knuckles.

Oh, hell no!

That is so not going to happen!

Before I realize it, I'm stalking across the space. It only takes a handful of strides for me to pull up alongside their table. Alyssa blinks out of her Jamison-induced haze as her gaze flickers in my direction. Ever since that girl turned fifteen, she's been after me. I've never seen her so much as look at another dude. A potent concoction of jealousy-infused anger vibrates through every cell of my being. It takes all of my self-control not to tackle this asshole to the ground and drag him away from her.

"Hey." I'm almost impressed at my own ability to keep my fury from bleeding through that one syllable. I want to rip off Jamison's head and shit down his throat. Alyssa needs to understand that she belongs to me. Whether we're together or not.

She's mine.

She's *always* been mine.

"Hi." Her gaze stays pinned to me as she leans against the chair and pulls off her glasses. The movement has her fingers slipping from his outstretched hand.

I release a pent-up breath the moment they're no longer touching. I'd hate to beat the shit out of one of my own teammates, but I'll do it. I don't like him touching her.

Hell, I don't like *anyone* touching her.

Anyone that is but me.

Fuck.

I plow a hand through my hair in agitation. Only now does it occur to me that I have no idea if she's been out with other guys. Whenever we run into each other, her attention is strictly focused on me. Even if I'm surrounded by other girls, she'll fight her way through the crowd to get to me.

And you know what?

That's exactly the way I like it. I enjoy knowing that even though I'm holding her at a distance, it's me that she wants.

Does that make me an asshole?

Probably, but I can live with that knowledge. What I can't tolerate is Alyssa going out with other guys. Fear and panic flood through me until I'm nearly drowning in it. Here's the problem—I can't have this girl for myself, but I don't want anyone else to have her either. I have no idea what to do.

Whether Jamison realizes it or not, he's treading on my territory.

"Daniels," I bite out.

Reluctantly, he sits back and folds his arms across his chest. His biceps pop with the movement. Is he seriously trying to intimidate me? I almost snort.

Not gonna happen, dude.

"What's up, Montgomery?"

Instead of responding to the question, I fire off one of my own. "Do you two know each other?" I wince at the bite of jealousy that threads its way through my gruff voice.

"We have psychology together," Alyssa cuts in, beating him to the punch and drawing my attention back to her.

I jerk my head toward the stacks where we can have a little more privacy. "Let's talk."

Her brows skyrocket across her forehead before she does the unthinkable and shakes her head. "Sorry, maybe another time? We're kind of in the middle of something."

Excuse me?

First of all, I'm well aware of what they're in the middle of, and that's exactly what I'm attempting to break up.

Second, is Alyssa really telling me no?

Me?

Is this the same girl who would have happily spread her legs any time I wanted?

"Look, Mont—"

"Shut the hell up," I glance at Jamison and snap, "this doesn't concern you. Do yourself a favor and stay out of it."

His jaw turns slack. I don't think he could be more surprised if I tackled his ass to the floor in the middle of the library. Jamison Daniels might be a senior, but I don't give a flying fuck.

Alyssa's eyes widen.

Since they're both in a state of shock, I drop the books I'm holding onto the table and take this opportunity to pull her away. Alyssa has always been something of a wildcard. I don't even bother to pretend it's not part of the attraction. Once she finds her bearings, she'll probably tear me a new one.

I grab her hand and yank her to her feet before flicking a glance at Daniels to make sure his ass stays glued to the chair. Even though I can tell he's tempted to get in my way, he doesn't move a muscle. The guy has always struck me as a pussy, so this isn't a total surprise. All bark and no bite.

"Colton," she says in weak protest.

"You've got two minutes, Montgomery," Jamison mutters.

Or what? What's he going to do?

Instead of jumping further down his throat and getting into a physical altercation, my grip tightens on her. That one touch has the brightest part of my anger and jealousy diminishing. Alyssa has always had this effect on me. She settles something deep inside. Something I've never wanted to examine too closely. Only now do I realize that I might have to. If my only alternative is to lose her, then there won't be a choice in the matter.

Ignoring Jamison, I wind my way through the stacks, searching for a place we can converse without interruption.

"Colton!" She tugs her hand, attempting to pull it free. "Stop! You can't just come here and hijack—"

Wanna bet?

When I grind to a halt, she slams into me from behind and stumbles. I swing around, my hands tightening on her slender shoulders before stalking toward her. She's left with no other choice but to scramble backward. Her eyes widen as her spine hits the bookshelf, and she realizes there's nowhere else to go. She's trapped.

And at my mercy.

Our gazes fasten as my lips hover over her parted ones. The scent of her is intoxicating. I've spent so much time keeping her at a distance that being this close to her drives me insane. It takes everything I have to hold myself in check. I want this girl in the worst possible way.

I always have.

Now that I've done the unthinkable and touched her, I'm finding it difficult to control myself. The floodgates have been opened, and there's no way to slam them shut again.

"What are you doing?" Her voice wavers as her hands press against my chest as if she's capable of holding me off. The heat of her palms burn through the thin cotton of my T-shirt, singeing the skin beneath it. The feel of them are tattoos that will forever be a reminder of the day I lost my battle.

"This."

I step closer, pressing our bodies together until I can feel every rise and fall of her chest against mine. Her breath catches at the contact right before my lips crash onto hers. For a heartbeat, maybe two, I wonder if she'll fight me. Her body stiffens before melting against mine as if she's wanted this for as long as I have.

When my tongue sweeps across the seam of her lips, demanding entrance, she opens, and I delve inside. Her fingers curl, sinking into the cotton fabric of my shirt. The crescent shape of her nails bite into my flesh, grounding me to the present, to the intimacy unfolding between us. Only now that I'm exploring her mouth do I realize how much I've craved this. How did I ever think that one taste of her sweetness, almost a year and a half ago, would be enough?

I lose all sense of time as our tongues tangle. I've missed the taste of her. No matter how many girls I've been with, they all paled in comparison. Needy little noises escape from her, and it only drives me on.

When I finally lift my mouth, we're both breathing hard.

A dazed expression fills her face. "I don't under—"

"Go out with me."

Every bit of haziness disappears as her eyes widen. I have to admit that the words shock the hell out of me as well. I stiffen and wait for the panic to crash over me. Instead, I'm flooded with relief.

"You want to go on a...*date*?" The question is forced out as if every syllable is foreign to her tongue.

Again, I steel myself for an avalanche of panic to bury me alive.

When that doesn't occur, I release a breath as the corners of my lips bow up. "Yup, I do."

Her brows draw together as she carefully searches my eyes. "You don't date." There's a pause before she tacks on in a steely voice, "You fuck around."

Guilty. That's what I've always done. Although, not for the reasons she assumes. I've spent years running away from the one girl I've always longed for, and I can't do it any longer. Only now do I realize that she might not give me a chance. I've lived the life of a manwhore, screwing whatever girl I wanted in an attempt to forget the one in my arms. It didn't work. And I can't bear the thought of her with anyone else.

For all I know, she's over it.

Over me.

It's a frightening thought.

I press closer before ghosting my mouth over hers. The way her breathing hitches, and her lips part, tells me that she wants me.

Wants this.

Instead of giving us what we both crave, I whisper, "Let me take you out."

Her teeth sink into her bottom lip as indecision flickers across her face. I loosen my grip on her shoulders before my fingertips drift along her bare arms. Once they arrive at her hands, I interlock our fingers together.

"Give me a chance."

She whimpers as I bury my face against the side of her throat, licking and nipping at her flesh. I'm so tired of fighting this deep-seated need I have for her.

"Okay." The word falls from her lips in a breathy little sigh.

It takes everything I have to beat back the beast inside and not take her right here in the library. I want to brand Alyssa as mine. I want every guy on this campus to know that she belongs to me.

"Good." My lips curve. "Now get rid of Daniels."

Chapter Five

ALYSSA

October of sophomore year...

Mia and I push our way through the crowded student section at the stadium, searching for a place to park our butts. It's game day, and I'm here to root on my man. Even though it's mid-October, the temperature is still seasonable, and I'm able to wear Colton's red and black jersey over a turtleneck. He gave it to me a couple of weeks ago. It's a huge deal. Only girlfriends get to wear players' jerseys to the games or around campus. After he left my dorm room, I screamed at the top of my lungs.

All the while wearing his jersey, of course.

Sometimes I have to remind myself that this isn't a dream I'll wake from. It's my reality. I'm dating Colton Montgomery. Every time I think about it, a little bubble of joy explodes inside me.

This relationship has come out of nowhere and taken me completely by surprise. Sure, I'd always hoped something would happen between us, but did I really think it would? No way in hell. How could I when Colton went to such great lengths to avoid me? First in high school, then at college. If we were paired up together for a class project, he found a way out. If I arrived at a party, he slipped out the backdoor. If he spotted me on campus, he'd take off in the opposite direction.

It might have taken a while, but I can take a hint. Just when I'd decided to put Colton Montgomery behind me and move on with my life, he came out of nowhere and swept me off my feet.

Honestly, I'm still in a state of shock. Colton can have any girl he wants. And he has. But he's never been one to get serious. He likes to play the field.

And yet...here we are.

Trust me when I say that I'm taking it slow. It's all about baby steps with this guy. Even though Colton came after me, he's like a skittish animal I need to approach with both caution and patience. So far, I've let him set the pace, and that seems to be working. I'm taking it day by day and letting our relationship unfold naturally. If I get too serious, too quick, he'll bolt. I can see it in his eyes.

"You're getting an awful lot of looks," Mia murmurs from beside me. "I wouldn't be surprised if one of these bitches shanks you in the bathroom just to wrestle that jersey from your cold dead body."

I snort. She's not wrong about that. I can practically feel the coveted stares and hear the whispers as we move up the stadium steps in search of seats. There are a lot of thirsty bitches around here waiting for an opportunity to steal my man. Especially now that he's done the unthinkable and committed to one specific female.

Me!

Yeah, I still can't get over it.

Any moment, I'm going to break out into a little happy dance. Although, I think Mia would slap me upside the head if I did.

Even though Colton is only a sophomore at Wesley, he's been a hot commodity since stepping foot on campus freshman year. Not only is he good-looking, but he's also a first-string wide receiver for the Wildcats. The idea of dating a guy like him is much akin to capturing a mythical unicorn. The girls who don't want to strangle me seek me out for advice. As if there's a secret formula to my success. If only they knew the truth.

I have absolutely no idea what happened to make him change his mind.

For the first couple of weeks, I was overly cautious, waiting for the bottom to fall out—waiting for him to wake up one morning and say that he's not interested in being tied down when there are a ton of groupies willing to spread their legs. I was almost afraid to sleep with him, figuring that's when he would break things off.

Instead, six weeks have slipped by, and we're still going strong. Gradually, I'm figuring him out. I'd always assumed he was just a guy who enjoyed screwing as many girls as he could. After spending time with him, I suspect there's more to it than that. He's surprisingly guarded. It's almost as if Colton puts up a façade for everyone around him. Only now am I beginning to peel back the layers to the man lurking beneath the surface. It makes me wonder what happened in his past for him to erect so many walls. It's tempting to ask. Instead, I've remained silent in hopes that he'll open up on his own when he's ready.

Mia points to two open spots in the middle of the row. We slide past a dozen people before settling on our seats with our drinks and popcorn. We wave to a few friends before the band performs the school song and the players jog onto the field in a wave of red and black. Even though there are ninety guys on the team, my gaze cuts right through them, locking on number twenty-five. My heart flips over in my chest as I watch him. The pads only accentuate the broad set of his shoulders. My gaze drops to his ass. I'm not going to lie, the red stretchy pants do wonders for it.

Mia bumps into my shoulder with her own. I tear my gaze away from Colton and glance toward her in question, only to find a grin simmering around the corners of her lips.

"I know what you're staring at, perv."

I snort out a laugh. "Can you blame me?"

She straightens in her seat and tilts her head as if giving serious consideration to the question. "Objectively speaking, the guy has a mighty fine ass."

Yes, he certainly does.

The ref flips a coin, and Tennessee will kickoff. I munch my popcorn and settle in to watch the first play of the game. My father is a die-hard football fan. It doesn't matter if it's the NFL, college, or high school. It's more of a religion. Friday, Saturday, and Sunday are days of worship in the Williams household. That meant loads of BBQ chicken wings, pigs in a blanket, chips, and cold bottles of beer. Not exactly dancer-friendly food. But Mom always made sure to have a veggie platter with hummus and lots of fresh fruit for me.

After about fifteen minutes, a ref blows a whistle, throws up a flag, and stops the play.

"What happened?" Mia asks, brows drawing together as she watches the guys standing around.

"There's a penalty for holding," I explain.

When she continues to stare in confusion, my lips twitch. "It means that one of our guys grabbed hold of the other team's defensive player while trying to block him. They're not allowed to do that. Now there's a penalty, and we lose ten yards."

Her brows pinch together. "It's almost as if you're speaking English, but I still can't understand a word you're saying." She lifts a hand to her face before touching her mouth. "Am I having a stroke? Is that what's going on?" There's a pause. "Wait a minute...aren't I the one who shouldn't be making sense if I'm stroking out?"

I burst out laughing. "Neither of us are stroking out. Although, if these refs don't get their heads out of their asses, I just might." I point to the field and explain, "Now we're further from the end zone, which makes it more difficult to score a touchdown."

She nods, continuing to look baffled. "Why does football have to be so complicated?"

I pat her shoulder. "It's a good thing you're pretty."

"Shut up. You know I've never been a fan of the game. Too slow and boring."

"Yup. Which is exactly why I appreciate you tagging along with me today."

She flashes an evil grin that sends chills scampering down my spine. "Don't worry, I'll come up with something torturous for payback."

I don't doubt it. She'll probably force me to stay in for the weekend and binge-watch Gilmore Girls. Mia knows I can't stand the show.

Usually, I'm the one dragging her butt to parties when she would much rather stay home.

An hour and a half later, the buzzer sounds, ending the second quarter of the game and signaling halftime. My attention stays trained on Colton as he jogs off the field. His gaze coasts over the student section before zeroing in on me, and I feel the connection straight down to my toes. He grins before tapping his fist against his chest and pointing toward me.

A sigh escapes from my lips before I can stifle it. Are there little red and pink hearts dancing above my head? Because I think there might be. If I'm not careful, I'm going to fall head over heels in—

"Oh God, you're falling for him, aren't you?"

It's not a question. More like a statement. And not one filled with happiness either.

As tempted as I am to downplay my growing feelings, I don't want to do that. Mia has been my best friend for nearly a decade. We've always been straightforward with one another. Even though she won't like the answer, I can't bring myself to lie. "Yeah," I track his movements until he disappears inside the tunnel, "I am."

Mia worries her lower lip before gnawing on it. Concern flickers across her expressive features.

When she remains silent, I blurt, "He's not the guy you think he is."

"So, what you're telling me is that he's only been *pretending* to be a player, out for one thing all these years?"

I wince as my shoulders slump and some of my pleasure drains away. It's a complicated question. One I don't necessarily have an answer for. "I don't know." That's what I'm trying to figure out.

Instead of meeting Mia's inquisitive stare, I focus on the band marching in formation on the field for the halftime show.

After a few minutes of silence, her arm snakes around me as she leans her head against my shoulder. "I'm just worried you'll get hurt. That's all."

I huff out a breath as some of my defensiveness melts away. It's not like I don't understand her concern. Colton is the king of hookups. The guy is nineteen years old, and this is the first time he's been in a relationship. I would be an idiot not to be cautious where he's concerned. But that doesn't mean I can hold back my feelings or pretend they don't exist.

"I won't get hurt." When it comes down to it, I realize that Mia has my best interest at heart. All she's trying to do is protect me. "We're taking it slow."

"Girl, please," she says with a snort, "you don't know the meaning of the word slow."

My lips tremble around the corners. She's not wrong about that. Where my bestie carefully weighs every decision she makes, I've always been a leap-before-looking kind of girl.

Has it gotten me into trouble over the years?

You bet it has. But that's the way I live life.

"I think you're already in love with the guy." There's a beat of silence before she adds in a serious tone, "You've always been in love with him."

Instead of acknowledging the truth, I press my lips together and remain silent.

This is the problem with having a best friend who knows you so well. She's able to figure out all your dirty little secrets. Even the ones you try to hide from yourself.

Chapter Six

COLTON

February of sophomore year...

Alyssa is wrapped up in my arms as my mouth roves hungrily over her neck. She arches, allowing me better access to her delectable flesh. A little moan escapes from her as she shoves the key into the lock.

Once.

Twice.

After three failed attempts, she whispers, "You need to stop that, or I'll never get this door open, and we'll end up having sex in the hallway."

I don't care where we screw, as long as I can get inside her. My cock is so damn hard that it's all I can focus on. The moment I slide deep inside her is always one of pure nirvana. I've never experienced anything like it before. There's a little voice inside my brain that wonders if I ever will again. Since that's not an entirely comfortable thought, I shove it away before I can examine it too closely.

"Colton."

My name comes out sounding more like a breathy sigh, and it does the impossible and makes me harder. I'll be honest, I couldn't stop even if I wanted to. Her skin is too damn sweet. I'm tempted to gobble her up in one tasty bite. I've had my fair share of chicks over the years, but I've never craved anyone the way I do her. She's like a drug pumping wildly through my system. Sometimes it feels like way too much, way too soon. And that scares the shit out of me. There are times when I'm struck with the urge to pull away in an effort to regain my bearings, but I always stop short of actually doing it.

My teeth sink into the delicate skin of her bared throat as my fingers graze her ribcage before sliding upward to her breasts. I glance down the hall to make sure it's empty. Since the coast is clear, I tweak her nipples through the thin shirt she's wearing beneath her jacket. "What's wrong, baby girl? Is there a reason you can't focus?"

She whimpers in answer as I continue playing with her body. Alyssa is so damn responsive to my touch. Sex with her is like...

I don't even know how to describe it.

There's a high I get when I'm inside the heat of her body. This must be what addiction feels like—craving something all the time even if it's a person. Even when you're balls deep, you can't help but wonder when you can be there again.

"If you keep that up, I'll come."

She's not kidding either.

So.

Damn.

Responsive.

Her whispered words go straight to my dick, making me throb even harder than I already am. Why the hell did I ever fight against this in the first place? Hands down, getting together with this girl was the best decision I ever made.

"Hey," someone yells from a couple of doors down, breaking into the thick fog that has descended, "get a room!"

"What do you think we're trying to do?" Alyssa bellows in response, unapologetic about our PDA.

My lips quirk as a chuckle slips free. Reluctantly, I lower my hands until my thumbs can graze over the soft outer swells of her breasts and my index fingers settle beneath the band of her bra.

Once upon a time, I'd thought her breasts were too small. Needless to say, I was mistaken about that. Maybe her cup doesn't runneth over like some girls, but it doesn't matter. Alyssa's tits are fucking perfect.

Everything about her is.

"Colton," she groans for a second time, writhing against me, all the while trying to jam the metal in the lock.

"What, baby?"

"You're killing me."

"Good. I want to ruin you for all other guys." The words slip free before I can stop them. My heartbeat jackhammers. It's the closest I've come to declaring my feelings for her.

"I think you already have."

On the fifth attempt, the key slides home, and the door handle turns.

"Thank God," she mutters as we stumble inside the space.

I've been dying to get my hands on her for days. Since we both have roommates, carving out time to be alone has become a challenge. I'm not going to lie, we've done it in my car and at the library. The potential thrill of getting caught turns us both on. She's definitely a girl after my own heart.

Next year, the plan is to move into an apartment or off-campus housing. I'll have my own room. Then I can sleep with her wrapped up in my arms every damn night. If the thought leaves me slightly shaken that I'm actually thinking that far ahead into the future when it comes to a girl, I ignore it and refocus my attention.

"Are you sure Mia won't be home for a while?"

A smile curves her lips as her eyelids lower to half-mast. "Yup, she's in class for another two hours."

"Perfect."

"I know."

"Hey, Alyssa," someone hollers from down the hall, "do you have—"

"Nope!" she responds without even glancing in their direction, "I'll catch you in an hour."

"An hour?" I grumble, nipping at her earlobe, "is that it?"

Her lips twitch. "Make it two," she corrects, slamming the door shut without waiting for a response.

The moment we're shuttered away in her tiny dorm room, we tear at our clothing as if starving for one another. Jackets are the first to be shed. Then shirts and her bra. Shoes and socks come next. Somewhere in the mix, jeans and leggings are added to the pile. It's a frenzy of fabric thrown in every direction until we're both stripped bare and falling onto the single twin bed.

Alyssa chuckles as my mouth lands on hers. She opens immediately until our tongues can tangle. It's like this every damn time. It never gets old. I'm so fucking hot for this girl. After we got together earlier this year, I half-expected that we would screw a couple of times before monotony set in. If I'm being completely honest, I'd secretly hoped for it. All I really wanted was to fuck Alyssa out of my system so I could move on, and she'd stop lurking in the back of my brain.

But that hasn't occurred. If anything, it's been the complete opposite. I can't get enough of her. The more I have, the more I want. It's a vicious cycle I can't seem to break. Hands down, being inside her body is the best damn feeling in the world.

Nothing else compares.

Hot licks of need spike through my veins, making me impatient. With the way I'm feeling, there's no time for foreplay. Alyssa understands this and widens her thighs until I can settle between them. As I thrust my tongue inside her mouth, my dick sinks simultaneously inside her.

An appreciative groan rumbles up from deep in my chest. There is no greater feeling than her welcoming heat squeezing me tight. She always laughs when I tell her how much I love her pussy. The truth is that I fucking revere it.

Eight strokes later and I'm coming with a vengeance.

Thankfully, she's right there with me.

Half a year later, and every time feels like the first. How the hell will I ever get enough of this girl?

Her teeth sink into her lower lip to stifle her moans. I keep my gaze pinned to hers and watch as wave after wave of pleasure crashes over her delicate features. I don't think I've ever seen anything as beautiful as the look on Alyssa's face when she orgasms. Her ecstasy only intensifies my own. I'm ashamed to admit that in the past, it was my satisfaction that came first. I've always been a selfish bastard when it came to sex. As long as I got my rocks off, it was all good.

Alyssa changed that. Her pleasure means everything to me. It's my first priority.

With a huff of exhaustion, my muscles loosen, and I collapse on top of her. Slender arms slip around my neck as she drags me close.

A chuckle fills my ears as her body shakes with silent laughter. "More than an hour, hmmm?"

Yeah...that didn't go according to plan. I'm lucky if that lasted five minutes.

Maybe four.

"That was round one," I grunt. "I've got a few more left inside me."

"Well," her lips feather across the side of my face, "I certainly hope so."

"Give me a few minutes to recover, and then I'll be ready to go." I roll to my side and take her with me, which is no easy feat in the narrow bed. Somehow, we manage to switch positions so that my back is to the mattress, and her naked body is sprawled across my chest.

Lying here with her in my arms is the second-best feeling. As our harsh breathing fills the dorm room, an unexpected contentment settles over me. I wrack my brain, trying to remember the last time I felt this at peace. As if all was right in the world.

But I can't.

I don't think I've ever felt like this.

If so, it was when I was a kid, around four years old before Mom decided to cut and run. As soon as that ugly thought mushrooms up in my consciousness, I squash it and blink back to the here and now. Alyssa grazes my chest with her fingers before lazily circling my nipple. I glance down, surprised to find her watching me from beneath her lashes. There's a sleepy look in her eyes and a softening around her mouth as if she doesn't have a care in the world.

At this precise moment, I feel the same. The crack she's managed to find in my heart opens wider.

Our gazes lock and hold as she whispers, "I love you."

And just like that, those feelings of peace and contentment vanish into thin air as if they had been a figment of my imagination the entire time. Everything inside me stills as my breath gets clogged at the back of my throat. It's as if I'm being suffocated from the inside out. My heart thumps a painful staccato, filling my ears like the roar of the ocean until it drowns out everything else.

There's a hopeful look on Alyssa's face. I open my mouth to say something.

Anything.

But nothing comes out.

One heartbeat passes.

Then another.

The happiness filling her eyes drains away before dying an agonizing death.

As much as I want to echo the sentiment, the words refuse to budge from my lips. Instead, my mouth turns cottony. Deep down, I knew this conversation was inevitable, and I'd even hoped I would be able to parrot it back to her.

But I can't do it.

When I remain mute, she turns her head away before resting her cheek against my chest so I'm no longer able to see her expression. The movement isn't nearly quick enough for me to miss the pain my silence has caused.

Chapter Seven

ALYSSA

One week later...

Seated on the floor of the studio, I cross one leg over the other and fold my upper body to my thighs, stretching my arms until they can sweep across the wood. Gradually I inhale, filling my lungs with oxygen and expanding my chest to capacity. I hold it for a couple of seconds before forcing every molecule from my body. Repeating the process, I focus on my breathing. I can almost feel the breakdown of lactic acid that had built up in my muscles during the intense sixty-minute rehearsal. After a few more deep breaths, I sit up and shift my legs before crossing the left over the right and bending forward to deepen the exercise. Once my calves and thighs have been properly stretched, I extend my legs in front of me and fold at the waist before widening them and moving through a second series of exercises.

Francois Dupre, our instructor, is a French import. His pedigree is impressive. He's classically trained, has danced as the lead with the French Ballet, and traveled the world. Most of the female dancers have a massive crush on him. A few of the males do as well. I can't blame them. He's dreamy with black wavy hair and intelligent cocoa-colored eyes. His body is long, lean, and muscular from years of rigorous training.

As if he hasn't already commanded everyone's attention, he claps his hands. "Excellent work," he says in lightly accented English. "We meet again on Friday."

A few sighs escape as three girls pop gracefully to their feet before rushing toward him. Once he's flanked on all sides, tittering laughter rings throughout the spacious room.

I glance at Zoe, who is finishing up her stretches beside me, and roll my eyes. "What a bunch of whores," I mutter under my breath.

The corners of her lips tremble before she spears a glance toward the growing swarm outfitted in Lycra. "Apparently, they haven't figured out that Monsieur Dupre has no interest in someone with lady parts."

I snort and shrug. "Perhaps they're hoping to persuade him differently?"

"It won't work." She leans toward me before admitting, "I already tried."

"You did not!" I gasp.

"Of course, I did." Her gaze slices to him as she lifts a slim shoulder. "I mean, come on. Just look at the man." Her voice turns wistful. "Can you even imagine what he looks like beneath his clothes?"

An image of Colton pops into my head. As delicious as Monsieur Dupre is, I only have eyes for one man. And it's not our dance instructor. "He turned you down?"

"Yup. He said his boyfriend would have a problem with it," she admits with a laugh. "I told him that I'd be more than happy to be the star of that little show."

"Shut up!" I swat her arm as my eyes pop wide. *"You didn't!"*

"Please, girl. You know me better than that." She grins and shoots another glance in our teachers' direction. "Do you have any idea how hot that would be?"

Umm...maybe?

"Anyway," she continues blithely, "it was a no-go."

I rise to my feet and extend my arms above my head before bending to the left, holding the pose, and then repeating it on the other side until my muscles feel limber.

Zoe slips off her beaten-up shoes before stuffing them inside her dance bag. I do the same, grabbing a bottle of water and lifting it to my lips. Once the container has been drained, I stuff it in the bag and pull on an oversized T-shirt. Black leggings come next before shoving my feet into a pair of boots and stuffing my arms into my jacket. "Ready to go?"

The willowy brunette nods as we wave to our instructor, who is still surrounded by a handful of students, and exit the studio. Even though I'm tired from a full hour of dancing, I feel revitalized. My muscles are fatigued and pliable.

No matter what happens in my life, dance is the one thing I can count on. When my parents went through a rough patch and were at each other's throats, dance is what got me through the hard times. If I couldn't escape to the studio, I was able to shove earbuds in, crank up the music, and lose myself in the choreography while locked in my bedroom.

What would I do if I couldn't dance?

Who would I be without it?

I don't have an answer to that. It's such an integral part of who I am.

Even though I'm nowhere near good enough to dance professionally, my dream is to one day open my own studio. During high school, I started teaching ballet and jazz classes. It's something I enjoy. I've been lucky to find an academy here in town where I can pick up a few classes to teach on the weekends.

Am I under the delusion that it will make me rich?

Nope, but I don't care. Dance makes me happy.

As we move through the crowded corridor, Zoe chatters about the upcoming annual showcase. Each performer choreographs a three-minute routine to highlight their talent. Wesley has a fierce program with dancers from around the world. Guest instructors are brought in from the most prestigious programs and academies. A number of students go on to perform in companies, on Broadway, or dancing backup. I feel fortunate to be here, studying alongside and learning from such a talented group of people.

"Hey, you want to grab lunch?" she asks. "After such a grueling rehearsal, I'm starving."

I pull on my fingerless gloves. "Sure. I could eat." Truth be told, I can always eat. It's a continuous battle.

What can I say? I'm part Italian and have a serious love affair with pasta. And chicken parmesan. One day, it will be my downfall.

As we push through the glass doors into the bright January sunshine, my phone chimes with an incoming message. I slip the cell from the pocket of my white puffer jacket and glance at the screen.

My heartbeat quickens as Colton's name pops up.

Six months.

It seems almost unbelievable that we've been together that long. Last week, unable to hold the feelings inside any longer, I'd dropped the *I love you* bomb after sex. I couldn't help myself. It had needed to be said, and I'd wanted Colton to know how much he meant to me.

It had been disappointing when he didn't return the sentiment, but it's fine. I know he cares. He shows me in a hundred different ways each and every day. Little things that make my heart beat into over-drive—like opening the car door for me, stroking his fingers gently through my hair, clasping my hand when we walk across campus, or turning up at my dorm in the morning with a steaming cup of coffee.

Even though we've been together for half a year, we're still taking baby steps. At some point in the not-so-distant future, I'm hoping Colton will come to the realization that what we have is special, and he loves me. Just like football, it's all about the long game with Colton. I'm nothing if not patient and persistent.

I swipe my finger across the screen as my gaze skims over the message. Zoe and I jog down the cement stairs until we're in front of the William Dutton Fine Arts building. It takes a moment for his words to sink in. As they do, my footsteps falter, and I stumble to a halt. My attention stays glued to the text as all of the oxygen evaporates from my lungs, leaving me to feel as if the wind has been knocked from my body.

"Alyssa?" With her brows pinched together, Zoe swings around before hoisting the strap of her bag onto her slender shoulder. "Are you coming?"

People knock into me in their haste to flee the building. A few grumble and tell me to get out of the way. When I remain silent, Zoe's fingers lock around my wrist before she drags me off the busy pathway and out of the rush of student traffic.

She waves a hand in front of my face to capture my attention as concern floods her voice. "Alyssa?"

I blink and refocus on the words—willing them to morph into something else—before giving my head a little shake.

This has to be a joke.

"Are you all right?" Zoe's voice softens as she searches my face for an indication as to why I've fallen into a semi-catatonic state.

Even though I'm splintering apart on the inside, I force myself to remain calm. "Um, sorry to bale," I mumble, unable to stop staring at the screen. It's like a horrific car accident I'm unable to look away from. "There's something I need to take care of. Go on without me, okay?"

Her lips sink further into a frown as she shifts her weight and cocks her head. "Are you sure?"

"Yeah." I glance up as my head continues to spin. "Sorry to flake on you like this."

"I don't know what's going on, but if you need backup, I'd be more than happy to tag along. I've got nothing better going on."

Her offer brings a slight smile to my face as I shake my head. "Thanks, but no."

"All right," she says, sounding dubious, "if you're sure."

"I am," I reiterate.

"I'll see you on Friday?"

"Yup." Barely am I aware of Zoe walking away and leaving me alone. Instead of reading over the message again, I stab the call button and hold the phone to my ear. A pit the size of Texas settles in my belly as it goes straight to voicemail.

What the fuck?

Is Colton really doing this to me?

After six months together, it seems almost unfathomable. Anger crashes over me as I stab the red end button and hit redial. When it goes straight to voicemail for a second time, I realize with a sinking heart that he has no intention of picking up my calls.

He's really doing this.

It's as if he lit a match, threw it over his shoulder, and burned our relationship to the ground.

And there's not a damn thing I can do about it.

Chapter Eight

COLTON

With my elbows perched on my knees, I sit on the bench in the locker room and stare sightlessly at my clasped hands. They're clenched so tightly together that the knuckles have turned bone white.

Did I do the right thing?

Or was it all a fucking mistake? One I can't take back, because let's face it, there's no way to smooth over a situation when you break up with someone through text. That's signed, sealed, and delivered.

Here's what I know—relief flooded through me as soon as I hit the send button.

That's got to mean something...*right?*

I straighten my shoulders, all the while trying to convince myself that I did what needed to be done. That, unfortunately, doesn't stop the self-doubt from mushrooming up inside me. I feel like the world's biggest asshole for handling it in this manner. I damn well know that Alyssa didn't deserve this, but I also realize there's no way I could have pulled the trigger if I'd stood in front of her and forced myself to look her in the eye.

So, yeah...I pussied out and shot her a text instead. And now, I'm acting like a little bitch by not picking up her calls or responding to her messages. She's attempted to contact me half a dozen times, asking what the hell is going on. Each one has escalated in both tone and disbelief. I can barely stand to read or listen to them. Her pain is palpable.

A heavy hand lands on my shoulder and knocks me from those thoughts. Blinking away the melancholy, I glance at Beck as he loiters beside me. He's already dressed and itching to leave, and here I am, sitting with a towel draped around my hips. I drag a hand over my face and attempt to pull my shit together.

"Everything good?"

The two of us have been friends since elementary school. We played on Pop Warner football teams together, then in high school, and now in college. Beck is one of the most talented quarterbacks in the country. He's been breaking state and NCAA records for years. Even as a sophomore, there's no doubt in my mind that he'll end up playing in the NFL. If Beck had his way, he would enter the draft next year, but his father has other ideas. And in the Hollingsworth household, Archibald rules the roost.

I shrug off his hand. "Yup."

My world is only imploding...no biggie. Although, it's by my own hand, so I'm not sure if that's something I can complain about.

"Then move your ass, and let's go. Collins is having a little get-together. I need to chill out for a while."

A party?

No, thanks. There's no way I can deal with a large group of people right now. Not with all this emotion ripping me up inside.

"Go on without me," I mumble, reluctant to reveal what's really going on. "I've got some shit to take care of."

He smirks. "Is that what we're calling getting laid nowadays?"

It's doubtful that will be happening any time soon. Instead of forcing out the words, I rise to my feet and yank a pair of boxers out of my locker before dragging them up my thighs. Joggers and a red Wildcats T-shirt come next. Once dressed, I grab my sweat-shirt and athletic bag, ready to take off. All I want to do is go home and lick my wounds in private. Sure, it's a self-inflicted injury, but that doesn't make a damn bit of difference. Beck and I are the last ones to leave as he pushes out through the heavy locker room door. I follow behind, sucked back into the chaotic whirl of my thoughts.

The whole did-I-or-didn't-I-make-a-mistake is eating me alive. The bitch of it is that I'll probably never know.

"Oh," he says, moving into the corridor of the athletic center, "hey, Alyssa."

My head snaps up so abruptly that I nearly give myself whiplash as my gaze collides with icy-blue eyes. All it takes is one look at the fury vibrating off her in heavy, suffocating waves to know that I won't escape this confrontation unscathed. I swallow down my growing nausea. This is exactly the kind of altercation I'd been hoping to avoid.

When she remains silent, lips pressed together in a tight line, Beck's quizzical gaze flicks to mine. Whatever he sees painted across my face is enough of a tipoff for him to abandon this sinking ship post haste. Can't say I blame him for it. I'd probably do the same if I were in his position. He jerks a thumb over his shoulder and takes a swift step in retreat. "So...I'm going to take off."

Instead of glancing at Beck, Alyssa's gaze stays pinned to mine.

"I'll catch you at the dorm," I mutter, dread pooling at the bottom of my gut.

"Yup." With pent-up longing, I watch as he disappears down the hallway like the hounds of hell are nipping at his heels.

An uncomfortable silence falls over us.

One heartbeat passes.

Then another.

Now that we're alone, I mentally brace myself for the oncoming explosion. Except Alyssa doesn't do the expected. Instead, she stares mutely, scouring my face for answers I refuse to give voice to. Hurt seeps into her eyes, mingling with the fury. A fresh wave of guilt crashes over me, nearly swallowing me whole. It would be so much easier if she'd just go off the deep end. Then I could mentally shut down and tune out the theatrics while she got everything off her chest.

But this?

The unspoken recriminations aimed in my direction?

The pain that radiates off her as if it's a living, breathing entity?

That's impossible to tune out.

How can I when I'm the architect of her agony?

When I'm the one to blame for giving in and allowing this to get out of hand?

Ever since middle school, I've yearned for this girl. Longed to reach out and stroke my fingers over her. Be close to her. Make her mine. Although, she would have never guessed it from my behavior. I've done everything in my power to ignore Alyssa. To keep her at a distance. To push her to the outer recesses of my brain so I wouldn't have to think about her. So I'd finally stop wanting her—dreaming about her.

It didn't work.

Nothing worked.

Even when I broke down and asked her out, I knew this is how it would eventually end between us. When it comes down to it, I can't give Alyssa what she craves. What she deserves.

No matter how tempting it is, I can't love her the way she needs me to.

So where does that leave us?

In a place that neither of us wants to be.

More than anything, I wish Alyssa had just been a fuck. One I could forget about. But she was never that. Whether she realizes it or not, that's the problem.

"Why?"

One shaky word falls from her lips, but it's more than enough. It's like a burning arrow shot right through the center of my heart. Even though it's tempting to look away, I force myself to hold her gaze. It's vital to bear witness to the harm I've inflicted. It'll serve as a permanent reminder to never let my guard down again. The damage rippling in its wake isn't worth it.

My gaze roams over her. So badly do I want to close the distance and pull her into my arms. She might only be five foot six, but Alyssa is a towering pillar of strength. I don't think I've ever met another girl like her. It's doubtful I ever will again. She's brave, confident, and ballsy. It's a wicked combination that drew me in from the very beginning.

It's the only reason she's standing before me now.

Had I really fooled myself into believing this girl wouldn't track me down and demand answers?

I should have known better.

More than anything, I wish everything could be different between us. I wish I weren't so fucked in the head. But, like everything else in life, wishes don't mean jack shit.

"Colton?" she bites out, thrusting out her phone. "Why would you do this?"

I jerk my shoulders. There's no way I can divulge the truth. That would mean opening up and letting her in—kind of like slitting my wrists and bleeding out emotionally. And that, I'm unwilling to do. So, I go with something believable. "I dunno, just kind of feels like this relationship has run its course." When her eyes widen, I force out the rest, needing a clean break. I can't have her coming back and trying to repair this. I need to blow it up. "There's only so much monotony I can deal with."

Her mouth tumbles open as she sucks in a sharp breath. *"What?"*

When her eyes turn glassy, I glance at the cement block wall beyond her. If I don't, I'll drop to my knees and beg for forgiveness. And I can't allow that to happen. There's no other choice but to soldier on.

"We had a good run. Six months is practically an eternity as far as I'm concerned. But I'm over it. I need to mix things up. Explore my options."

"You're doing this because you," there's a beat of silence as if she's having a difficult time wrapping her lips around the words, *"want to sleep with other people?"*

No.

"Yeah." I shift my weight, impatient to get this over with. Bile rises in my throat as I toss the question back at her and hold my breath. "Don't you?"

Any color filling her cheeks drains away as she shakes her head. "No, I don't."

I tighten my hands into fists to stop myself from reaching out and consoling her. My words are ripping her apart, and it's excruciating to watch. Any moment, I'm going to crumble. "Look, Lys—"

"Don't you dare call me that," she growls from between clenched teeth. "I will *never* be that to you again."

I jerk my head into a terse nod. "It's better to walk away before someone gets hurt."

A gurgle of strained laughter bubbles up from her throat. "Yeah, it's too late for that."

As much as I fight to keep the words locked deep inside, I blurt, "I'm sorry." It's probably the only thing that's come out of my mouth that bears any resemblance to the truth.

"Are you?" She tilts her head and stares at me as if she has no clue who I am. It's the first time she's ever looked at me that way. It takes effort to keep my expression carefully blank. Almost bored. "You know what hurts the most?"

All of it.

There's nothing that doesn't hurt.

I brace myself before shaking my head.

"That you thought so little of me and my feelings that you couldn't be bothered to have an honest conversation." Again, she holds up the phone. "Instead of acting like a man, you sent me a lame-ass text." Alyssa falls silent, almost as if digesting what she's just expressed. "If I hadn't hunted you down, you probably would have ghosted me."

As much as I hate to admit it, she's right. That's *exactly* what the plan had entailed.

"It seemed easier that way," I mumble, feeling like a grade-A asshole. It's almost impressive the depths I've managed to jackhammer down to.

"Easier for who?" she snaps, voice escalating, echoing off the cavernous cement walls.

Since that seems more like a rhetorical question, I don't bother with a response.

"Where did this come from?" Her brows draw together in bewilderment as if mentally reviewing the autopsy of our doomed relationship. "I thought you were happy."

"I was." The emotion churning in her eyes is enough to break me. I hate myself for doing this to her. "And now I'm not."

"Just like that." There's a pause. "Like a light switch. Happy." She snaps her fingers as the brightness in her eyes returns. If she loses the battle with her tears, I won't be able to stand it. "Unhappy."

"Yeah," I force out glumly, edging closer to my breaking point.

"I don't know what to say." She shakes her head. "Just...wow."

When I remain mute, Alyssa inches forward, closing the yawning distance that separates us. Sorrow is etched across every line of her expression. "I realize there's nothing I can say that will change your mind." She forces out a brittle laugh. "And I won't bother to try. I refuse to beg and grovel for some guy who is willing to throw me away like a dirty Kleenex."

No, that's not Alyssa's style. She has way too much pride and self-worth for that.

Instead of allowing the tears to trek down her ashen cheeks, she blinks back the wetness and glances away. "You know what sucks the most?" Before I can answer—not that I was going to—she continues, "I really loved you. Even though you didn't say it back to me, I thought you might feel the same."

A thick lump of emotion settles in the middle of my throat, making it impossible to breathe. Death would be preferable rather than witness the way she's laying herself bare.

A frown tugs at the corners of her lips as her gaze slices to me. "That's the reason, isn't it?"

I gulp down the icy shards of dread and try to keep it all buried deep beneath the surface before it can undo the chaos I've unleashed on this relationship. "What are you talking about?"

Understanding dawns across her face as she carefully examines my eyes. If she searches hard enough, deep enough, she'll unearth all of my secrets, and that can't be allowed to happen. "That scared you, didn't it?"

The floodgates open, and panic rushes through every cell of my body. I shift impatiently, tempted to flee from not only this building but her. My chest tightens, and pain throbs through me with every sharp intake of breath.

Maybe Alyssa believes that she loves me, but she doesn't.

How could she when my own mother wasn't able to?

There has to be something seriously wrong with me if Candace could walk away without a second look.

Doesn't Alyssa understand that I can't be the man she wants me to be?

I'm incapable of giving her what she needs—even for the short-term. She deserves better. I realize it, even if she doesn't. It's only a matter of time before she comes to the same conclusion and leaves. And that, I won't be able to withstand.

Once was more than enough.

The fear of this happening again has the blood running through my veins turning to ice. It also gives me the little nudge I need to end this once and for all. "Come on, girl, you had to know this was a long shot when we got together. It was a gamble." I shrug, wanting to appear nonchalant. "You rolled the dice, and it came up snake eyes. You should be giving me props for remaining faithful for this long. As much as I've enjoyed your unicorn pussy, this whole exclusivity thing isn't for me." I reach out and stroke my fingers along the curve of her jaw. It doesn't escape me that this will be the last time I touch her. "I wouldn't mind keeping you in my back pocket and having a taste of it every once in a while."

As the last word falls from my lips, she bats my hand away before shoving both palms against my chest and knocking me back a step with an angry grunt.

"Fuck you, Colton! You really are an asshole, you know that?"

Yeah, I do.

And now, thankfully, she knows it, too.

Chapter Nine

ALYSSA

There's a gentle tap on my arm.

"Lys?"

I blink out of the frenzied whirl of my thoughts and refocus my attention on Mia. "Hmmm?" I dredge my brain. If she fired off a question, I have no idea what it was. I really need to snap out of this funk.

Sympathy flashes across her face as she loops her arm through mine and tugs me closer. "Aww, girl. I'm sorry. I know this must be tough." There's a pause. "You want me to beat Colton's ass? For you, I'll do it."

Even though it takes effort, I force out a snort. It feels like my entire body is riddled with pain. "Nah. He's not worth it." My lips quirk at the corners at the idea of Mia getting into any kind of physical altercation. She's never so much as had a disagreement. She's always walked the straight and narrow, but that behavior intensified after her sister, Brianna, died in a car accident. Sometimes I get the feeling that Mia is trying to distract her parents with all of her accomplishments. Straight A's, tennis tournaments, and a squeaky-clean reputation. It must be exhausting to be so perfect.

I wouldn't know. I'm far from it. More than that, I have zero inclination to pretend I am.

"Damn right, he's not," she agrees.

I glance up at the sun as it shines brightly. There's not a cloud in sight. Even through my sunglasses, the harsh illumination hurts my eyes. Normally, a day like this would make me want to tip my face to the cerulean-colored sky and soak up all the glorious rays.

That's not the case today.

If I didn't have dance class, I would be buried beneath a mountain of blankets in my bed. It's been more than a week since Colton blew my world to smithereens. And here I am, continuing to pick out the jagged pieces of shrapnel embedded in my skin. I'm still blown away that he had the audacity to break up with me.

Through text message.

Text!

The lousy bastard.

Who the hell does that?

Colton Montgomery, that's who.

I give my head a shake, needing to banish him from my brain. Dwelling on the situation won't do me any good. And it won't make the pain magically disappear. Although, it would be kind of nice if it did. I'm tired of thinking about it. Tired of being depressed and pissed off.

Mia squeezes my arm, and I realize that I've once again become ensnared in my own thoughts. "Sorry," I mutter, embarrassed by my inability to pull myself out of this misery, "what did you say?"

"I was wondering if you wanted to grab dinner tonight. Maybe pizza?" Her voice escalates with growing excitement. "Oh! There's a new Thai restaurant downtown that just opened. I've been dying to try it."

I grimace at the idea of eating either of those options. It's enough to make my belly revolt.

"No." Instead of admitting that I don't have much of an appetite, I say, "I'll probably hang out at the studio for a while and work on chore-ography. The showcase will be here before you know it, and I need all the extra rehearsals I can squeeze in."

It doesn't escape me that without dance, there wouldn't be a reason to drag my ass out of bed in the morning.

Or ever.

"Listen," Mia's voice turns hesitant, "I know you said you didn't want to talk about—"

"Good," I cut in promptly before she can meander too far down this pain-ridden road, "then we understand each other perfectly."

Her face falls, and her shoulders wilt. A heavy silence descends as we continue along the cement path that winds through campus.

It's on the tip of my tongue to apologize when she murmurs, "It might help you get over the breakup if you talk about it."

Absolutely not. Revealing just how much Colton hurt me won't help matters. It'll only make me look like an idiot for believing he was anything other than a player. Mia is my closest friend, and usually, I tell her everything, but I couldn't bring myself to share his parting words with her. It was way too humiliating.

Fuck him and his unicorn pussy comment.

Even the memory is enough to bring a hot sting of embarrassment to my cheeks.

Relief floods through me as the fine arts building comes into view. I appreciate Mia trying to be supportive, but the best thing I can do is put this whole ugly mess behind me. I want to forget we were ever together or that I gave him the time of day. The only way that will happen is to stop talking about him. And thinking about him. I want to focus all of my energies on things that matter. Like dance. Even the thought of losing myself in the choreography is enough to loosen the constriction gripping my chest, making it easier to breathe.

I keep my attention locked on the brick building in the distance. "I appreciate the offer, but I'm good."

"Okay," she mutters, not sounding the least bit convinced. "If you're sure."

"I am." Somehow, I manage to hoist my lips into a thin semblance of a smile. It's not one that stretches across my face, but still, I deserve credit for the effort.

A sigh escapes from Mia before she shrugs, hopefully giving up the crusade she's so intent on. "If you change your mind, I'll be here to listen." Just when I think that we've put the whole ugly matter behind us, she adds, "Bottling all that emotion up inside isn't healthy."

"Maybe not, but it's a hell of a lot better than sitting around and crying over a guy who isn't worth one damn tear."

I wouldn't mind keeping you in my back pocket and having a taste of it every once in a while. No strings attached, of course.

"That's not what I learned from Dr. Haskel."

Those quietly spoken words have everything inside me softening. Mia attended therapy with her parents after Brianna's death. Even though I would never ask, I can't help but wonder what good it did. It sure as hell didn't bring her sister back. And her family, for all their plastic smiles and pretending, are still fractured at the core. Her dad works a gazillion hours a week and is barely around. Julia, her mother, drowns herself in alcohol, anti-depressants, and shops like there's no tomorrow. Maybe she secretly wishes there wouldn't be. I can't necessarily blame her for that. What could be worse than losing a child?

Guilt explodes in me like a gunshot as I pull Mia into my arms and hug her tight. She's like my sister from another mister, and nothing will ever change that. Not time, distance, or assholes masquerading as boys with good intentions. "I realize you're trying to help, I really do, but I don't want to talk about Colton. Let me work through this breakup and process it in my own way."

Her muscles loosen. "But you're not working through anything. All you're doing is pretending that Colt—"

When I give her a steely-edged glare, she rolls her eyes and flattens her lips before doubling down on her stance. "All you're doing is pretending that the jerk who shall not be named was never in your life. How is that healthy?"

Healthy?

I want to laugh. Or maybe cry.

Dealing with this breakup in a *healthy* manner is the least of my concerns. I'm worried about spiraling into a deep depression I won't be able to claw my way out of. The truth of the matter is that I'm hanging on by my fingernails. I've crushed hard on Colton for years. That's not something you work through in a weekend. I'd given him my love, and it hadn't been enough. Instead, he'd tossed it back in my face and decided that he'd rather screw as many girls as possible.

Yesterday, I'd spotted him across campus by the Union, surrounded by a fawning crowd of groupies. Clearly, they were all celebrating his newly minted single status. I'm sure panties have been dropping left and right in jubilation.

I'd caught him mid-laugh with a smile curving his lips. Unconsciously, my feet had stopped moving as my heart cracked wide open. For the briefest of moments, our gazes had collided before he glanced away, dismissing me on the spot. The rejection, along with the way he'd moved on so effortlessly, cut right to the bone. How I'll get through the rest of this year—not to mention the next two—I have no idea.

I never thought I'd say this, but graduation can't come soon enough. I need to get as far away from him as possible. I'd briefly flirted with the idea of transferring universities, but that's not feasible. Wesley has the best dance program in the state, and I don't want to bale on Mia. More than that, I refuse to let him chase me away.

So, for the foreseeable future, I'm stuck here with the jerk who shall remain nameless.

"I'm not pretending," I mutter. "I'm choosing to move on and forget about him."

"Same thing."

"Not at all." Before she can argue, I add, "I really need to get to class." I give her a quick kiss on the cheek. "I'll see you tonight, all right?"

She nods. "Yup. Whatever I end up ordering, I'll make sure there's enough for both of us."

"You're the best." With that, I haul ass toward the fine arts building. Mia might think that I'm running away from my feelings, but she's mistaken. I'm simply putting them behind me and moving forward. What else am I supposed to do?

Once inside the studio, a puff of relief leaves my lips, and my shoulders loosen from around my ears. I didn't realize how tight my muscles had become until they relaxed. I drop my bag along the wall and peel off the scarf and jacket. I'm twenty minutes early, and there is only a handful of students in the room warming up at the barre or rehearsing steps.

The next to come off are the leggings and shirt until I'm stripped down to a black leotard and tights. I grab my shoes from my bag and slip them on my feet before settling on the floor and stretching. There's something comforting about the routine. Dazzling sunlight pours through the floor-to-ceiling windows as a tinge of sweat hangs in the air.

"*Bonjour*," Monsieur Dupre greets as he saunters through the entryway. He's dressed entirely in black from head to toe. And yes, he looks hot as fuck in a way that only attractive European men with an overabundance of confidence can pull off.

My hand rises in a wave as a smile trembles across my face when I think about Zoe propositioning him.

And his partner.

One of the girls on the floor hisses my name, and I blink back to awareness. She jerks her head toward the corner of the studio, where our instructor unwinds a scarf from around his neck. "Sorry." I press a hand to my chest and raise my voice. "Did you call me?"

"A word, *s'il vous plaît*."

"Of course." I pop to my feet and pad over to him.

A slight frown tugs at the corners of his lips as he scrutinizes my appearance. "You are well?"

I shift uncomfortably under his relentless stare. "Umm, yes." I'd rather shove bamboo beneath my fingernails than admit I'm upset over a guy. The number one rule in the studio is that outside bullshit stays where it belongs. *Outside*. We don't bring it into this space, allowing it to taint the creative energy of the dancers.

"*Très bien*." Before I can return the question, he says, "I assume you have submitted an application for the London Contemporary Dance School study program."

I draw my lower lip between my teeth and shake my head as embarrassment stains my cheeks. "No, I didn't." When he mentioned the highly sought-after program a few months ago, I'd kicked around the idea but never bothered to apply. I'd been drunk on my relationship with Colton, and the idea of leaving Wesley—and him—for an entire year hadn't even been a consideration. I'm ashamed to admit that I'd prioritized him above dance. Considering how we ended, that had been an epic mistake on my part.

Especially since all I'd been was unicorn pussy.

My fingernails bite into my palms as I straighten my shoulders.

His perfectly sculpted brows pinch together. "Why not?"

There's no way I can reveal the truth. The man would probably mutter in French before banishing me from the program altogether. "I didn't think I stood much of a chance against the competition." It's not a lie.

"The deadline is next week," he clips out with a glare that makes me feel three inches tall, "submit your application."

Properly chastised, I bob my head. "Yes, Monsieur."

When he remains silent, I scurry back to my spot on the floor. My heart pounds a steady tempo as I give serious consideration to the program in London.

Do I really have anything to lose by throwing my hat into the ring?

Not really. The odds of making it through the selection process are minuscule, and it'll give me something other than the obvious to focus on.

So...I guess in that regard, it's a win-win.

Chapter Ten

ALYSSA

One month later...

The muscles of my belly contract as I click on the email and skim over the first line. I'd mentally prepared myself for a—*we regret to inform you...blah, blah, blah.*

Instead, it reads—*Congratulations! You have been selected...*

I blink and scrutinize the first line for a second time, but the words remain the same. It still says congratulations.

Holy shit! How did this happen? I didn't think I had a snowball's chance in hell of being selected to attend LCDS. There were only a handful of spots, and the competition was killer. Without Monsieur Dupre practically forcing me to apply, I wouldn't have bothered. A potent concoction of excitement and fear bubble up inside me. As those thoughts swirl through my head, the dorm room door swings open, and Mia steps inside.

Her lips lift into a smile when she spots me at the desk near the window. "Hey! I didn't expect you back so soon."

"The professor cut our class short," I tell her. "I just walked in ten minutes ago."

With a huff of breath, she tosses her bag onto the bed before pulling off her jacket. "It's freezing out there." Her cheeks have pinkened from the walk across campus.

"Yeah," I agree, gaze flicking to the window and the thin blanket of snow that covers the ground, "it is." As far as I'm concerned, spring can't come soon enough.

Mia drops onto the bed next to her bag before pulling out her phone. "I'm glad your here. I found a few more apartments for us to check out. I know it's early, but we should try to find something before all the good ones get snatched up."

Shit.

Mia and I have discussed living off-campus since we were freshmen. We've already looked into a few places, but they were located further away from the university than convenient. It has to be within walking distance since parking on campus is a nightmare.

My gaze darts to the laptop screen. Only now do I realize that I haven't mentioned the LCDS exchange program to her.

I mean, why would I?

I'd assumed nothing would come of it. Except...now I've been accepted. And I'm supposed to leave in July. That's less than four months away. My belly drops to the bottom of my toes. It's like I'm sitting at the tippy top of a roller coaster, waiting to take that first plunge. Unconsciously, my hand settles over my lower abdomen.

There's no way I can turn down such an amazing opportunity to dance. Honestly, this couldn't have happened at a better time. Escaping from Wesley for the year is exactly what I need to get my head on straight and stop thinking about Colton. I can finally purge him from my system once and for all. There's got to be a few hot guys in London who can help with that, right?

Excitement bursts inside me like a bubble.

My gaze settles on Mia again, and some of my enthusiasm recedes.

How am I going to break the news to her? I feel like a real jerk for baling. We've had these plans for years. But...I can't stay here. For my own mental health, I need to get away from Colton.

"There's something I need to tell you," I blurt, unable to hold the news in any longer.

"You still want to look for something off-campus, right?" With a frown, she glances around the confined space. "Because I seriously don't think I can live in the dorms for another year. I need out."

"Yeah." I fall silent, unsure how to bring up the exchange program. "I mean, no."

Her brows snap together as she straightens on the bed. It's obvious from her expression that she has no clue where I'm going with this. "Oh my God, you want to live in the dorms again? Aren't you tired of such cramped quarters? It's like we're on top of each other all the time." Mia stares at me like I've grown a horn on my head. And why wouldn't she? I've been bitching about this place since day one. If we could have moved off campus immediately, I would have done it in a heartbeat, but it's university policy that freshmen and sophomores live in the residence halls.

Ugh. I'm making a complete mess of this.

I draw in a deep breath and hold it in my lungs for a moment before slowly releasing it back into the atmosphere. Maybe it would be easier if Mia reads the email for herself. Before I can rethink the decision, I grab my laptop from the desk and plop down next to her. "I received this today."

She shoots me a quizzical look before her gaze settles on the computer screen. A few beats of silence pass as her eyes widen, and she glances at me. I can almost see the wheels in her head spinning. "Wait a minute," her voice rises with each syllable that flies out of her mouth, *"you're doing a study abroad program next year?"*

My shoulders collapse under the heavy weight of her words. "I only applied because Monsieur Dupre insisted. I didn't actually think I'd make it." Steeling myself for her response, I force out the question, "Are you angry?" This month has been difficult enough. I don't think I can bear adding Mia's ire to the list.

"Angry?" As she shakes her head, some of the surprise falls away. "Of course, I'm not mad. Although, I wish you would have given me the heads up when you applied."

"Honestly, I didn't think I had a shot."

She frowns, annoyance sparking to life in her eyes. "That's the most ridiculous thing you've ever said. Why wouldn't you get accepted?"

Barely does she give me a chance to open my mouth before continuing, "You're an amazing dancer. They're lucky to have you."

Thick emotion wells in my throat as I set the computer aside and pull Mia into my arms. This right here is exactly why this girl is my bestie. I couldn't ask for a more supportive friend.

"As much as I'm going to miss you, I think it's an incredible opportunity."

"Really?" Hope rises inside me like a phoenix from ashes.

"Hell, yeah! I wish I could come with you. I'm so jealous!"

"You can visit!"

"Damn right I will," she says with a laugh. "Maybe I'll squat in your apartment. Or dorm. Or flat. Or whatever the heck they call it over there."

That would be so much fun. I wish it were a possibility. A pang of sadness fills me when I think about not seeing Mia's smiling face everyday. It's funny, my mother tried to dissuade me from living with my bestie when I announced during our senior year of high school that we were going to room together at college. She said that it was a good way to lose a friend. But that never happened. Instead, we're closer than ever.

And a year of separation won't change that.

As much as I've insisted that I'm over Colton, it's more wishful thinking on my part than anything else. It's been five weeks since the blond football player dumped my ass, and he's been spotted at several parties with his harem. Every time one of my so-called *friends* catches sight of him, I'm sent a barrage of photo evidence regarding how easily he was able to move on from our relationship. I finally told them to knock it off. Every damn picture was like a paper cut. Painful, yet not nearly enough to kill me.

Mia reaches over and lays a hand across mine before giving it a gentle squeeze. "Even though I'll miss the hell out of you, it's too amazing of an opportunity to pass up."

She's right. It is.

Now that all of this is out in the open, a fresh wave of excitement crashes over me.

I can't believe that I get to dance in London for an entire year!

With any luck, when I return, the blond football player will be nothing more than a distant memory.

Chapter Eleven

COLTON

Summer before junior year of college...

I pull my metallic gray 840i convertible BMW into Beck's circular driveway before shifting into park and leaving the car to idle. I shoot him a text to let him know that I'm outside waiting before drumming my fingers impatiently on the sleek leather steering wheel.

A couple of minutes tick by, and there's no sign of Beck. His truck is parked in the drive, and there are lights on inside the house, so I know damn well he's here. We've got plans tonight, and I'm impatient to get to them. We're supposed to meet up with a couple of chicks from high school. I fire off another text.

Let's move!

When there's nothing but stereo silence from his end, I slam out of the vehicle and stalk up the wide stairs to the massive front door before rapping my knuckles against the mahogany.

No answer.

I ring the bell and listen as it echoes throughout the house.

This is seriously ridiculous.

I peek in the side window but don't see any signs of life. My fingers go to the ornate handle and wiggle it, but it doesn't budge. Beck's parents are out of town for a couple of weeks, traveling somewhere in Europe.

Honestly, it would serve him right if I took off and left his ass sitting home. I would have zero problems entertaining the girls on my own. Wouldn't be the first time. Won't be the last.

As soon as an image of Alyssa pops into my head, I shove it away and curse under my breath. The girls are supposed to help me forget, not remind me of her.

It's totally messed up.

I glance around the darkened front yard before stalking around the side of the house. For all I know, he's hanging out by the pool. The guy's got a pretty sweet setup out back. As I step through the black iron gate, a splash of water catches my attention. No wonder Beck didn't respond to the texts. I open my mouth to tell him to get moving when I realize he's not alone.

He's got company of the female persuasion.

Looks like someone started the party without me.

Fucker.

Since the couple in the pool are going at it pretty hot and heavy, they don't notice me stalk closer. Close enough to get a good look at who he's making out with.

Well, well, well...isn't *this* an interesting turn of events.

Since I'll be damned if Beck is the only one who gets a little action this evening, I say obnoxiously, "Dude, I thought we had plans."

They splinter apart before Mia Stanbury blinks, looking all sorts of dazed and confused. I can't help the shit-eating grin that slides across my face. Not in a million years did I ever think I'd see the day that she willingly allowed Beck to lay hands, not to mention lips, on her.

The emotion that tumbles across her expression when she realizes she's been sucking face with her archnemesis—and that I'm here to witness it—is almost comical.

At least, I'm entertained by it.

"Why, hello there, Mia," I say, humor simmering in my voice, "can't say I expected to find you here."

When I was with Alyssa, I couldn't get the dark-haired girl to join us if she thought there was a remote possibility that Beck would make an appearance, and now look at her...

I'm a huge fan of irony. And this situation is chock-full of it.

Beck keeps his arms locked around her. Clearly, he's not in any hurry to let go.

"Colton," she mutters through stiff lips. Even with only the pool lights for illumination, hot color blooms in her cheeks. Any moment she'll burst into flames.

I stuff my hands in the pockets of my shorts and rock back on my heels as if I've got all the time in the world to stand around and shoot the shit with them. "So, what have you crazy kids been up to?"

As if I don't know...

I didn't think it was possible for her face to grow any rosier, but that's exactly what happens.

"Wait in the car," Beck snaps, "I'll be out in ten."

I have no idea what prompts me to say it, but the question shoots out of my mouth before I can stop it. "You gonna come out with us, Mia?" I pause for a beat. "I doubt the chicks we're supposed to hookup with tonight will appreciate that, but, oh well." I shrug. "Sucks for them."

Her eyes widen as she slaps her hands against Beck's chest, attempting to escape from his embrace. Fury flashes across his face as he levels a steely-edged stare at me.

Fine, I'll admit that it was a dick move.

"Dude," Beck growls, clearly pissed that I just dropped a bomb, "get the fuck out of here before I beat your ass."

I hold up my palms in a gesture of surrender. "Whatever. Don't get your panties in a bunch." Now that my work is done here, I swing away and head for the car. I can't resist calling over my shoulder as I pass through the gate, "You got ten. Wrap this shit up, and let's go."

Not waiting for a response, I stalk to the front of the stone mansion. He gets fifteen minutes, and then I'm out of here. Anger simmers in my veins as I slide onto the butter-soft leather. I'm not oblivious. I know Beck has been carrying a torch for Mia. I'm also well aware that he'll make good on his threat to give me a beat down for jacking up his night once he gets out here. There's a part of me that's spoiling for a fight.

After ten more minutes, I fire off a third and final text. I'm losing my patience. Scratch that, I'm fresh out. Hell, for all I know, he and Mia are still going at it. Although, she was pretty pissed off when I walked away, so that's doubtful.

You know what?

Screw this, I'm out of here.

I jam the key in the ignition as Beck yanks open the door and slides onto the seat beside me. "Took you long enough," I bite out. "I was just about to take off."

"Too bad you didn't do that when you realized I was busy," he shoots back, clearly irritated.

"Give me a fucking break," I snort. "We both know Mia can't stand your damn ass. What were you gonna do? Fuck her in the pool? You might not realize it, but I did you a solid. That girl would have hated you even more than she already does."

He presses his lips together and glares in stony silence.

Here's the thing—he knows I'm right. The tension gathered inside me loosens when he fails to respond.

A grin slides across my face as I cup my fingers to my ear. "I'm sorry, what's that?" I pause for a beat. *"You're welcome, Colton? Thanks for saving me from myself?"*

"I wouldn't go that far," he mutters, slouching on the leather and staring straight ahead.

"Please. I couldn't get Mia to come out with us if there was even a slight chance you would show up." I cock my head. "Doesn't that tell you something?"

Of course it does, but Beck is nowhere near ready to acknowledge it.

"Just drive," he mutters.

"You know I'm right," I say smugly, starting up the engine and squealing out of the driveway before punching the gas. "I hate to be the one to break it to you, but it's never gonna happen with that girl. You need to move the fuck on."

He slumps further into the black leather. "Maybe," he bites out, "you should do yourself a favor and take your own advice for a change."

My jaw tightens as I stare at the dark ribbon of road stretched out in front of us. "Don't think I'm not trying," I mumble. "Every damn night, I'm trying to get over that girl." There's no point in specifying which one I'm talking about.

He knows. Just like he knows why I've been in a shit mood for the last five months. It doesn't take a rocket scientist to figure out.

"You screw so much," he says, "that I'm surprised your dick hasn't shriveled up and fallen off. Remind me to buy you some balm for your birthday."

A hint of a smile lifts my lips, although it doesn't quite reach my eyes. "Don't I know it, brother."

A heavy silence falls over us as I crank the steering wheel and turn onto the main stretch of road. It's on the tip of my tongue to ask about Alyssa. I haven't seen her around for a while. And she blocked my ass on all her socials. Which...I can't exactly blame her for. But tell me how I'm supposed to stalk that chick if I can't see what she's up to?

I try to swallow down the words, but they refuse to budge. It's only a matter of time before they burst free.

One second slips by.

Then another.

"Did Mia mention Lys at all?"

Fuck me. I've done my best to scrub that girl from every part of my life. Evicting her from my head and heart has turned out to be more complicated than I assumed.

Beck scrutinizes me silently before tossing a crumb my way. Not that I deserve it with the bullshit I just pulled. He's a better friend than I am. "Guess she's studying abroad in London for the year."

His answer takes me by surprise. I blink and stare straight ahead as my lips tug down at the corners. "No shit?"

"Yup."

My heart constricts. It's like there is a vise squeezing it.

"Huh." That's all I'm capable of forcing out.

It's weird to think of Alyssa not being here. At the same school. In the same town. In the same damn state. Hell, the country. Even when I was trying to ignore her, she was here. I could keep an eye on her. I caught glimpses of her around campus when she didn't know I was looking.

And now she's gone.

A heavy pit settles in my gut. I'm so fucking tempted to pelt him with more questions. This time, I keep them buried deep inside. In the months since our breakup, I've done my damnedest to move on. It hasn't worked. So maybe...maybe this is for the best.

Out of sight, out of mind...right?

Let's hope that turns out to be the case.

Chapter Twelve

ALYSSA

March of junior year...

Jack grabs hold of my hand and laces our fingers together before flashing me a cheeky smile as we take in the shops on Oxford Street. The skies are overcast, but the weather is seasonable for this time of year in London, which means it's about fifty degrees. We're both bundled up in jackets. I can't help but return his easy expression.

Effortless.

That would be the perfect word to describe my relationship with him.

He's handsome, charming, and so very British.

I've turned into something I never expected to be—a cliché. I could listen to him talk all day long. And I flipping love when he uses words like—*bullocks, bloody*, and *knackered*. It makes me laugh every time. And the guy knows it, which is exactly why he does it. He gets a little twinkle in his dark eyes when my lips start to twitch.

And he's a footballer.

Well, I mean soccer player. In England, it's called football, and it's huge. Like nothing I could have imagined. One of the big rivalries is Arsenal versus Tottenham. Having been born and bred on American football, I never paid much attention to professional soccer. A few high school games here and there, but that was the extent of it.

When Jack realized I was totally clueless about the sport, he took the time to explain the rules, and over the months, I've grown to enjoy it. It's fast-paced, and the fans are rabid. I would pit them against the most diehard football fans any day. He even bought me a scarf to hold at the matches we've attended when the team jogs onto the pitch.

And watching him sprint across the field certainly isn't a hardship. He's thick and muscular and reminds me nothing of a certain someone else.

We met at a pub while I was out with my roommate. Much to Jack's chagrin, I friend-zoned him almost immediately. After that, I noticed we would end up at a lot of the same parties, and slowly, we started spending time together.

It's been...nice.

Different than what I'm used to. I don't have to chase Jack to get his attention. I already have it. He seems to have eyes only for me. From the very beginning, he's made his intentions clear. He doesn't play games, and he's not out screwing every girl who spreads her legs.

It's a refreshing change of pace.

We've been teetering on the brink of...*something* for the last couple of weeks, but I'm not ready to delve into another relationship just yet —especially when my time in London will be drawing to a close. Even though I try not to dwell on Colton, there are times when he invades my brain, slyly wrapping himself around my heart and squeezing tight. He's turned out to be a difficult habit to kick—even when we're an ocean apart.

But then again, what did I really expect? I've had feelings for the guy ever since my sophomore year of high school. It's unrealistic to assume they would vanish over night simply because I wanted them to.

The moment I realize the direction my mind has wandered, I shove those thoughts away and squeeze Jack's hand, wanting to ground myself in the moment. Colton has been relegated to my past, and that's exactly where he needs to stay. Jack, on the other hand, is my present.

Possibly my future.

Even though everything remains uncertain, I'm excited to figure it out.

Chapter Thirteen

COLTON

August of senior year...

"Hold the elevator!" I call out, forcing myself to jog through the lobby of our apartment building. Sure, I could take the stairs, we only live on the third floor, but I'm wiped. We've been practicing on the turf under the blazing, hot sun twice a day for the last couple of weeks. Every muscle in my body is screaming for mercy. A fifteen-minute soak in an ice bath wasn't nearly enough to undo the damage Coach inflicted this morning.

The man is a total sadist.

Just as the metal doors are about to close, they bounce open again. I hasten my step, jumping on board, as a huff of relief escapes from my lips. My plans for the afternoon involve my queen-size bed and a long nap to recharge before heading back to the field for round two.

"Thanks." I glance at the lone occupant inside. There are three oversized boxes stacked in her arms, concealing her face. All I'm able to make out are curvy hips and long, sun-kissed legs peeking out from the bottom of her black athletic shorts.

A quick glance at the control panel reveals that the button for the third floor has already been hit.

"No problem," she says, shifting the boxes around in her arms to get a better grip.

As weary as I am, I can't just stand here and let her struggle with the containers. Without a doubt, I can be an ass, but my stepmother, Jenna, did attempt to drill a few manners into my head. "Looks like you've got quite the load there. Want some help?"

"Nah," she says with a soft grunt as she moves the boxes again, "I'm in the home-stretch."

"You sure? I don't mind giving you a hand," I offer for the second time.

"Don't worry about it. I've got them."

I lean against the wall of the elevator and fold my arms across my chest. "Must be moving day." Over the past week, there have been a number of Wesley students getting situated in the building for the upcoming academic year.

"Yup, I've been at it now for a couple of hours," she confirms.

I glance at the panel on the wall next to the door. "You're on the third floor?"

"Right again," she says with a laugh. It's deep and throaty.

There's something oddly familiar about her voice. My brows draw together as I wrack my brain. Fuck...I really hope we haven't hooked up. That always makes for awkward run-ins. Before I can investigate the situation any further, the elevator jolts to a halt and the doors slide open, spitting us out onto the third floor. I slap my palm against the frame of the elevator so the doors can't slide shut as she steps off the platform and into the hallway.

As she takes a few steps, the top box wobbles, and I spring into action, grabbing it from her. Maybe she doesn't want my help, but she's getting it.

"Thanks!"

Our gazes lock, and my footsteps falter, surprised at who I find buried behind the containers. "Mia?"

She looks equally stunned as her gaze widens and her body stills. "Colton." There's a pause as she forces out a greeting. "Hey."

Silence descends as we stare. It's like neither of us know what to say. Just when the situation turns awkward, she clears her throat. "So...you live here?" An unenthusiastic note tinges her voice, and I realize she's probably praying that turns out not to be the case.

Unfortunately, I'm going to have to burst that bubble.

"Yeah." I point to the end of the hall. "Last door on the left."

Her lips sink at the corners as she reluctantly stares in that direction. *"Oh."*

Mia and I grew up together. I've known her since elementary school. We've never had a problem, although she definitely became more standoffish after my breakup with Alyssa. It's not like I can blame her for feeling that way. I guess that's what happens when you dick over someone's best friend. You become a permanent fixture on their shit list.

I jerk my head in the same direction. "Your place is over there, too?"

"Yeah." Her lips do more than just sink at the edges. They bow into a full-blown frown. Every thought and emotion is there to see as it flickers across her expressive face.

We both realize why this has the potential to be a powder keg of a situation.

Don't ask about her, asshole.

Don't you dare do it.

It's been eighteen months since our breakup, but who's counting?

By now, I should have moved on. Alyssa Williams should be nothing more than a blip in my past. One of the many girls that I've screwed. But that's the last thing she'll ever be. No matter how much I've tried to eradicate her from my brain, she's still there, gnawing away gleefully at the back of it. What I've come to understand during the time Alyssa has been gone is that she will never be *just* a girl.

She'll always be *the* girl.

The one I forced away because I was too chicken shit to open myself up and risk being hurt again. If I have any brains whatsoever, I'll assist Mia to her door and pretend there isn't a past sitting uncomfortably between us.

Easier said than done.

"So...Alyssa?" I wince as the words shoot from my mouth. "Is she back yet?" The possibility of her staying in London for our last year at Wesley has my heart constricting painfully in my chest. I hate to admit it, but I've been mentally counting down the weeks until her return. I'm not even sure what the point is. After the way I blew up our relationship, it's doubtful she'll ever look at me again, much less engage in idle conversation.

It's not a surprise when Mia's expression becomes shuttered, and she glances away. Her lips press into a tight line, and I wonder if she'll brush off the question.

Hell, maybe she'll tell me to go fuck myself.

Anything is possible.

After a long stretch of silent moments, she finally grumbles, "Not yet."

"But she'll return to Wesley for the fall semester?"

She huffs out a breath. "Yeah."

If Mia thinks I'm at all deterred by her begrudgingly given responses, she's mistaken. "Is she living here, too?"

The dark-haired girl's brows slide together as she glares. "Yeah. Are you finished with your grand inquisition? Can I move on with my life now?"

Once I've confirmed Alyssa's living arrangements, everything inside me loosens, and I can finally breathe again. Air rushes into my lungs. Until this very moment, I didn't realize how oxygen deprived I'd become. It feels like I've been submerged beneath the water indefinitely. Only now am I able to fight my way to the surface and break through to the other side.

Mia mutters something indecipherable under her breath and stalks down the hallway before I can grill her for more information. Since my legs are almost twice as long as hers, it only takes a moment to catch up. She stops one door short of mine before shifting the boxes in her arms and attempting to dig around in her front pocket.

"Here, give them to me."

"No, thanks," she huffs, clearly irritated by my presence. Usually, this kind of ire is reserved solely for Beck.

"Come on, Mia. Don't be stubborn. Let me help."

She shoots me another steely-eyed glare. "I suppose giving in is the quickest way to get rid of you."

"There you go." I flash her a grin. "Just focus on the positives."

She snorts before rising to her tiptoes and stacking the containers on top of the one I'm already holding. Then she slides the key from her pocket before shoving it in the lock and turning the handle.

With her back propping open the door, she stretches out her arms. "I'll take it from here."

"I got it. Just tell me where you want them." Feeling nosy as fuck, I saunter into the apartment.

She points to the living room/dining room combination. "Set them down anywhere over there."

I do as she asks before straightening to my full height and glancing around. There are boxes stacked everywhere. I'm overwhelmed just looking at the place. It will take weeks to put away all this stuff. Even though I know she'll turn me down flat, I can't resist throwing out the offer. "You want some help with all of this? I've got a few hours to kill before I need to head back to the stadium."

She releases a long breath, all the while surveying the cardboard shantytown that has sprung up on the outskirts of the living room. For a moment, I almost wonder if she's actually considering the question. But then she shakes her head. "No, it's fine. I'll just take it a little bit at a time."

I shift my weight from one foot to the other. "You sure? I'm willing to lend a hand."

Her voice softens, losing some of its rigidity. "I appreciate the offer, but no."

Since I wasn't expecting a different outcome, I shrug. Hell, I'm kind of surprised she didn't toss me out on my ear as soon as I set the boxes on the floor. "All right then." I meander to the door. "Guess now that you live here, I'll see you around."

As I cross over the threshold, Mia's voice stops me in my tracks. "Colton?"

I turn and meet her steady gaze. "You should know that Alyssa has moved on."

And just like that, I'm shoved beneath the glassy surface of the water again and can't breathe. Mia's words shouldn't cause me a moment of heartache. If anything, relief should be pumping through my body.

That's the outcome I was hoping for, right?

It's the reason I pushed her away in the first place.

But...that's not the way I feel.

Unable to utter a sound, I jerk my head into a tight nod before slipping from the apartment and into the hallway.

Chapter Fourteen

COLTON

"We're late," Beck mutters, hastening his step as we move through the lobby of our apartment building before pushing through the glass doors and into the sunshine, "and I'm in no mood to run suicides."

That makes two of us. We've done more than enough of that this summer. My body already feels battered and bruised, and it's only August. Coach came back in July when training camp started up with all these new workout regimes. I'm not sure if he's trying to intimidate the freshman, but I don't like it.

Not one damn bit.

Added to that, it's hot as hades out here. And it will feel a thousand degrees hotter when we're running plays on the turf. There are times when the field actually looks hazy in the afternoon sun. A few of the guys have already passed out. That's Division I football for you. Pussies need not apply.

I'll tell you this, deciding not to enter the draft was the right decision. As much as I love football, and I'll miss the sport, I'm ready to move on to the next phase of my life. I glance at Beck, knowing he doesn't feel the same way. He'll enter the NFL draft this year and, more than likely, be a first-round pick. I can't wait to see what team he signs with. I'm stoked for the guy.

I'm knocked out of those thoughts when a female voice catches my attention. My head whips up, knowing exactly who it belongs to.

Alyssa.

My footsteps falter as my gaze locks on her. That's all it takes for the air to get clogged in my lungs. I don't know how it's possible, but she's even more beautiful than I remember. My gaze roves over every part of her. From the top of her blond head to the tips of her toes, I catalog all the little details that have changed. The sleeker haircut that frames her face. The willowy form that somehow looks longer and leaner. She doesn't resemble the same girl who carved out a place in my heart. The one who chased after me throughout high school and the first couple of years of college. There's something different about her. An air of sophistication that wasn't there to begin with.

From all the luggage being dragged up the walkway, my guess is that Mia just picked her up from the airport.

"Well, this should be interesting," Beck mutters under his breath.

It's almost laughable that I'd thought our time apart might have dulled the feelings that have always festered beneath the surface where she's concerned. If anything, they're stronger than ever and trying to break free. For the first time in eighteen months, my blood pumps through my veins with renewed energy.

A heartbeat later, she becomes aware of my presence. Her gaze settles on me, and the easy-going expression falls away from her face as if it had never been there to begin with. Her blue eyes turn stormy. If my feelings haven't softened over time, neither have hers. That realization is slammed home when Alyssa grabs hold of Mia's arm and yanks her to a halt.

There's no disguising the wrath in her voice as she snaps, "What the hell is *he* doing here?"

My unrelenting stare leaves her bristling with anger.

"Right," Mia glances nervously between us before admitting quietly, "I, ah, meant to tell you about that."

"About what?" Her jaw locks as if bracing herself for catastrophic news. "What didn't you tell me about?"

"They also live here," her friend blurts, shifting her stance.

There's a beat of silence before Alyssa says through stiff lips, "I really hope you're joking."

"Sorry, Lys," the dark-haired girl whispers. "When I signed the rental agreement, I had no idea they lived here or that we're neighbors."

Alyssa's eyes widen. Any moment, they're going to fall right out of her head and roll on the ground near her feet. *"What?"*

Mia winces as Alyssa's sharp voice cracks through the air.

I don't realize I'm on the move or that I've closed the distance between us until I grind to a halt a few feet from where she stands. The temptation to reach out and pull her into my arms is almost overwhelming. It's been way too long since I've touched her. Unfortunately, I know exactly how that would go over, and it's not well.

Alyssa glares through narrowed eyes. Color flares to life in her cheeks, giving them a flushed look. When she remains silent, it occurs to me that if I want our relationship to be different, I need to make the first move. In a way, it feels like I've been waiting for this moment for a long time.

"Hey, Lys." Everything inside me warms as her gaze flicks to mine. I have no idea if I can make this right between us, but I want to try.

If it were possible to wipe away the past and start over again, I would do it in a heartbeat. Am I delusional enough to think that a simple conversation will undo the pain I inflicted?

Hell, no.

This is Alyssa Williams we're talking about. The girl has a temper. What I'm fully expecting is that she'll bite my head off—kind of like a female praying mantis after they've mated. But I'm willing to swallow my pride and allow it to happen. Anything that will get us on the rocky road to making amends.

Much to my surprise, that's not what transpires.

Instead, she says, voice full of ice, "Did you hear that?" Eyes wide, she glances around as if searching the area. "It almost sounds like a ghost from boyfriends' past."

My brows rise as a frown pinches my expression. She wants to give me the silent treatment and pretend I don't exist?

Fine, I deserve it.

I glance at Mia to get a read on her thoughts. She jerks her shoulders and for a second, my heartbeat stutters as her words from two weeks ago ring unwantedly through my head.

You should know that Alyssa has moved on.

What if that's true?

All this girl wanted to do was love me, and I stomped all over her heart and ran away like a little bitch. Looking back, I'm embarrassed by my own immature behavior. My tongue darts out to moisten my lips as I make another attempt to break through her icy veneer. What I don't know is how deep her cool exterior runs and if it's possible to drill down past it.

"It's really good to see you, Lys." When she continues to avoid eye contact, I decide to take my life into my own hands by stepping closer and pulling her into my arms. For a sliver of a moment, my mind tumbles back to what it felt like to hold her any time I wanted.

Her body goes whipcord tight as a growl of protest emanates from deep within her chest, and then she's fighting her way out of my arms like I'm a serial killer trying to wrestle her to a white van. Once Alyssa breaks free, she shoves me away before straightening her shirt and spearing me with a steely-edged glare that would shrivel the balls off most guys. With a huff, she turns her attention to Beck, who watches the show we're treating him to with an amused expression.

My guess is that he's loving this. Usually, he's the one intent on making an ass out of himself. And yeah, when the shoe is on the other foot, I derive a lot of enjoyment out of it.

"Hello, Beckett. It's nice to see you." Now that Alyssa is no longer addressing me, her voice softens considerably as she flashes a megawatt smile in his direction.

A kernel of unwanted jealousy explodes in the pit of my belly even though I know damn well I have nothing to be concerned about. Alyssa and Beck have been friends for years. But still...I don't like her looking at him like that—especially when she can't be bothered to give me the time of day.

"Did Mia happen to mention the welcome home party I'm having this Saturday at Bang Bang?" she asks.

The temptation to lay hands on her pounds through me. Instead of giving in to the urge, I keep them to myself.

"Feel free to stop by if you're not busy," Alyssa adds.

Humor flares to life in Beck's green gaze as he slants a look toward the dark-haired girl. "Nope, she didn't mention it." Yeah, there's a reason for that. Mia can't stand Beck. It's doubtful she would spit in his mouth if he were dying of thirst. Then again...I did catch them getting it on in Beck's pool a year ago. So, it's altogether possible I'm mistaken about that.

Mia's lips sink into a frown as she gives her best friend a bit of side-eye. Alyssa doesn't bother to glance in her direction. I have a hunch the invitation is payback.

"Hmm," Alyssa continues with a small frown, "that's strange. She must have *forgotten* to mention the party to you the same way she *forgot* to mention that a certain someone who shall remain nameless is my new neighbor."

Yup, most definitely retribution.

Mia's eyes narrow as if she, too, has arrived at the same conclusion.

Unable to remain silent any longer, I blurt, "Hey, what about me? Don't I get an invite?"

By the sparks of blue anger that flash in her eyes, I'm guessing that would be a negative. When she remains silent, I give her my most charming smile—the one that can melt the panties right off a girl—and attempt to put the past behind us. "How about for old times' sake?"

I get zero reaction.

Any power I'd once wielded over her has vanished. It's a frightening realization. Even though I'm the one who opened my hand and let her slip through my fingers, all I want to do is reel her back in.

Alyssa tilts her head and glances around owlishly. "It's so strange the way I keep hearing something."

Frustration bubbles up inside me. Maybe I have no right to feel it or be irritated by her behavior, but that doesn't stop the hot licks of emotion from flooding through me.

Tired of being ignored, I say, "Really, Lys?" I pause for a beat before adding something I *know* will solicit a reaction from her. "You're acting like a child."

Boom. Mission accomplished.

If I'd wanted her attention, I now have it in spades. She goes off like a firework on the fourth of July. Thunderclouds erupt on Alyssa's pretty face as she wheels around to face me. Two steps bring her close enough to drill a finger into my chest.

Well...at least she's touching me of her own volition. That's got to be a step in the right direction.

Then again, maybe not.

Fury vibrates off her in heavy, suffocating waves. "*I'm the child?*" Her voice escalates with every word that she bites out. "That's rich! You dumped my ass because you couldn't keep your dick in your pants! Don't you *dare* turn this around on me!" The people passing by on the sidewalk in front of the building stop and stare. "You and I are *not* friends. We will *never* be friends! I was an idiot for thinking you were anything other than a *manwhore!*"

When I remain silent, the atmosphere around us crackles with explosive energy. It's like an impending lightning storm. Any moment, I'm going to get fried.

Remorse nearly swallows me whole as tears prick Alyssa's eyes, giving them a glassy appearance. She blinks back the moisture and glances around as if only now realizing that her outburst has drawn unwanted attention. A dull red color seeps into her cheeks.

She meets their inquisitive stares with a snarl. "Move it along! Show's over. There's nothing to see here."

An apology sits on the tip of my tongue. Before I can push it out, Mia grabs Alyssa's luggage and drags it to the building. Beck scrambles to open the glass door before the two girls disappear inside the lobby. And I'm left standing there like a slack-jawed dumbass.

Once the door closes firmly behind them, Beck glances at me with a raised brow.

"Well," he says, running his fingers along his shadowed jaw, "that could have gone better."

I grimace at the understatement. Any hope that my past transgressions might be forgiven go up in flames.

Or, more accurately, a dumpster fire fueled by a drum of gasoline.

Chapter Fifteen

ALYSSA

Oh my God!

What the hell just happened?

Emotion churns through me as Mia shoves the key into the lock and twists the handle before dragging my bags inside our brand-new apartment. The confrontation with Colton has left me shaken and out of sorts. Was I really under the delusion that it would be possible to ease back into life at Wesley? That I could take my time, adjust a bit, and find my bearings before having to come face-to-face with him? I glance at my phone, noting that I haven't even been on American soil for a full hour before we had a blow-up.

Ugh.

That encounter couldn't have gone any worse.

After my time in London, I'd convinced myself I was over him—that I'd detoxed the guy from my heart. Only now do I realize that it was nothing more than wishful thinking on my part, or I wouldn't have gone off the rails like a complete psycho. I wince, remembering the avid faces watching from the sidelines. A few spectators had been on the verge of grabbing a bowl of popcorn and pulling up a lawn chair to enjoy the show.

On a positive note, it's doubtful I'll have to worry about Colton pestering me in the near future. Or anyone else who witnessed that debacle. I'm sure my new neighbors will give me a wide berth and avoid me like a case of the clap.

One year. That's all I have to endure until graduation. Then we'll go our separate ways, and I'll never have to see him again.

The adrenaline pumping through my veins dissipates, leaving exhaustion behind to fill the void. It takes every last ounce of strength to muscle my luggage into the small entryway and slam the door closed.

With a huff of breath, I glance around our new digs. I'd been so excited by the photos and virtual tour Mia had sent. It seemed almost unbelievable that we had all this space to ourselves. No more dorm life! Or teeny tiny flat.

Although, given what just transpired outside, I would happily exchange this place for a dorm. How am I going to coexist in the same building with Colton Montgomery?

I trudge into the sun-filled living room before collapsing onto a chair. Another wave of exhaustion crashes over me. I don't think I've slept for a solid twenty-four hours. There had been so much that needed to be packed up and too many people to hug and kiss goodbye. As excited as I was to return to Wesley, I was sad to leave all the new friends I'd made behind—especially since I have no idea when I'll see them again.

Almost gingerly, Mia settles on the couch across from me. A flicker of unease fills her expression as concern gathers in her eyes. "I'm really sorry, Lys. I meant to tell you about Colton on the ride home from the airport, but I didn't know how to do it." She jerks her shoulders. "When I toured the building and then signed the rental lease a few weeks later, I had no idea he lived here."

My gaze meanders to the patio door that leads to a small balcony. I'd been over the moon when she'd stepped outside with her phone and panned the area. The idea of being able to sit outdoors on a balmy night and study in the fresh air seemed almost extravagant.

And now?

Not even that little perk can bring a smile to my lips because all I can think about is that Colton will be here, too. I'll run into him in the hallways. I'll have a first-class seat to the groupies he entertains. That thought is enough to make me nauseous. A humorless chuckle bubbles up in my throat. It seems ridiculous that I'd actually convinced myself I was over him. Or that I'd moved on with my life when clearly that is not the case.

"It's fine." Now that the brightest part of my anger has drained away, guilt rushes in to swamp me. "Sorry for being such a raving bitch and inviting Beck to the party."

She shakes her head as a groan slips free.

It only makes me feel worse. Mia renting an apartment in the same building as Colton was an unfortunate coincidence. Me inviting Beck to the welcome home party, however, was not.

I clear my throat and add in a hopeful tone, "It's always possible he won't show up."

Mia snorts before leveling a disbelieving stare in my direction. "I think we both know he'll be there."

She's right, we do.

Beck has always had a not-so-secret thing for my bestie. Mia, on the other hand, wants nothing to do with the guy, which is a challenge since they grew up together, live next door to one another, and their parents are good friends, which means they end up spending holidays and vacations together.

As easy on the eyes as Beck is, I can't blame her for keeping him at a distance. He's a player, and Mia has experienced enough pain in her life to willingly invite more. I might have been gone for a year, but I can't imagine that much has changed where Beck Hollingsworth is concerned.

Unlike me, Mia knows better than to try and tame a bad boy.

"We could always look for another apartment and, if we find something, try to get out of the lease," she says, breaking into my thoughts.

I glance around the newly decorated space. I like what Mia has done with the place. Already, after only being here for two weeks, the apartment looks homey. It would be such a pain in the ass to move again. Not to mention, I really do love that balcony.

Am I really going to allow Colton Montgomery to chase me away from here?

Nope. I refuse to give him the satisfaction. Decision made, I blow out a breath and shake my head.

Mia's shoulders loosen from around her ears as a tentative smile curves her lips. "Don't worry. I'm sure we'll barely see him. You're busy with dance, and his season is just beginning. You'll be like two ships passing in the night."

You know what?

She's probably right. I've got nothing to worry about.

And if Colton has any brains whatsoever, he'll avoid me like his life depends on it.

Because guess what?

It does.

Chapter Sixteen

COLTON

"Montgomery, get your ass off the field!" Coach barks when I fumble yet another pass. "Kwiatkowski, take his place!"

Fuck.

I need to get my shit together before I get pulled permanently from the line-up. Instead of making eye contact with Beck, I stare at the turf and jog off the field. I already know what I'll find in his eyes, and that's a—*what the hell is going on with you* look. I can't blame him for it either.

The last couple of practices have turned out to be a shitshow. Passes I should be catching with ease are getting dropped, missed, or slipping right through my fingers. On one of the last plays, I actually tripped over my own damn feet. If you didn't know better, you'd think I had never seen a football, much less held one in my hands.

Ever since I stepped foot on the field when I was a kid, my game has been consistent. I don't have high-highs or low-lows. I'm a solid player. Dependable. Coaches know this. My teammates know it. Beck knows it as well. I'm always in position, ready to catch whatever my QB throws my way.

Except today.

And yesterday.

Not to mention the day before that.

Now that I think about it, my game has been off for the last week —specifically since my run-in with Alyssa. I can't stop thinking about her or searching for her. I'm like a stalker, hanging around the building, trying to catch sight of her.

Most people, the ones who know jack about football, think the game is all brute strength and physicality, but that's not true. There's a mental component. And that's where I'm falling short. My head is no longer in the game. It's wrapped up in my ex. Unless I can turn things around on the field, I'll be riding the pine for the foreseeable future. And that's never happened before.

Coach ignores me for the remainder of practice while Kwiatkowski, our second-string wide receiver, runs through a handful of plays with Beck. And wouldn't you know it, the junior receiver catches every damn pass thrown to him. It only compounds the feelings of powerlessness already wreaking havoc on me. I've been first-string since I stepped foot on campus freshman year. My spot has never been in question.

Now it feels like I could lose everything I've worked for in an instant. By the time Coach blows his whistle at the end of a two-hour practice, my head is a mess. I need to get out of here and figure out how I'm going to fix this problem.

Once in the locker room, I keep to myself. I'm not in the mood to joke around with these guys. Even though I remain silent, Beck doesn't take the hint. Instead of giving me a wide berth, he drops onto the bench and peels off his jersey before tossing it in the locker.

I feel the heaviness of his gaze burning a hole through me. He might not give voice to all the questions swirling through his brain, but I hear them loud and clear. Beck and I have been playing ball together since we were kids. We recognize each other's tells and quirks. Half the time, I know what play he'll run before he does. The guy never has to seek me out on the field. I instinctively know where I need to be and get into position. As far as football is concerned, we have some kind of weird mental connection going on. It's what makes us so good together.

It's just another reason the last couple of practices are screwing with my head even more than Alyssa. Sure, everybody is entitled to an off day. It goes with the territory. But this has turned into more of a slump, and that scares the fuck out of me.

Especially with the season looming right around the corner.

What if I can't turn it around in time?

This is my last year at Wesley. The goal has always been to go out on a high note with a winning season. I want to bring home a conference championship before taking my rightful place alongside my father in the personal finance company he founded. These are my glory days, the ones I'll look back at with longing and fondness when I'm stuck sitting behind a desk for twelve hours a day, trading stocks and shoring up client portfolios. At this rate, I'll be relieved they're over.

I keep my gaze focused straight ahead. The last thing I want to do is field any questions or talk about the obvious elephant in the room. Everyone knows that once you do that, it becomes real. There's no shoving the genie back in the lamp. With rough fingers, I rip off my jersey and toss it on the bench. Agitation wafts off me in heavy, suffocating waves. I'm all but choking on it.

The rowdy locker room turns quiet as Coach stalks through with his Wesley Warriors ball cap pulled low over his eyes and a clipboard clenched in his hand. Air gets wedged in my lungs as I wait for what's coming down the pike.

As if I don't know...

"*Montgomery*," he barks, "get your ass in my office as soon as you're dressed."

I jerk my head into a tight nod but keep my lips pressed together.

Well, shit. This isn't good.

Coach Taylor glares at the group of half-naked guys and barks out a few more victims. When he's done, he slams the door to his office with so much force that it rattles on its hinges.

Devon Baker, a three-hundred-pound lineman, laughs, "Better bring some lube with you, Montgomery. Doesn't look like he's in the mood to give it to you gently."

Like I don't know that?

I glare at Baker before giving him the finger.

Our first game against Tennessee is in two weeks. If I can't pull my crap together, there's no way Coach will allow me to step foot on the field. They're a tough team with a powerhouse of an offensive line. The thought of cooling my ass on the bench while Kwiatkowski takes my place makes me gut sick.

Beck clears his throat, drawing my attention to him. "So—"

"Don't even say it, man." I fall silent and rip off the remaining pads. It's like they're choking the life out of me. I've never felt that way before. I don't understand why I'm failing at something I've always excelled at.

"Say what?" he asks nonchalantly, continuing to strip off his sweat-soaked apparel.

Even though it's uncomfortable, I admit through stiff lips, "That my game is off." Acknowledging the truth is like a punch to the gut. Expected, but still a surprise.

For the first time since we've entered the locker room, I give Beck a bit of side-eye to get a read on his expression. It's just as I suspected. Concern mingled with confusion. Exactly what I don't want to deal with. I've always found it easier to suppress my feelings and shove them deep down inside where they can't see the light of day.

Keep it moving.

That's my motto.

I do my best not to dwell on the reason this is happening. My hope is that if I ignore the problem long enough, it'll work itself out. That's what I've done all my life—ignored the bad shit and focused on the future, and I've been just fine. So why isn't it working now? Why are the wheels falling off when I need them to stay put? This can't be how I go out.

It just can't be.

I need to get this situation figured out and fast before it becomes any more of an issue.

Beck shrugs, downplaying my plunging spiral. "Wasn't going to mention it."

I almost snort.

Yeah, right.

"Good," I say with a grunt. Unable to help myself, I shoot an anxious glance toward Coach's office. My voice drops before I reluctantly admit, "For once in his life, Baker is right. I'd better grab some lube. Coach is going to ream my ass."

Beck flicks his gaze toward the inner sanctum.

Nik Taylor is one of the toughest coaches you'll find in Division I football. He runs his program like a tight ship. If he's willing to give one hundred percent to his team, he expects his players to do the same in return. If you're not willing to bleed for the guys standing shoulder to shoulder with you on the field, there's no place for you on this roster. Even though I have no intention of entering the NFL draft, I wanted to play for the best. With the best. Against the best.

Now I don't feel worthy of playing alongside these men. It's the worst fucking feeling in the world.

"Please," Beck snorts. "Baker is a bonehead. Don't listen to a word that comes out of his yap."

That might be true, but I have a hunch that he's spot-on about the lube. Coach isn't going to put up with stupid mistakes on his field. I'm scared shitless that he'll pull me. If Coach doesn't believe in me—a man I've played for my entire college career—how can I believe in myself?

"Look, man," Beck continues, interrupting those depressing thoughts, "we all have off days. Don't stress about it."

I think that by now, we both realize this is more than just an *off day*. It's a string of unfortunate events.

"Easier said than done," I mumble.

With nothing else to say, we silently strip off the rest of our gear before hitting the showers. Now that Coach has cloistered himself in his office, the locker room once again turns rowdy. Everyone has caught their second wind. Guys are talking about all the parties happening off-campus this weekend. The team has been at Wesley, practicing twice a day since the beginning of July. We've spent hundreds of hours running through plays on the field, lifting in the gym, scrimmaging, and watching game film. With the start of school next week, this is the final hoorah. Everyone wants to cut loose and party their asses off before we have to buckle down for the season.

Once Beck hits the showers, I slump onto the bench with a huff and stare pensively at my hands. I want to get this ass-chewing over with and move on with my life. Best case scenario, this will be a pep talk. Worst case, Kwiatkowski is moving up in the world. A cold sweat breaks out across my brow at the possibility. A couple of guys have already come and gone from the enclosed space and yet, I remain paralyzed on the bench.

"Get a move on it, bro," Beck prods, returning with a towel slung around his waist. "I got shit to take care of."

"Go on without me," I mutter. "I have a feeling this is gonna take a while."

Beck pulls on a pair of boxers and athletic shorts before shoving his feet into slides. "Does this have anything to do with Alyssa?"

"Fuck if I know." I drag a hand over my face, not wanting to admit my suspicions.

There's a long pause before he says, "You could always try talking to her."

Ha!

The only problem with that bit of advice is that I actually value my life and am not looking to end it prematurely.

"Yeah, I don't know about that. It didn't go so well the first time." For fuck's sake, he was there. He witnessed the shitshow that ensued when I tried to make nice. At one point, I'd actually thought she might inflict bodily harm. "That girl could give Coach a run for his money in the ass reaming department."

One side of Beck's mouth quirks with humor.

"You heard Alyssa," I add, just in case he's a little slow on the uptake. "She wants nothing to do with me. In fact, she'd rather I not breathe the same air as her." I shake my head, chuckling grimly under my breath. "If Lys had her way, she'd rather I didn't breathe at all."

It's funny, I can't remember a time when Alyssa *wasn't* chasing after me. Throughout high school and then college. I'm sure I sound like a giant dick, but there was something comforting about the knowledge that she would always be there, waiting in the wings.

And now?

Now she wants nothing to do with me. If it were possible for her to smote me on the spot, she'd do it in a heartbeat, without a single thought or care. Then she'd step over my cold dead body on her way out the door.

Beck interrupts the whirl of those thoughts. "Can you blame the girl?"

He knows how everything went down between us sophomore year.

Maybe sending a text message to break up with her wasn't the smartest idea. Actually, there's no *maybe* about it. Alyssa had confessed her love, and I freaked out and cut her loose. At the very least, I should have sat her down and had an adult conversation. Instead, I'd taken the easy way out, and it backfired in my face.

I focus on my clasped hands instead of meeting his curious stare. "Not at all." Only now, as the uncomfortable silence settles around us, do I realize the locker room has thinned out. Most of these guys are ready to get their weekend started. This is the last place they want to hang out.

Even though I don't want to give voice to the words, I'm powerless to stop them from escaping. "You going to Alyssa's party?"

Beck shrugs as guilt flickers across his expression before his gaze skitters away.

Why did I even bother to ask? Of course, he's going.

"You could always crash the party," he says with a chuckle.

I snort out a laugh.

Can you even imagine?

"Somehow, I don't think that would go over well." The only thing my presence would accomplish is to piss Alyssa off even more than she already is. Just like football, I need a little time to figure out the best course of action.

"Have you considered giving her a gift she really wants?" When I raise a brow in question, Beck smirks. "Like your balls on a silver platter?"

I grab my sweaty practice jersey and throw it at Beck's face. He bats it away before it can make contact.

"You're a dick," I laugh, my muscles loosening.

He grins, and the thick tension holding me captive finally dissipates. "Tell me something I don't know."

Chapter Seventeen

ALYSSA

"Welcome home, bitch," Mia shouts, attempting to be heard over the pulsing beat of techno as we clink our shots of Fireball and toss them back. The smooth liquor slides down my throat, warming me from the inside out.

"Holy shit, that's terrible!" my bestie sputters, coughing as tears gather in her dark eyes. "No more shots. I'm tapping out."

Undeterred by the declaration, I laugh and order another round. I'm nowhere near done. Everywhere I look, there are friends who have shown up to help celebrate my return to Wesley. I'll admit that while packing up my bags and preparing to leave London, part of me was tempted to extend my student visa for another year, but in the end, I decided the best course of action was to come home, finish out my degree, and graduate on time. Maybe, if I still feel the same way in the spring, I'll return.

And then there's Jack. Even though I'd taken everything at a glacial pace where he was concerned, it had only begun to heat up between us. I'm not sure what will happen with that situation. Probably nothing. We're an ocean apart. It's difficult enough to maintain a relationship when I'm on the same continent with a guy, let alone a six-hour international flight away.

I glance at my best friend, the girl who planned this amazing night, and realize that coming home was the right decision. Even though I met some amazing new people—ones I hope will be in my life forever—I'd missed my bestie something fierce. We've been friends for as long as I can remember. There's a history between us that can't be denied or erased. I was there when her sister died and the subsequent challenges her family faced. She was the shoulder I leaned on when I broke my ankle freshman year of high school and questioned if dancing would ever be the same.

We have one last year together before we head in different directions. I'm both excited and scared by the prospect. Above all, I'm glad Mia is by my side. I have no idea what I would do without her. Luckily, I'll never have to find out.

My gaze runs over the length of her. She looks smoking hot in a black dress that hugs every single curve. Unlike me, the girl has an hourglass figure. And tonight is all about showcasing it.

The drinks have already gone to my head, and I'm in my element. When the music changes and the bass starts to thump, reverberating off the walls, I squeal and grab Mia's hand, dragging her to the dance floor. "I freaking love this song!"

This night is all about having fun. I want to let go and enjoy the drinks, music, and good friends who have come out to celebrate my return. I shove my way through the press of writhing bodies before carving out a tiny space for us. My hands go in the air as I lose myself in the beat. It's not difficult. The DJ has some serious skills. Each song bleeds into the next as we shake our asses, singing along with the lyrics. Mia grabs my hand and twirls me around. A smile stretches across my face as I laugh, enjoying myself like I haven't in a long time. Friends come and go as the music plays on. I have no idea how long we stay out on the dance floor. The only way I realize time has passed is by how parched my mouth becomes.

I close the distance between us and shout, "I need to use the bathroom."

Her cheeks are pink from all our exertion, but I can tell she's having a blast. Sometimes Mia has a difficult time cutting loose. She wants to be the perfect kid and student, forever walking the straight and narrow. It's good for her to let go and have fun. If anyone needs it, it's her.

"Want me to come with you?" she asks.

"Nah." With a shake of my head, I wave her off. "I'll be back in a sec, stay here so I can find you again."

A strobe light of color bounces off the walls as I push my way through the thick crowd. I catch flashes of people I know and wave as I continue on my way. It turns out to be a five-minute wait for the restroom. I chat with a few friends in line and catch up on their lives. Once inside, I do my business and touch up my lip gloss before fluffing my hair. It's long and loose, floating around my shoulders. I probably should have put it up with all the ass shaking I'm doing, but I'm having way too much fun to care.

On the way back to the dance floor, I detour to the long stretch of bar for another drink. I'm dying of thirst. If I were thinking clearly, I'd get an icy cold bottle of water and hydrate. But tonight, I'm not going to be smart. I'm going to suck down as many drinks as I want and keep the party going until the wee hours of the morning.

As I shoulder my way through the throng, I prop my elbows on the smooth surface and catch sight of a smoking hot bartender mixing cocktails with the precision of a professional. His hair is inky black in the dim lighting, and his eyes are dark, almost onyx in color. He must feel my perusal because he glances in my direction and flashes an easy smile before handing over two bottles of beer and making his way toward me.

The closer he gets, the sexier I realize he is. Physically, he ticks all the boxes.

Tall—*check*.

Easy on the eyes—*check*.

Large hands—*check*.

Knows how to make a cocktail—*double-check*.

If I were in the market for a one-night stand, this guy would fit the bill perfectly. And with his dark hair and eyes, he doesn't remind me of—

Nope. Not even going to go there.

I refuse to let him ruin my night.

The sexy bartender lays his palms on the counter before leaning toward me. "What can I get for you, birthday girl?" His voice is deep and smooth but does nothing for me.

"Birthday girl?" I echo, wondering if he has me confused with another chick. There are certainly enough of them vying for his attention. Looks like he has a lot of options for the evening, although I'm not one of them.

"Sure. People have been buying you shots all night long." He flashes a beguiling set of dimples as he grins. "Props to you. I'm surprised you're still standing. You must have one hell of a tolerance."

"Oh." I laugh and shake my head, realizing that he's had his eye on me for a while. "It's not my birthday. Just a little party to celebrate my return to Wesley. I spent last year studying abroad."

"Well then," his dark eyes sparkle as they rove over me, "welcome home."

"Thank you." While his attention is flattering, I'm still not interested. Even though Jack and I parted ways as friends, I'm not looking for a relationship anytime soon.

"Sounds like it might be my turn to buy you a shot."

"No more shots," a deep voice grumbles, interrupting our conversation. That's all it takes for my good vibes to disappear. "She will, however, take a bottle of water."

I stiffen and swing around. Even though I know exactly who I'll find standing beside me, it's still a surprise when my gaze collides with his bright blue eyes. A reluctant shiver of awareness scuttles down my spine at his proximity.

The last time I saw Colton outside our apartment building, I was too damn furious to notice all the little changes a year of separation had wrought. As much as I loathe to admit it, he looks better than ever. The maroon T-shirt he's wearing hugs his biceps before stretching tautly across his chest. Somehow, his shoulders are even broader than they were a year ago. My mouth dries as an avalanche of unbidden memories crash over me. I remember what it felt like to slide my fingers across all that steely strength. I tighten my hands in an effort not to reach out and touch him.

What the hell am I doing?

It takes effort to jolt myself out of those insidious thoughts. For as long as I can remember, Colton has had this effect on me. I lose all conscious thought when he's nearby. I'd hoped my year spent in London would help me to forget about him—or, at the very least, get over him—but that doesn't appear to be the case.

When it comes to Colton Montgomery, my heart and body have a mind of their own. With punishing force, I crush the fragile emotions attempting to take root inside me.

Never again.

I will never willingly give my heart to another man who is unable to hold it carefully in the palms of his hands.

You know that saying—when someone shows you who they are, believe them?

Yeah...I need to take that expression more seriously.

Fool me once, shame on you. Fool me twice, and I deserve everything I get for being a naive dumbass. I'll be damned if I allow Colton to ruin this night for me. He no longer has a place in my life. He made sure of that when he dumped my ass and walked away.

"You don't get to tell me what to do," I snap before turning my full attention to the guy behind the long stretch of counter. The hunky bartender's gaze bounces cautiously between us. I grit my teeth, hoping my ex-boyfriend will slink off now that I've put him firmly in his place.

"Hey, Shane," Colton says. "How's the knee holding up?"

"It's better. Went under the knife at the end of May and have been rehabbing it ever since." He adds, "Pretty sure my football days are long gone."

"That sucks, man. Sorry to hear it."

I press my lips together until they feel bloodless as Colton continues to commiserate with the bartender. Even though I had zero interest in a hookup, I suspect my ex is attempting to cock block me. It's almost enough to make me snort, except...he has no right to interfere in my life.

Hunky bartender shrugs. "It is what it is."

"Truth," Colton agrees.

This is the point where I wonder if there will be a moment of silence in memory of Shane's knee.

Instead, the bartender slants a tentative look in my direction. "Is she with you?"

I open my mouth to tell him that I'm my own person and can answer that question for myself when Colton beats me to the punch.

"Yup."

Is this guy being serious right now?

We aren't together.

We will never be together again.

"Got it." Hunky bartender doesn't bother to spare me another glance. All flirty banter has now ceased. "One bottle of water coming right up."

My mouth hangs open. Before I'm able to gather my wits, the drink is set in front of me, and then he's moving on to greener pastures. Or, in his case, readily available one-night stands.

Anger bubbles up inside me like a geyser.

Who the hell does Colton think he is?

He can't just saunter in here and attempt to jack up my night. He wasn't even invited to the party! It's a struggle to keep all of my riotous emotions in check. The last thing I want is to lose my shit and create yet another spectacle.

Been there, done that. Not interested in a repeat performance.

A week later and there are still a few apartment residents throwing cautious glances in my direction when our paths happen to cross in the lobby or elevator. I've been dubbed the psycho chick who should be avoided at all costs.

When I finally have a thin veneer of civility in place, I growl, "What are you doing here?"

Colton shifts his stance, angling closer. "I came to see you."

"Why?" Did I not make myself perfectly clear the other day? We have nothing more to discuss.

"I hate what happened when we ran into each other. It shouldn't be like that between us."

A gurgle of disbelief bubbles up in my throat as my eyes widen. "Did you really think it would be any different?"

Guilt flickers across his expression before he plows his fingers through his blond hair. "I don't know. Maybe I'd hoped that enough time had passed, and we could start over with being friends."

You know what I think?

That he's lost his damn mind. A year isn't nearly enough time to dull the pain he carelessly inflicted. I had loved him with all my heart, and he'd stomped it to smithereens as if I hadn't meant anything to him. The painful truth is that I probably hadn't. Him settling down had been an experiment—an epic failure, at that.

Why bother pretending? So he can absolve himself of guilt?

No, thanks.

Hard pass.

"You and I will *never* be friends." The air gets clogged in my throat, making it difficult to breathe. I take a hasty step away, needing distance. I'm not usually one to retreat from a skirmish, but in this instance, it's all about self-preservation. I'm making a tactical decision. The sooner I get away from Colton, the better off I'll be. The sight of him dredges up too many unwanted emotions.

Just as a breath of relief slips from my lips, Colton's hand shoots out. His fingers wrap around my forearm, halting me in my tracks, making escape impossible. His touch sends a jolt of electricity sizzling through my veins.

There used to be a time when I melted beneath his calloused hands. All he had to do was flick those gorgeous blue eyes my way, and my insides turned to jelly. It takes every ounce of resolve to fight the unwelcome desire growing inside me and remain strong. Even though he's sent me spiraling into chaos, I'll be damned if I give him the satisfaction of seeing how easily he's able to affect me.

Still.

Still!

It's disheartening.

When Colton's tongue darts out to moisten his lips, my core clenches in response. I'm like one of Pavlov's dogs salivating at the dinner bell. The amount of pleasure he was capable of giving with that mouth...

My guess is that he took the year I was gone to further hone those skills.

That disturbing thought is like a bucket of frigid water dumped all over my libido.

"Isn't it possible for us to sit down and hash this out?" He tugs me closer, reeling me toward him. "What I did to you was wrong. Give me a chance to explain what was going on inside my head."

Explain?

Ha!

I have zero interest in hearing any of his lame-ass excuses.

My gaze drops to his fingers. It feels as if the imprint of them is being singed into my flesh. I don't understand how I can still have feelings for someone who threw away our relationship like it was nothing more than a dirty Kleenex. I need to cut this off at the knees. I'm all too aware that an innocent conversation with Colton has the potential to lead to other things, and I can't take a chance of getting sucked back into his orbit.

"There's nothing for us to discuss. You broke up with me sophomore year." I throw in a careless shrug, wanting him to think that I'm indifferent. "We've both moved on."

If only that were true.

Emotion flares to life in his eyes. He drags me so close that I have to crane my neck in order to meet his gaze. "You sure about that?" Tension ratches up in the air. "Because it kind of feels like we might have some unfinished business to take care of."

"You're mistaken. There is absolutely nothing between us." I gulp down the rising turmoil attempting to break loose inside me. "You made damned sure of that."

A soft puff of breath leaves his lips as sorrow wells in his eyes. "I'm sorry, Lys. I got scared and hurt the one person I shouldn't have."

No, no, no.

I refuse to listen to his bullshit. More than that, I won't allow him to burrow beneath my skin again. He had his chance, and he blew it.

It takes all of my strength to twist out of his hold. Relief floods through me when his hand falls away, sinking back to his side. Aware of his ability to spring forward and detain me at any moment, I take a hasty step in retreat. When he remains still, eyes locked on me, I take another. And then a third. The more distance I put between us, the better off I'll be.

"It doesn't matter. None of it does." Even though my whispered words are drowned out by the music and chatter that surrounds us, I know he hears them loud and clear. I see it in the sadness that flickers across his expression.

Before he can take up any more of my time, I swing around, shoving my way through the thick press of bodies. I need to get as far away from Colton Montgomery as possible.

But will it be enough?

Somehow, I don't think so.

Chapter Eighteen

COLTON

That went about as well as I expected it to—straight down the tubes.

Although, she didn't lose her shit like the other day, so I guess that's progress.

If I had any brains whatsoever, I'd chalk this endeavor up as a lost cause and walk away before I make matters any worse. Hell, had I been thinking clearly, I wouldn't have crashed her party in the first place. I'd leave the past where it belongs and allow Alyssa to move on with her life which is what she insists she's trying to do.

But I can't. Not when I sense that buried beneath all the hurt and anger are emotions fighting to break free. Until I make sure that there's nothing I can do to rectify the situation, I won't be able to let go of our past.

Decision made, I hang out at the bar. Shane keeps me well stocked with water. As tempting as it is to guzzle down half a dozen beers, or a few shots, I've become enough of a shitshow without inviting more problems.

Two hours later, Alyssa is still on the dance floor, getting her groove on. I can barely take my eyes off her. She's mesmerizing. That girl has enough moves to give a corpse major wood. The lights flicker, and the music continues to pump as she rolls her hips and lifts her hair with slim hands as if putting on a private show for some lucky bastard.

Just to be clear, I'm not the lucky bastard.

I drag a hand over my face. It's killing me to watch her out there. And yet, looking away isn't possible. Every time some asshole slides in front of her, I have to grit my teeth and talk myself out of stomping over and ripping her away. I've lost track of how many shots she's tossed back, but it's a lot—too many. It's a surprise that she's still able to stand upright, let alone twerk in that tiny silver dress that barely covers her ass.

Alyssa hasn't glanced at me once since stalking away. It's like I don't exist. A large pit settles at the bottom of my gut at the realization that there might not be anything I can do or say to mitigate the damage I inflicted.

"You want another?" There's a pause. "Although, I'll be straight with you, man—you toss back anymore drinks, and I'll have to take your keys away. I can't allow you to drive home in your inebriated condition."

I snort out something that barely passes for a chuckle. "Nah, I'm good."

Shane leans against the bar as his gaze cuts through the crowd to Alyssa. Her blond head is like a halo glowing under the strobe lights. I reluctantly pull my attention away from her and glance around the club. Unfortunately, I'm not the only one who has taken notice. Dudes are circling like hungry sharks.

"How long have you two crazy kids been together?" he asks casually, breaking into my thoughts.

Instead of admitting the truth, I narrow my eyes and glare. "Long enough."

Shane played football until an ACL injury knocked him out of commission last season. He's always been a fan favorite with the ladies. As much as we're friends and teammates, I'm not an idiot. The interest was apparent in his eyes when he was talking to Alyssa earlier.

He nods toward the dance floor. "You sure she knows that?"

"It's complicated," I grumble, not wanting him to get any ideas. By the looks of the guy, it's much too late for that. I don't want to knock them from his head, but I will if I have to.

"It always is, brother."

Before I have a chance to respond, he takes off, heading down to the opposite end of the bar to help a customer.

Alyssa's friends come and go. There's dancing and more shots. I caught sight of Beck earlier in the evening, but now he's nowhere to be seen. I look around and realize Mia is also conspicuously absent from the festivities.

Hmmm. Interesting.

An hour and two more bottles of water later, Alyssa hugs a few girls and gives them a quick wave. A happy light fills her eyes as a smile stretches lazily across her face. She looks pleasantly buzzed as she saunters past the bar. Her feet grind to a halt as her gaze collides with mine, and all of the lightheartedness filling her expression dissolves. The edges of her pink slicked lips sink into a frown as her brows jerk together. "You're still here?"

I straighten to my full height before closing the distance between us. Alyssa might be tall, but I've got a good ten inches on her. The closer I get, the more she has to lift her chin to maintain eye contact. "I wasn't sure if you needed a ride home." And it sure as shit wasn't going to be with another guy.

"I don't. There are plenty of friends I can catch a ride with." She waves toward the people still filling the club. "So, feel free to take off."

I shake my head. "I'll head out when you do."

A puff of exasperation escapes from her lungs. "Then you can go now because I'm leaving."

The physical pull is more than I can withstand, and I take another step in her direction. We're so close that I could reach out and yank her into my arms. The temptation to do exactly that pounds through me like a steady drumbeat. Except I know exactly how it'll end. And that's not well. It'll only piss her off more than she already is. "I'll take you home." I just want to get her into my car and away from all the dudes scoping her out.

"No, thanks." She searches the crowd for an alternative. "I'd rather Uber it."

Sorry, that's not happening.

"We're headed to the same place. It's a ten-minute drive. I think you can withstand that much time alone with me."

"Wanna bet?" When she attempts to slip past me, I mirror the movement and block her escape.

Anger sparks to life in her eyes, banishing the mellowness that had been filling them minutes ago. "Get out of my way, Colton. I'm serious!"

"We can do this the easy way or the hard way. It's your choice." Already I can tell how this interaction will unfold. Although, I'm still holding out a glimmer of hope that she'll surprise me.

Her lips form into a snarl. "You're out of your damn mind if you think I'm going anywhere with you! I'd rather—"

"The hard way it is," I say with resignation, stepping closer before hunkering down and hoisting her up. She grunts as my shoulder connects with her midsection.

For one blissful moment, she falls into silence as her slender body hangs stiffly over mine. Knowing the surprise will wear off quickly, I hightail it to the exit. Two steps later, all hell breaks loose.

"Colton Davidson Montgomery!" She pounds on my back, trying her damnedest to inflict as much damage as possible with her fists. "Put me down this instant, or I'll scream my head off!"

Thankfully, the club is dark, and the music is still pumping around us. Other than a few drunken glances speared in our direction, no one pays us much attention as I stride toward the door.

Which is for the best. This would be a difficult situation to explain.

The second I hit the paved lot, I beeline toward my BMW parked half a dozen rows away.

"Goddamn it! You have no right to kidnap me!" Even though she continues to pound her fists against my back, she's not inflicting any real injury. Hell, the hits I take in practice are worse than this.

When she wiggles against my shoulder, nearly falling off, I smack her ass with the flat of my hand. "Stay still before you get hurt."

"Ow!" She sucks in a sharp, disbelieving breath. "You son of a bitch!"

"Then stop fighting me. All I'm trying to do is make sure you get home safely."

"Ironically, you're the one causing me pain!" There's a beat of silence before she growls, "You do realize that you just accosted me, right?"

Maybe.

With one hand holding her firmly in place, I reach into the front pocket of my jeans and grab my keys before hitting the button on the fob.

Now comes the tricky part—how to maneuver Alyssa into the vehicle without her fighting me and possibly getting hurt. I yank open the door and lower myself down until her heels scrape against the pavement. With my breath wedged in my lungs, I release her before straightening to my full height. My gaze stays locked on her. It wouldn't surprise me in the least if she attempted to run—even in those heels—or sucker punched me in the face.

A gentle breeze slides through the riotous tangle of her blond hair, blowing it around her shoulders as a wild light fills her eyes. I can't help but think that she's gorgeous in her towering rage. Even though it's totally perverse, my cock stiffens to half-mast.

The slinky silver dress clings to every slender curve. Barely does it hit mid-thigh. I'm sure if she bent over, I'd catch a glimpse of her panties.

And she better damn well be wearing panties.

"How dare you!" she growls. The words are low and menacing as her body shakes with barely contained fury. "You have no right to pick me up and cart me out of a club like a sack of potatoes." Her gaze arrows to the two-story brick building across the parking lot.

Her face is so easy to read.

"Don't even think about it," I tell her. "You won't get far." There's a pause as I tilt my head. "Unless you're looking for me to lay my hands on you again."

She gnashes her teeth before baring them like a rabid animal. *"I hate you!"*

All of the sexual tension simmering in the air between us dissipates. "I know, Lys. There's nothing else for me to say other than I'm sorry."

Wetness pricks her eyes. Instead of allowing the tears to fall, they pool in her blue depths, shimmering like crystals in the darkness.

That's all it takes for my heart to crack wide open.

"I don't give a fuck about your apologies," she snaps. "You can shove them right up your ass for all I care." As she takes a hasty step in retreat, her heel hits a crack in the asphalt, and her eyes flare wide as she falters.

When her arms pinwheel, I spring forward, wrapping my fingers around her shoulders in an attempt to steady her. "Are you all right?"

"No." Before I can ask what's wrong, she whispers, "Do you have any idea how much you hurt me?"

My throat closes up until it feels like I can't breathe.

When I remain silent, she continues, "Any at all?"

The pain that seeps into her vivid blue depths is enough to kill me. "Yeah, I do. I wish it were possible to go back in time and change everything about the way we ended." The truth is that I wish I hadn't ended it at all.

"That's not possible. You can't rewrite history. You can only put the past to rest and move forward. That's exactly what I've done."

"I don't believe you." More like I don't want to believe her. "I think you still want me."

My gaze drops to her mouth. Those pouty lips that were made for all kinds of sin. I miss kissing them. I miss them wrapped around my cock as she stared adoringly up from her knees. Even dredging up the memories makes me throb with arousal.

It's as if she can sense the thoughts running rampant through my head. "Don't."

Her tongue darts out to smudge her lips. Everything in me tightens as I lower my face to hers. We're so close that I can feel her warm breath drift over me. It only drives the fierce need I've always had for her.

"Don't what?" I murmur, ghosting my lips over her soft ones. It takes every ounce of self-control not to close the distance between us and take what I want.

"Kiss me."

"Why not?"

She tilts her head toward mine, almost as if angling it for better access. "Because...I don't want it."

Losing the battle with myself, I nip at her lower lip before sucking the fullness into my mouth. A whimper escapes as I tug her to me until her breasts are smashed against my chest. A sultry taste that is distinctly hers explodes on my tongue. After all the time and distance that I forced between us, having her this close is like a wave crashing over me, dragging me to the bottom of the ocean. I'm drowning in the taste and feel of her, and I don't give a damn. I don't care if I ever make it up to the surface again.

Even though it goes against every single impulse pounding through me, I pull away enough to say, "Are you sure about that?"

Chapter Nineteen

ALYSSA

Why is it that all rational thought falls to the wayside anytime he lays his hands on me? Colton Montgomery has been my kryptonite for as long as I can remember. It's disheartening to realize that nothing has changed in that regard. No matter how strong I think I am, this is all it takes for me to crumble.

I've kissed a handful of boys since our breakup, and none made me forget myself or feel as if I would shrivel up and die if they didn't take my mouth.

But that's exactly the way it is with Colton.

A year and a half of separation did nothing to lessen the attraction that churns within me. I want him now as much as I ever did. And I have no idea how to change it. Or kill the emotion that simmers beneath the surface.

"Tell me to stop," he growls against my lips. "If that's what you want, you need to say the words."

My lungs fill with air as my head swirls from a potent concoction of Colton-infused alcohol. It's dizzying. I open my mouth to tell him exactly that, but the words die a quick death on my tongue, refusing to be summoned. I need him to step away and give me a little bit of breathing room so rational thought can once again prevail. When he's this close, corrupting every sense, sending every nerve ending into chaos, it's impossible to think straight.

My guess is that he won't give me the time or distance to find my bearings and come to my senses.

In fact, I know he won't.

Not unless I demand it of him.

And...I'm unable to do that.

After all this time apart, not only do I secretly crave his touch, I need it. With a groan, I tilt my face toward his. That's all the signal he needs to proceed. His hands slide from my shoulders to my face, where they cup my cheeks. His thumb strokes against my lower lip before his mouth captures mine. One sweep of his tongue is all it takes for me to open. The first taste of him has fireworks exploding inside my head before sinking like a heavy stone to my core.

One kiss, and it feels like I could self-combust from the pent-up desire churning beneath the surface.

"You have no idea how much I missed this," he mutters against my lips.

Oh, but I do because I feel the same.

His fingers disappear from my face, slipping over the tops of my shoulders, grazing my arms and ribcage, before settling on my ass. He cups each cheek in the palm of his hands before squeezing them as if testing the weight and feel. Electricity sizzles through me at the intimate contact. A groan bubbles up inside me, fighting to break free.

I haven't felt this turned on since...

Colton.

And that is all kinds of depressing.

The intrinsic knowledge that this will end badly isn't nearly enough for me to push him away. It's nothing more than a fleeting thought. Here and gone before I can fully grasp it.

Or act on it.

I'm so caught up in the feel of his hands and mouth wreaking havoc on my body that I don't realize he's walking me backward until my spine hits the shiny metal of his BMW. The thick length of his erection digs into my belly, leaving me to gasp for breath. I remember all too well what it felt like to have Colton driving deep inside my heat.

The mere thought is enough to weaken my knees. If he weren't pinning me in place, I'd fall to the ground before melting into a puddle of goo.

Why does something so bad have to feel so damn good?

He nibbles at my mouth before drawing away. Without thinking, my fingers dig into his T-shirt, attempting to drag him closer. His mouth hovers over my ear, ghosting over the curve of it. Shivers scamper down my spine before he sucks the lobe into his mouth. His teeth sink into the soft flesh, and a whimper of need escapes from me.

The fire he ignited so easily in my core bursts into flames as his lips caress their way down the column of my neck. Sucking and licking at my sensitive skin, drawing it into his mouth, and feasting on it. He singes a hot trail across my collarbone before nipping at the tops of my breasts. My chest rises and falls in rapid succession as his hands sweep along my sides before settling on the gentle swells. With a flick of his wrist, he tugs at the slinky material until one breast is bare to the warm night air that swirls around us.

A deep groan rumbles up from his throat as his mouth fastens on my nipple. Not once do I consider the possibility that someone could exit the club and spot us at the back of the parking lot.

How can I when Colton is attacking every single one of my senses?

I tilt my head toward the bright star-filled sky and allow the pleasure to crash over me like a tidal wave. Once he's licked and sucked at one tiny bud, he pulls the material up and covers me before lowering the other side and showering it with the same ardent attention.

"I fucking love your tits."

His words echo in my head.

This isn't the first time he's made the claim. Whenever he said it, I would laugh because my breasts are fairly non-existent. Wesley's campus is overflowing with girls who are, well...overflowing in that department. But Colton never seemed to mind. When we were in bed together, he spent hours worshipping them. And I loved it. They might be small, but they're incredibly sensitive and easily stimulated.

I have no idea how much time elapses before he lifts his mouth and slides the material back into place before popping to his feet and pressing against me.

"I've missed you, Lys."

The deep rasp of his voice as he uses the nickname leaves me melting. It always has. But especially now with his hands all over my body.

"I've missed *this*," he adds, his mouth descending. As he pushes into me, forcing me to flatten against the metal of the vehicle, my spine curves. Each vertebra bends under his strength. His fingers lock around my wrists before dragging them over my head and pinning them to the roof. I'm so cognizant of his thick erection digging into me. Of my breasts pressed beneath the steel of his chest. I'm overwhelmed by his masculine presence.

More than anything, I wish I didn't revel in the dominance, but I do.

So much.

Just because I can be assertive and know what I want doesn't mean that I don't enjoy submitting and made to feel as if I've been rendered powerless. To have my senses eclipsed by physical strength wielded in a manner that isn't an attack but one that makes me feel emboldened by my own sexuality. It's nothing more than an illusion. A trick of the imagination. It requires a man to walk a fine line, and Colton knows exactly how to do it.

And that, like everything else he does, is a major turn-on.

As much as I hate to admit it, there were too many nights since our breakup when I laid awake in my bed, unable to find sleep, as thoughts of him crashed unbidden through my head. The way he touched me. Stroking my flesh to life and sliding deep inside my heat until there was no other choice but to shudder with orgasm. Inevitably, my fingers would slip beneath the elastic band of my panties before caressing my lower lips and circling my clit until I was gasping out his name.

Every time I caved to the temptation, I told myself that it was because I would never feel Colton's touch again. He was like a ghostly specter hovering over me, dredging up painful yet delicious memories, which is precisely why this feels more like a dream than anything else. Tomorrow morning, I'll be chock-full of regrets and recriminations but tonight?

Tonight, I'm going to blot out common sense and enjoy this experience to the fullest.

By the time he pulls away to nip at my chin with sharp teeth, my lips feel bruised and swollen. As reluctant as I am to admit it, Jack's kisses were *nothing* like this. They didn't stir anything beneath the surface. They were a pleasant distraction I'd hoped would flourish into something more. As soon as that thought bursts into my brain, I force it away.

Jack is sweet, kind, and nice. He's one of the most caring and considerate people I've ever met. We built a solid friendship before it grew into something more. And even then, when it turned romantic, I insisted on taking my time and easing into a relationship. But we never generated this kind of...

Combustible energy that feels like it has the potential to destroy everything in its path.

That's exactly how it feels when I'm with Colton. There's no other way to describe it.

He's all I can see.

All I'm able to think about.

It's addictive.

It's the rough scrape of hands sliding beneath the hem of my dress as it rides up my thighs that grounds me in the here and now. The tips of his fingers dance across my flesh, inching their way beneath the fabric. Air gets trapped in my throat when they stroke over my panties.

The warm August air wafting over my flushed cheeks isn't nearly enough to cool them. I'm not sure if anything can extinguish the heat that has exploded to life in my core. As he drops to a crouch in front of me, I know exactly how this scenario will play out. I also know that I'm not going to prevent it from happening. I don't have that kind of strength. If I'm being completely honest with myself, I don't want to stop it.

I want him.

And I want this.

Tomorrow will be soon enough to deal with the ramifications of my stupidity.

Colton's hands inch their way upward, lifting the dress until my underwear is exposed. He leans forward, brushing a soft kiss against the cotton. His fingers hook into the elastic band on each side of my hips before dragging the fabric down my thighs, past my knees, until it's stretched taut between my ankles. I expel a shaky breath from my lungs as anticipation coils like a spring deep in the pit of my gut.

Actually, the excitement unfurling inside me is much lower.

Carefully he lifts one foot, removing the material that serves as protection before repeating the movement on the other side. In silence, he stuffs the flimsy scrap into the pocket of his jeans.

His face hovers no more than six inches from the heat of my core. Every inhale has him breathing me in before exhaling a warm puff of air against my bare flesh. A thick shudder works its way through me as his gaze stays focused straight ahead.

"You're so fucking beautiful," he rasps.

My heart jackhammers a painful staccato against my ribcage. My gaze stays locked on him, watching every move, taking in every detail about this moment. Wanting to etch it into my memory so that I'll be able to take it out anytime I want to revisit it.

Time stretches between us until it becomes unbearable, and I shift restlessly beneath his hands. When he finally leans forward, I expect him to attack my aching flesh in much the same manner he assaulted my mouth a handful of minutes ago, devouring me in one hungry gulp. Instead, he buries his nose against me before inhaling deeply. It's as if he's trying to breathe in my very essence.

"No matter how much pussy I attempted to lose myself in after we broke up, it was never you."

My breath hitches at the admittance.

With unhurried movements, as if we're not standing in the back of a crowded parking lot, he rubs his face against me. The slight stubble on his cheeks abrades my delicate flesh, releasing a thousand tiny shivers inside the confines of my belly.

My spine arches as I give in to the chaos he's created.

Just when I don't think I can take another moment of this sweet torture, his lips feather against me. My skin is so over-sensitized and achy. I want to scream with the impending storm that pushes its way to the surface. The first flick of his velvety softness sends me soaring, and I groan, my head rolling back as my eyes shutter so I can focus on his touch.

He draws one plump lip between his teeth and nibbles at it before repeating the maneuver on the other side. His tongue thrusts into my throbbing heat, falling into a devastating rhythm. When I begin to spiral, he backs off, allowing his soft breath to drift over me as if attempting to cool my lust. Before I can utter a word, he circles my clit with his tongue, pushing me once again relentlessly toward orgasm.

I'm moments away from splintering apart when he eases back for a second time. Frustration explodes inside me. I can't take much more of his teasing. My fingers curl with the need to claw at him, to pull him against me and finish what he started. I open my mouth to protest when he lifts one heeled foot from the ground and plants it on his shoulder so that I'm spread impossibly wide. Even though the night air is warm, it cools my damp flesh, and a shudder works its way through me at the erotic image we must make.

"Fucking gorgeous." As he presses forward, my leg bends, exposing every delicate inch for him to feast upon.

The first swipe of his tongue nearly sends me hurtling over the edge of insanity. My fingers tangle in his hair to hold him in place as he nibbles at me. With his face buried against my heat, he drives me ruthlessly toward oblivion until I have no choice but to hurtle blindly over the edge.

Stars explode behind my eyelids as my heart beats wildly. Wave after wave crashes over me, threatening to suck me under. If I die like this, I would have zero regrets. My pussy continues to pulse as he devours my clit. I have to pin my lower lip with my teeth to keep all the sound buried deep inside where it will never see the light of day.

It's only after Colton has wrung every last drop of pleasure from me does he rise to his feet and crush his body to mine. If he weren't pinning me to the side of his car, I would slide to a boneless heap on the pavement.

"You're even more delicious than I remember."

With that, his mouth slants over mine. Unwilling to focus on what just transpired, I allow myself to get lost on a riotous sea of emotion.

Chapter Twenty

ALYSSA

A groan escapes as I roll onto my side. The motion has my head throbbing to life behind my eyelids.

Correction—my entire body throbs to life.

What the hell went down last night?

It takes a moment to jumpstart my brain.

Ah, that's right...welcome home party at Bang Bang. That much, I remember. And shots. My God, the shots. What the hell had I been thinking?

Apparently, I hadn't been.

I crack open an eye and glance around.

Thankfully, I'm in my own bedroom. That, in and of itself, is a huge relief. I remember flirting with a couple of guys on the dance floor. The music had been on point—one amazing song bleeding into another.

Wait a minute...

My brow furrows.

Colton.

The party crasher.

We'd had words at the bar when he'd attempted to cut me off. If only I could have ignored him, but that's never been an option. Even though I'd spent the night dancing, I had been acutely aware of his brooding presence. From the corner of my eye, I watched him stare at me with a single-mindedness that had shivers careening down my spine.

I'd made sure to put on a show so he could see exactly what he was missing. Guess I pushed it too far because I remember him hoisting me over his shoulder and carrying me out of the club caveman-style. Maybe if I hadn't put up a fight, everything smoldering in the air between us wouldn't have detonated.

A groan of embarrassment slips free.

Oh my God! Did I really let him go down on me in the parking lot?

Yup, sure did.

I search the murky depths of my brain. I don't remember anyone stumbling across us but let's face it, I'd been out of my mind. There could have been a full-on crowd cheering us on, and I wouldn't have been cognizant of it.

Even thinking about the orgasm that had streaked through me is enough to make me throb to life with painful awareness.

Oh, the horror of it all.

I grab my pillow and drag it over my head before letting loose a scream. I've done exactly what I promised myself I wouldn't. I allowed Colton to lay his hands on me.

Needing to escape from the onslaught of memories that continue to flood into my brain, I throw off the covers and ease my way from the bed before staggering out of my room. I make it a few steps into the short hallway before spotting Mia as she shovels a spoonful of cereal into her mouth. She looks none the worse for the wear, which is the complete opposite of me. I feel like a steaming bag of dog shit some derelict teenager lit on fire.

Bitch.

I lift my hand to my hair and realize that it's sticking up from every conceivable angle. And I didn't bother washing off my makeup last night either. I probably bear a striking resemblance to a rabid raccoon.

"Hey," she chirps, spoon paused midway in the air, "how are you feeling?"

"Stop shouting," I wince before grabbing my head so that it doesn't roll off my shoulders. "Please, I beg of you."

"That good, hmm?" A smile simmers across her lips as a teasing light enters her eyes. "Let me guess—you're looking for a little hair of the dog that bit you?" There's a pause. "I'm sure we have a bottle of tequila around here somewhere. Want me to get it?"

"God, no." Even the thought is enough to make my stomach heave. "I'm never drinking again."

Mia snickers as if she doesn't believe me. Hell, I'm not even sure *I* believe me but, with the way I'm currently feeling, it seems like an excellent idea moving forward.

Once my belly stops spasming, I point to the kitchen. "I need massive amounts of Tylenol and Gatorade." With that, I stagger into the other room before returning with a humongous bottle of the orange sports beverage. My fingers tremble as I fumble with the cap.

"Why did you let me drink so much," I accuse, successfully prying off the top and chugging a quarter of it. Instead of settling my gut, it only makes it churn even more. I press my fingers against my mouth before releasing a loud belch.

"If memory serves, I told you several times to slow down, but you weren't in the mood to listen. At one point, you called me a buzzkill." Leave it to Mia to throw that in my face. When I fail to respond, she asks, "Exactly how many shots did you have?"

"I lost count after eight." That thought is enough to make me nauseous. I shake my head to clear it before frantically waving a hand. "Please, I can't even think about that. It'll make me sick. Never mind, I'm already sick." Getting up was a mistake. I point to my room. "I'm going back to bed. Wake me up tomorrow. Or maybe the day after that. Hopefully, I'll have bounced back by then."

I stagger a few steps when an image materializes in my brain, and I swing around. "Wait a minute. Were you busting a move on the dance floor with Beck, or was that a tequila-induced dream?"

Because at this point, anything is possible.

With a wince, she averts her eyes. But not before I catch the guilt that flickers in their dark depths. Instead of answering, she busies herself by shoving another spoonful of cereal into her mouth.

Well, isn't this an interesting turn of events.

Seconds tick by without a response. My hangover dissipates as I take another step and jab a finger in her direction. I wrack my brain for anything more. The images are fleeting and blurred at the edges, but there's no way they're a figment of my drunken imagination. "Yeah," I pipe up, instantly warming to the subject, "you two were *definitely* dancing. His hands were all over you. And you, *ya little hussy*, were totally enjoying it."

Her face goes up in flames as she squirms on the couch. Her eyes turn a little hazy, and I'd give anything to know what's running through her brain.

I wave a hand in front of my bestie's face. "Hello? Earth to Mia. Come in, Mia."

She blinks, snapping back to attention and our conversation. "Sorry."

"Please tell me I wasn't hallucinating. Because if that's the case, I really *am* going to lay off the booze."

Silence stretches between us before she begrudgingly admits, "No, we danced together." As tempting as it is to give her the third degree, I'm in no frame of mind to do it. I'll just tuck this bit of information away for safekeeping.

She raises a brow and attempts to turn the tables on me. "Is there anything *you* would like to tell me about?"

"Huh?"

Her gaze turns knowing. "I saw you at the bar with Colton."

Instead of admitting the truth, I grumble, "Can you believe that guy had the audacity to show his face after I purposefully went out of my way *not* to invite him?"

"Umm, maybe?" She pauses. "Any interesting conversations?"

I wish it had only been *conversations* that had taken place between us. As far as I'm concerned, what happened was nothing more than a momentary lapse in judgment. My guess is that the shots didn't help with that. If Colton thinks one orgasm has smoothed everything over, he's woefully mistaken. I have zero interest in getting my heart annihilated for a second time.

I force my feet into movement before dropping onto the armchair and squeezing my eyes shut. "He wants to be friends," I mutter, remembering the conversation from the bar. "Don't worry, I was extremely clear about where he can shove his friendship."

Although, let's face it, spreading my legs wide for him probably didn't do much to convey that point as firmly as I wanted.

Mia's lips bow into a smile. "Maybe that was the closure you needed to move on. Feel any better about getting it out of your system?"

Guilt floods through me for misleading her as to what really transpired. "Surprisingly, no."

"I'm proud of you for giving him a piece of your mind. That took balls."

Clearly, she assumes that I gave him an encore performance of my psycho tirade. Unfortunately, nothing could be further from the truth.

That being said, I'm not going to set her straight. It's best to forget the matter entirely. "As far as I'm concerned, he can shove those up his ass as well."

"Sounds like his ass is a crowded place," she says with a chuckle.

Unable to help myself, I crack open an eyelid. My shoulders shake before we both burst into laughter. "Yeah, it does."

Chapter Twenty-One

COLTON

The apartment door closes with an audible click as I hitch my backpack onto my shoulder. As I turn, ready to head to campus for the next couple of hours, my gaze collides with Alyssa's as she steps into the hallway.

For a split second, time stands still as we both freeze in place. Memories from Saturday night crash through my brain at the speed of light. Alyssa in my arms, backed up against my BMW as my mouth feasted on hers. Her long legs splayed wide as I pushed her relentlessly toward orgasm in the parking lot of Bang Bang.

It had all happened so damn fast. One minute, she's raging at me, and the next, my hands are on her with our mouths fused together. The energy we always seem to generate had exploded upon impact. Whatever this is between us, it's so much more than sexual chemistry. If that's all it was, it would be a simple matter to relegate her to the past and move on with my life. She would be like all the other girls I've slept with and promptly forgotten about. With Alyssa, it goes so much deeper than that.

Unsure what to do, I lift my hand in a cautious wave.

Even from a distance, Saturday night sits uncomfortably between us.

As I give her a tentative greeting, she jerks out of her paralysis and flees down the carpeted hallway like the hounds of hell are nipping at her heels.

It's tempting to huff out a laugh. Had I really assumed that kissing her into submission would be enough to thaw the icy veneer encased around her?

Maybe.

Although, I should have known better. If I'm brutally honest with myself, pushing her against my vehicle and going down on her in a public parking lot probably didn't help matters.

What am I saying?

Of course, it didn't. Just look at her—she can't escape from me fast enough.

What I should do is cut my losses and leave her alone. By all indicators, that's what she wants. And yet, I can't do it. After holding Alyssa in my arms again and kissing her, I'm unable to fool myself into believing it's possible to move on without a fight.

Decision made, I do the only thing I can and give chase.

Instead of waiting for the elevator to stop on our floor, Alyssa slams through the metal door and disappears into the stairwell. I pick up my pace and shoulder my way through the opening before it has a chance to close. As I peer down the cement stairs, she glances up, and our gazes collide before she flicks them away and hastens her step. With my hand wrapped around the railing, I speed up. A few steps down, my shoe slips, and I tighten my grip around the metal to steady myself. I can just picture it now—breaking my neck in an ill-fated attempt to catch up with my ex. Knowing Alyssa, she'd probably think it was sweet irony for past misdeeds.

And maybe she'd be right.

Thirty seconds later, I throw open the door and glance around the empty lobby. Not that I expected her to wait for me—hell would have to freeze over in order for that to occur, but it certainly would have simplified matters.

As I push through the glass door into the fresh air, I catch sight of her striding down the walkway. She waves to another girl before accelerating her pace as I jog to catch up with her. Her long blond hair is pulled up into a ponytail that swings from side to side as she continues to speed walk. My gaze roves down the slender line of her back before arriving at her ass. My fingers itch to palm the supple cheeks like I did the other night, and my cock stirs, warming to the idea.

Since the direction of those wayward thoughts isn't helping matters, I jerk my attention away. Manhandling the girl probably isn't going to help win her over. What I need is to employ a different tactic.

As I pull up beside her, Alyssa slants a look in my direction. Her lips sink at the corners before she focuses straight ahead and pretends I don't exist. If she thinks that will deter me, she's got another thing coming.

"So," I say, testing the waters, "long time, no see."

She presses her lips into a flat line before muttering, "Not nearly long enough."

Well...at least she offered up a few begrudging words. That's got to be something, right?

Since she hasn't bared her teeth and growled, I ask, "Did you have a good time Saturday night?"

A tick or two passes by before she finally says, "Yup. It was nice to see everyone again."

Wow. Look at us, communicating like adults.

Since I'm unwilling to drop the conversational ball now that it's rolling, albeit slowly, I add, "I had a great time, too."

"Did you now?" Her narrowed gaze slices to me. "Didn't you spend the night sitting at the bar all by your lonesome?"

"What I meant is that I had a good time after I carted your ass out to the parking lot." The way her eyes flare tells me that I probably should have restrained myself and kept the comment locked deep inside. Although that knowledge doesn't stop me from tacking on, "I'm pretty sure you enjoyed it, too."

She draws in a sharp breath before hissing, "We're not going to talk about Saturday night because absolutely nothing happened."

Like hell, it didn't.

"Oh, I'm pretty sure it did."

A punch of color flags her cheeks. "You're mistaken about that."

"Am I? Cause I'm pretty damn sure I took off your panties and spread—"

"*Enough!*" She grinds to a halt before wheeling around to face me. Anger leaps to life in her eyes as she takes a step forward, closing the gap between us until she can drill a finger into my chest. "I don't want to talk about what happened in the parking lot! I want to forget about it. Understand?"

"That's unfortunate." My gaze settles on her parted lips, and I'm so damn tempted to remind her just how explosive it can be between us. Instead, I reach out and trail my finger along the soft curve of her jaw. With a grimace, she bats my hand away. "We were always good together."

"Maybe so," she concedes, "but that was a long time ago." I open my mouth to argue when she adds, "I will never be stupid enough to get involved with you again."

I almost wince at the pain that flashes in her eyes.

After our breakup, I did everything possible to push Alyssa to the outer recesses of my mind. I fucked every jersey chaser who would spread her legs. And yet, it was never enough. They were never Alyssa. Every girl was a paper-thin imitation of the only one I'd ever cared about. She's dominated my thoughts for more years than I care to admit. Laying my hands on her Saturday night only amplified the emotion coursing through me.

I have no idea if there's anything I can do or say to earn her forgiveness, but I have to make an effort. Believe it or not, my intention hadn't been to piss her off more than she already is. I'd only wanted her to acknowledge that there's still something between us. If I can get her to admit that, then there's a glimmer of hope we can pick up the pieces and move forward. "Lys—"

"Don't call me that," she snaps.

"Alyssa," I correct, only wanting to soothe the fire I've inadvertently stoked to life. She swings away before I can finish. Unwilling to throw in the towel just yet, I huff out a breath and jog to catch up with her as she stalks toward the university.

A heavy silence settles over us as we walk side by side before stopping at a crosswalk. Campus looms on the other side of the street.

Alyssa shifts impatiently. My guess is that she's counting down the seconds until she can shake me loose. As I wrack my brain for something that will turn the tide of this doomed interaction, her phone dings with an incoming text. Without sparing me a glance, she pulls the slim device from her bag before peeking at the screen. I crowd closer, trying to catch a glimpse of the message.

Jack.

Who the fuck—

"Who the fuck is Jack?" I grunt as a surge of jealousy rushes through me.

Alyssa scowls as if she legit forgot I was hovering beside her before pocketing the phone without responding to the message. "None of your damn business."

Wanna bet?

As difficult as it is, I keep that thought to myself. I don't need to aggravate her any more than I already have. It's almost impossible to believe there was ever a time she chased after me. You would never guess it from this disastrous interaction.

Even though I'm the one who fucked up our relationship, I don't want her dating other guys. Maybe Alyssa doesn't realize it yet, but she's mine. She's always been mine. Instead of holding her close and nurturing the love she had for me, I stomped on her heart and pushed her away.

There has to be a way for me to smooth this over. "Look, I—"

As soon as the light changes, Alyssa scrambles across the street. It only takes a few long-legged strides to catch up with her. It feels like that's all I've done.

Given chase.

"How about we meet for lunch," I suggest, knowing our time together is limited now that we've reached campus.

Her gaze stays focused on something in the distance only she can see. "Sorry, I'm busy."

"That's funny," I narrow my eyes, "but I didn't give you a specific time or date."

"It doesn't matter," she says in a clipped tone before scowling. "Where you're concerned, I'm busy for the foreseeable future."

Damn, but she's proving to be a tough nut to crack.

"Lys—" When she skewers me with a glare that could send a lesser man up in flames, I hastily correct myself. "Alyssa. I meant to say *Alyssa.*"

Impatience wafts off her in heavy waves as she grinds to a halt and swings toward me. She peers around before dropping her voice. "Whatever you're trying to accomplish here, I'm not interested. I'm really not." There's a pause as she steps close enough for me to feel the heat of her body. It takes everything inside me not to reach out and grab hold of her just to prove her wrong. She still wants me. I see it buried beneath the fury in her eyes.

For the first time since Alyssa returned to Wesley, I wonder if it's possible to break through the impenetrable walls she's erected. Doubt trickles in before I stomp it out.

"Here's the thing—you had me. I was all *yours*." Pain flickers across her face before it's once again masked behind a frosty exterior. "But you threw me away because you wanted to fuck your way through this campus."

No. That's not true.

"You need to move on and allow me to do the same. Just because you have regrets doesn't mean that I do. Or maybe this is all a game." She pops a shoulder. "Either way, I don't care."

Does she really think I'm capable of that kind of heartlessness?

That I could mastermind some kind of manipulative game to draw her in again before kicking her loose? Even though I can't necessarily blame her for being suspicious, her low opinion makes me gut sick.

When I remain silent, at a loss as to how to reach her, a pleading look enters her eyes, and for the first time, I truly wonder if there's any hope for us. Alyssa doesn't understand why I pushed her away. She believes the bullshit I spoon-fed her. What I need to do is tell her the truth. It had absolutely nothing to do with other girls and everything to do with the intensity of my feelings for her.

I open my mouth, ready to lay it all on the line. I don't give a damn if we're on the edge of campus, and there are a ton of people rushing past us on their way to class. I don't care about the curious stares we're collecting from onlookers. Our gazes stay fused together as everything around me falls away.

"Colton!"

The high-pitched voice has the moment disintegrating as I'm jolted back to reality. Alyssa blinks to awareness before taking a hasty step in retreat and flicking an uninterested glance at the girl waving frantically and calling my name.

"Seems like your fan club found you. Take a good look. That's what you dumped me for." With that, she walks away.

And there's not a damned thing I can do to detain her as I'm swarmed by a handful of girls.

Fuck.

Chapter Twenty-Two

ALYSSA

Hands down, this has been the week from hell.

All right, maybe that's a slight exaggeration.

My courses are going well. Most of them are dance which makes the day pass by quickly. And I was able to secure my old job at a small studio in town, teaching a few classes to four and five-year-olds. They're squirrelly and have way too much energy, but they're adorable as hell and make me laugh. And I need the cash. Unlike Mia, my parents don't have a fat portfolio filled with stocks and bonds.

So...if everything is going just fine, why am I not able to shake the feelings of irritability and discontent? It's almost as if something is brewing inside me, and I have no clue what it is. And that makes me nervous.

Jack has called a handful of times since my return, but our relationship no longer feels the same. It's almost as if I was able to blot out everything when I was away, and now that I've returned to Wesley, that's no longer possible. It only adds to my growing confusion.

What I will say is that it's nice to be back with Mia. I really did miss my girl. And dancing again for Monsieur Dupre has been amazing. I didn't realize how much I've learned and grown while studying in London. But he's taken notice. And that means everything to me.

My brain continues to spin as I yank open the building door and walk through the lobby. Instead of waiting for the elevator, I take the stairwell. As soon as I arrive at the third-floor landing and push through the metal door, the sound of music assaults me. My jaw unconsciously locks as I tighten my hands. The trimmed nails bite into my flesh, leaving little crescent-shaped imprints on each palm. Even though I'm at the far end of the hallway, I can already guess where the booming bass is originating from.

Colton and Beck's apartment.

In less than two seconds flat, the annoyance festering beneath the surface becomes full-blown anger.

The music grows in decibel with every step I take. By the time I shove the key in the lock, I'm ready to explode. With a slam of the door, I stalk into the living room. Mia is at the small dining room table with her laptop and earbuds. My guess is that they have to be noise-canceling, otherwise there is no way she could work through this racket. I shoot an irritated glance toward the thin wall we share with our neighbors. For a handful of seconds, I consider contacting the building manager to complain before reluctantly deciding against it.

That being said, if this continues much longer, I'll be more than happy to make that phone call. If that makes me a Karen, so be it.

Mia glances up from her computer screen and waves. The smile curving her lips disappears as she takes in my expression. She pulls out the earbuds and sets them on the table next to her laptop. "Hey! How was class?"

"It was fine." I send another glare toward our noisy neighbors before waving my hand in their direction. "How long has this been going on for?"

"Hmmm. Maybe an hour or so?" Mia shrugs. "It's not a big deal. It kind of goes with the territory when you're living in an apartment building with a bunch of college kids. The weekends get noisy."

My lips sink further into a scowl. "Someone should really talk to them about this." When her brows rise, I add, "It's so rude! I can barely hear myself think over that racket."

"I'm sure it won't last much longer. They're probably having a few drinks before hitting the parties."

"I don't give a damn what they're doing. They should have more consideration for the people who live next to them."

"Well," she says lightly, "I can see someone is in a mood."

I drag a hand down my face. Honestly, I don't know what's wrong with me. I spent two years in the dorms. The weekends were exactly like this, and it never bothered me in the least. Hell, most of the time, I was the one leading the charge. Even though I suspect the reason for my pissy mood, I'm not ready to acknowledge it to myself or Mia. Instead, I do my best to shake off the bad vibes before they can ruin my night.

"Sorry." I drop my bag onto a chair. "It's been a long week. I'm just tired and still adjusting to the time difference." That's a reasonable explanation for my behavior, right?

Mia pops to her feet before closing the distance between us and dragging me into her arms. Because my bestie knows me so well, she cuts right through the bullshit and gets to the heart of the matter. "I know it hasn't been easy living next to Colton, but I'm glad you're back. There's no way I would have wanted to go through senior year without you by my side."

Her earnestness makes the tension rushing through me evaporate. "Me, too." As tempting as it had been to stay in London, there's no way I would have actually gone through with it. Mia and I only have this year to spend together before we go our separate ways. Her to law school and me to...well, something with dance. I'm not nearly good enough to make a living as a professional, but I would love to open my own studio someday and teach.

"So, any plans for the night?" she asks before pulling away. "Isobel and Kara are going to Bang Bang. They didn't get nearly enough last weekend. Izzy said something about a hot bartender she wants to flirt with."

As soon as Mia mentions the club, an image of Colton pops into my brain. The way his lips had devoured mine before coasting over my body and settling on my—

Nope. There is no way I'm going there.

I quickly shove the memory away and shake my head. "I'm not in the mood to club."

"Really?" Her brows slide together. "Since when? You love shaking your ass on the dance floor."

She's right about that. Under normal circumstances, I enjoy getting out there and busting a move. It's the best feeling. Totally freeing. All my problems float away, and it's just me and the music.

I shrug, refusing to reveal the real reason. Bang Bang has officially been tainted. I don't know if I'll ever be able to go there again and not think about what happened in the parking lot. As much as I'm trying not to dwell on Colton, it's difficult when his music is reverberating off our walls.

"All right. I'm sure we can figure something else out. Let's see." She taps her finger against her chin. "I heard Lambda Chi Alpha is having a huge bash. We can always stop by and check it out."

"Yeah," I mutter, glancing away before sucking my lower lip into my mouth and chewing it thoughtfully, "maybe."

Usually, I'm the one attempting to cajole Mia into going out and cutting loose, not the other way around.

Disconcerted by the role reversal, Mia lays a hand across my forehead. "Are you feeling all right? You're not acting like yourself."

I snort out a laugh and try to shake off the strange emotions that have taken root inside me. It's become an all-too-common occurrence of late. As much as I don't want to admit it, this has everything to do with Colton. I hate that he wields so much control over my life when I want nothing to do with him. If only there were a way to purge the guy from my system once and for all. That's exactly what the time spent in London was supposed to accomplish.

Clearly, that turned out to be a major failure.

"I'm fine." I draw in a steady breath, trying to calm everything inside me before gradually releasing it back into the world. "You know what, maybe we should go to—"

My voice ends on a squeak when there's a loud crash against the interior wall that connects with the guy's apartment, and then the music is cranked up, which I didn't think was possible.

Mia raises her voice in order to be heard above the ruckus from next door. "Maybe we should go out and grab something to eat."

I grit my teeth and try to hold onto the last shred of my temper, but it's useless. "I'm not going to be forced out of my own apartment! I've had enough. I'm going over there to put a stop to this!"

"Oh, God." Even though she mutters the words under her breath, I hear them loud and clear. "This isn't going to end well."

"Not for them it won't," I agree wholeheartedly.

Before she can stop me, I stalk out of the apartment. Twenty steps bring me to their door. I raise my fist and pound on the wood. Now that I'm right outside their place, the music is almost deafening.

This is ridiculous!

Ten seconds tick by without a response. Why am I surprised? They probably can't hear it. I grit my teeth and rap my knuckles harder.

Fuck!

I hiss out a breath before shaking my hand.

Oh, I am so going to let them have it!

After another twenty seconds, the door swings open, and I find Beck standing on the other side. There's a cheerful smile lighting up his face. "Hey, neighbor! Wanna come in? We're pregaming it. Lotta parties happening tonight." He points at me. "You should really come out with us."

My eyes narrow before I bare my teeth. A low growl rumbles up from my chest.

There's a pause.

"Hold on and give me a sec." He raises a finger before turning away and bellowing into the crowded apartment, "Colton, it's for you!"

Instead of waiting, I push past Beck and stomp inside the tiny entryway. Jeez. There must be at least thirty people jammed in here. I recognize a number of guys from the football team. For each one, there are two girls hanging off them.

Unless you're Colton Montgomery—then you have at least four groupies pawing at you.

A punch of unwanted jealousy surges through me before I can stomp it out. The thought is so disturbing that I quickly shove it from my brain. As soon as our gazes collide, he rises from the couch he's parked on. Without a word to the chicks attempting to maul him, he cuts easily through the crush of people. His towering presence has them scattering out of the way. It only takes a moment for him to reach me.

Before he can say anything, I snap, "We need to talk."

Carefully he searches my face. "Okay."

When he doesn't move, I growl, "In private." Any moment, I'm going to totally lose it.

"All right." He locks his fingers around mine and tows me through the cluster of people laughing and drinking in the small apartment.

Even though I steel myself for it, the moment he makes contact, a little zip of electricity sizzles through my veins. If there's a way to turn off this unwanted attraction, I have yet to find it.

It's only after he shutters us away in the privacy of his bedroom and clicks the lock into place that I wonder if marching over to give him a piece of my mind was the best course of action. He leans against the door, barring my escape, before crossing his arms against the wide expanse of his chest.

It's official...this was definitely a terrible idea. I should have taken Mia up on her offer to grab something for dinner and gotten the hell out of here instead of taking matters into my own hands.

"What's up?" he asks, interrupting the frantic whirl of my thoughts.

My mouth goes bone dry as I try not to notice how good he looks in the fitted navy-colored T-shirt that hugs his biceps. It occurs to me that this is precisely how I got in trouble last weekend.

I clear my throat and glance away. "The music is really loud." Unconsciously, my gaze flickers to him. It's like I can't *not* look in his direction.

"Yeah, sorry about that. Things got a little out of control. I'll turn it down. It's not a problem."

His easy apology takes the wind out of my sails. I shift my weight, unsure where we go from here.

One brow hikes up across his forehead. "Is there anything else?"

"No." I shake my head as my teeth sink into my lower lip.

The room turns quiet as he pushes away from the door, eating up the distance between us. Every step sends my heart jackhammering against my ribcage until I'm positive he can hear it above the pumping beat of the music emanating from the other room. Every nerve ending inside me goes on high alert.

My eyes widen. As much as I've tried to convince myself that I'm over Colton, that's not the case. I hate the attraction that hums like a live wire between us. The callous manner in which he dumped my ass should have killed every fragile emotion inside me. It's disconcerting to realize that it hasn't. My feelings are as strong as ever. Even if they're tinged at the edges with fury, somehow that only makes them more potent.

What's worse is that every intention is clearly written across his face. And still, I'm powerless to stop it from coming to fruition.

My hands tighten. "Don't," I whisper, knowing that it won't stop this from happening. The moment he grabbed my hand and towed me into this room, the battle was already lost. I just didn't realize it until this very moment.

He gently cups my cheeks before tipping my head and searching my eyes. "You shouldn't have come here."

He's right. I'm already berating myself for my stupidity, but there's nothing to be done about it now. I walked right into the lion's den, thinking I would come away unscathed.

I'll be lucky to make it out alive.

Barely do I get a chance to suck in a breath before his mouth crashes onto mine. One sweep against my lips, and I'm opening until he can plunge inside. Our tongues tangle, and it's enough to wipe away the knowledge that this is a disastrous idea. My palms go to his chest. Instead of shoving him away, my fingers curl into his shirt, attempting to drag him closer. A growl rumbles up from his chest.

Our lips fasten, and teeth scrape against one another. All of the protests inside my head go silent as a barrage of sensations flood through me. As much as I try to convince myself that Colton is no different from any of the other guys I've been with, I realize deep down inside this is a lie. Colton is unlike anyone else. There is something elemental between us. Electric. Cataclysmic. Every time we come together, this knowledge is slammed home almost painfully, making it impossible to ignore.

I'm not sure how to go about altering this truth. It might not even be possible. All I know is that when I'm locked in his arms and his mouth is claiming mine, I feel more alive than ever before.

And that, in a nutshell, is the problem.

How do you go about eradicating an emotion so powerful?

I don't have an answer.

His hands fall from my face, gliding over my chest and belly before arriving at the button of my jeans where they hesitate. "I want you, Alyssa. Saturday night wasn't nearly enough."

A groan bubbles up in my throat because he's right. Even as I lay stretched against his car, the warm night air hitting my damp flesh, I had already arrived at the same conclusion. If that encounter did anything, it was only to stoke all those dormant emotions to life.

Guess the joke is on me. They're more alive than ever and clamoring to break free.

"Do you want this?" he asks when I remain silent.

Say no!

Push him away!

Do something!

"Yes." As soon as the word escapes from my lips, the snap of my fly is released, and the zipper tugged down. My fingers skim across his flat abdominals, hovering for a moment before dipping inside his athletic shorts and wrapping around his hard length.

Oh, God.

Memories of what it felt like to have him surging inside me bursts into my consciousness as the scrap of material between my legs dampens. We always fit together perfectly like two pieces of a puzzle.

As soon as the zipper is lowered, his hand delves inside my panties and parts my lower lips before thrusting deep inside. A gasp escapes from me as a second finger joins the first. My muscles contract around him as pleasure floods through every cell of my body.

"You're so fucking wet." He pumps his fingers, picking up the pace. "I've missed this so much."

Even as the words reverberate throughout my being, I refuse to parrot them back to him. Already I've given him so much more than I wanted.

My fingers tighten around his cock. Somehow, it becomes harder, feeling more like steel. Another punch of arousal hits me as I remember what it was like to take him in my mouth. To have his fingers tunnel through my hair and watch him spiral out of control.

"That feels so damn good," he whispers hoarsely as I stroke his shaft. "I need to be inside you, baby."

The endearment is like a fist tightening around my heart, squeezing until it becomes painful.

Don't do it! Allowing him inside your body will only make matters worse. It'll be like he's branding you all over again.

"I want that, too." I hear myself say the words as if from far away.

"Thank fuck."

He breaks free from me before crouching down and ripping away both the panties and jeans. Once they've been tossed aside, he brushes a kiss against my bare pussy before rising to his feet and lifting me off mine. A moment later, we're tumbling onto his queen-size bed, and he's landing between my legs. There's something comforting about his heavy weight pressing me into the mattress. If I close my eyes, it would be so easy to trick myself into believing that everything was the same.

That *we* were the same.

With his shorts in place, his thick erection presses against my heat, and a shiver of need careens through me.

His movements still. "Are you absolutely sure about this?"

Yes.

No.

Oh, God.

I jerk my head into a tight nod. For better or worse, this is happening. Colton and I are like two trains on the same track destined for a head-on collision. He slips his hand between us and yanks away the material covering him. In one swift motion, he thrusts deep inside me.

Yes!

A whimper falls from my lips as a feeling of fullness suffuses me. It's been more than a year and a half since Colton has been inside my body. A powerful concoction of pleasure infused pain jolts through me as he buries himself to the hilt. Once he bottoms out, he holds himself perfectly rigid. His girth stretches me impossibly wide. I used to tease him about having such a thick cock, but it's the truth. I feel owned when he's inside me, and my core is pulsing around him, attempting to adjust to his size. He brings every nerve ending to life.

"Shit," he grits between clenched teeth, "I forgot the condom."

"I'm protected," I quickly say. I've never allowed anyone but Colton inside my body without one. This is exactly what this guy does to me, and I wish with all my being he didn't. He makes me throw my better judgment out the window.

A grunt of relief escapes from him as he pulls out almost completely before thrusting home again. A tidal wave of pleasure crashes over me, and I forget there isn't a thin barrier of latex to separate us.

He repeats the movement. With each thrust of his hips, ecstasy swirls through me, building until I can't contain it.

"Fuck, baby," he growls, "I'm going to come."

As soon as he bites out the words, an orgasm streaks through me. His name is a fervent chant on my lips. Stars explode behind my eyelids, and for one glorious moment, it feels like I'm going to pass out. I can't remember the last time I experienced such an intense release.

Colton arches his back, continuing to move, riding out the wave until his muscles turn lax. As his head falls forward, he buries his face in the hollow of my neck. His warm breath wafts across my flesh as I squeeze my eyes tight.

Huffing out a breath, I force my eyes open and stare sightlessly at the ceiling. I've always taken responsibility for my actions. Colton didn't force me to have sex. Nor did he make me do anything I didn't want to in the parking lot of Bang Bang.

I allowed this to happen.

Wanted it, even.

And now I'll be the one who lives with the consequences.

It's almost as if Colton can sense the disconcerting thoughts crashing through my head as he props himself up on his elbows and watches me. "Am I hurting you?"

"No." I shake my head, realizing that if there's anyone inflicting pain, it's me.

His voice turns cautious. "Are you all right?"

Rather than meet his inquisitive stare, I keep my attention focused on the ceiling. I need to come up with an extraction plan. "I'm fine."

His cock is still buried deep inside my body. There's a part of me that doesn't want him to pull out. Even though I'm not looking at him, I feel the weight of his stare. There's no hiding from it. "You don't seem fine."

A sigh escapes as my gaze flickers toward him. Now that the ecstasy has faded, an odd kind of regret rushes in to fill the void. "This shouldn't have happened."

"Don't say that," he whispers, sounding almost wounded by my words, which is laughable considering that he's the one who threw me away. When he buries his face against the side of my neck for a second time, a shiver scampers down my spine as his warm breath feathers over my flesh. "Give me another chance."

My heart stutters.

No.

Sex is one thing, handing over my heart is an entirely different matter. "How can I do that when I don't trust you?"

His breath catches, but he doesn't offer up a response.

And that, my friends, is all the answer I need.

Chapter Twenty-Three

COLTON

I check my phone for the umpteenth time for any missed messages.

Unfortunately, it's just as I suspected.

Nada.

I reached out and texted Alyssa a few times, but it's been stereo silence from her end, which isn't a total surprise. Nothing I do seems to make a difference. If anything, my actions have only pushed her further away. At this point, I have no idea how to bridge the gap that now separates us.

It's been more than a week since she stomped over, and we had sex. I find myself hanging around the apartment building, trying to catch sight of her, but she remains elusive. Almost as if she's trying to evade me.

Actually, that's *exactly* the tactic she's employing.

That girl wants nothing to do with me, and there doesn't seem to be a damn thing I can do to change that. I hate to admit it, but I'm teetering on the verge of giving up. There are times in life when you fuck up and are able to fix the mess. This isn't one of them.

My head is full of Alyssa as I walk across campus on my way to my last class of the day. It's a business course and boring as hell. Although I suspect that has more to do with the professor than the material.

He's a middle-aged dude with a monotone voice. No matter how many energy drinks I guzzle, it's never enough to keep me from dozing off.

As I pass by Grinders R Us, the local coffee house on campus, a flash of long, blond hair catches the corner of my eye, and my head whips in that direction. My footsteps falter as I spot Alyssa sitting at a table inside. Her lips lift into a smile as she tucks a stray lock of hair behind her ear. A bolt of electricity surges through me as my attention zeros in on her, eclipsing everything around me. I wrack my brain, trying to remember the last time she looked at me like that.

It was more than a year and a half ago. Before I blew our relationship to hell. Back then, there were times when I would catch her staring at me like I was a fucking god. I loved it. Craved it. Reveled in it. In the end, I took her feelings for granted, thinking it would always be that way. Turns out that's not the case.

I don't realize I've sidled up to the picture window until my nose hits the glass.

"Fuck," I mumble, rubbing the tip with my fingers and taking a hasty step in retreat.

Is this really what it's come to?

Me stalking some girl in the middle of campus in broad daylight?

Don't answer that.

No one has ever twisted me up inside like this. Every instinct is screaming at me to go inside and claim my girl. But how can I do that when it's become increasingly clear that Alyssa wants nothing to do with me? The mature thing to do would be to respect her wishes and move on. As I force myself to take a reluctant step away from the window, a burst of laughter escapes from her lips as a large hand reaches across the table before settling on hers.

What the hell?

And then I'm right back where I started, pressed against the glass. Only now do I realize that she's not alone. There's a guy parked across from her. All thoughts of backing off and giving Alyssa her space evaporate as I hightail it into the coffee shop and stomp over to where the happy couple is lounging. Even the thought of another guy touching her is enough to set me off.

You know what scares me most?

That she actually might move on without giving me another shot.

As soon as I pull up alongside the table, Alyssa glances at me. The smile falls from her face as her eyes widen. "Colton."

"Hey." My narrowed gaze slices to the guy across from her.

A heavy silence blankets the three of us, turning the atmosphere oppressive.

Alyssa shifts on her chair before clearing her throat. "Levi, this is Colton."

Levi?

What the hell kind of name is that?

Unaffected by the way I glower, the dark-haired guy sits back in his chair as a relaxed smile lifts the corners of his lips. "Oh, hey. You're Colton Montgomery. Nice to meet you, man."

"Yeah," I mumble, even though I don't mean it, "same."

"The Wildcats are having a great season." He chuckles, "I probably shouldn't admit this, but I have a lot of money riding on you guys winning a conference championship."

"Is that so?" I grunt in response, tempted to tank the season just so this guy loses money.

Fuck him.

Of course, that's not going to happen. I'm still playing like shit, so my ass hasn't seen very much of the field lately. Kwiatkowski, on the other hand, is living his best life. I shove that thought from my head, not wanting to dwell on it. I've got more pressing matters to contend with.

Namely, this guy.

Levi.

I try not to snort.

"Yeah," he continues, "I was just telling my buddies that—"

Dismissing him, I shift my weight and focus on Alyssa. I don't give a damn what this guy was yapping to his buddies about. "Can I talk to you outside?"

"Oh." She peeks across the table at Levi from beneath the thick fringe of her lashes. "Well, I—"

"Great." Not taking no for an answer, I grab her hand and pull her to her feet. She rises with a small squeak of protest.

"Maybe you haven't realized it, but we're in the middle of some-thing here," Levi says, straightening on his chair.

No, douchebag, you're not.

I swear to God, if he gets in my way, I'm going to punch him. Now that I'm practically benched, I've got nothing to lose.

Alyssa must see the determination that has settled over my features because she quickly says, "It's fine, Levi. I'll be back in a minute."

Yeah, that's not going to happen either.

"Are you sure?" His gaze bounces reluctantly between the pair of us as a frown settles on his face.

No more easy-peasy smile, is there?

"Yup." Alyssa gives me a bit of side-eye. "It's all good."

Levi grumbles something indecipherable under his breath before slouching against the chair. It's like he realizes he should be making more of a fuss since I swooped in and hijacked the girl he was with.

Now that a decision has been made, I haul Alyssa out of the shop and around the corner away from the prying eyes of student traffic. Plus, I don't want the dude inside to come out and find us.

"Colton," she growls, "was that really necessary?"

You bet your ass it was.

When I advance on her, she scoots away until there's nowhere else to go. Her shoulder blades hit the brick building. My fingers lock around her wrists before dragging them over her head and shackling them against the wall.

The pulse beneath the delicate flesh of her throat flutters wildly as she whispers, "What are you doing?"

"This." And then my mouth is crashing onto hers. The urge to brand her as my own throbs through me.

For a moment, her body stiffens before melting beneath mine. The taste of her is the only thing powerful enough to calm the beast raging inside. It's desperate to claw its way from beneath my skin.

The irony is that I spent so many years not wanting to feel anything, afraid to let anyone in, including this girl. *Most especially this girl.* My deepest, darkest fear is that they'll disappear from my life. It's not something I'm entirely comfortable acknowledging. It's the reason I pushed Alyssa away after she revealed her feelings for me. I know what it's like to love someone completely. To have them walk away and not bother with you again is soul-crushing. I've gone to great lengths never to experience that kind of pain again.

Until this tiny female insisted on clawing her way inside me and burrowing deep.

And now she wants to walk away?

Move on without me?

Forget I ever existed?

No way. I refuse to allow that to happen.

It's only when she turns soft and pliant that I take the kiss deeper, so deep I have no idea where she ends, and I begin. When I finally lift my mouth away, we're both breathing hard. I rest my forehead against hers. The only time I feel sane is when she's in my arms.

Unfortunately, I'm the last person she wants touching her.

"Who's the guy?" I ask gruffly, unable to forget about him.

As if waking from a dream, she blinks away the thick haze clouding her eyes. "Just someone from class."

"Was it a date that I interrupted?" It better not have been.

Her body stiffens. Just when I think she'll refuse to answer, she admits in a clipped tone, "We were grabbing a coffee."

"Do you like him?" Unable to hold back, I can't stop myself from bombarding her with a spray of questions. Honestly, I don't know what I'll do if she's developed feelings for the guy. How can I combat that?

"We're just friends."

A puff of relief escapes from me.

Even though I have no right to tell her what to do, the words burst free before I can rein them back in again. "I don't want you with anyone else. And I sure as shit don't want any other guys touching you."

"Colton..." Emotion flickers in her eyes before she glances away.

"Look at me," I growl.

Her widened gaze slices to mine as I repeat, "I don't want anyone else touching you." When she remains silent, I run the tip of my nose along the curve of her jaw. "I don't want anyone else inside your body."

"Please," she whispers. Not only is she intent on fighting me, but herself as well. I hear the struggle in her voice. And I get it. Truly, I do, but still…

"Give me another chance, Lys." Before she can shoot me down, I add, "That's all I need to prove that I've changed. That I'm not the same guy you left behind."

A rush of air escapes as her body wilts against mine. "I don't know."

Her wrists are still pinned against the brick wall as I ghost my mouth over hers. "Just one."

When I make another pass, never quite touching her lips, she groans and tilts her head as if silently offering them up to me.

"You've got my word that I won't fuck it up this time."

"I can't go through that again, Colton. I just can't."

Thick emotion bleeds through her voice, and it nearly breaks my heart. I'm the one who did this to her. And I'll have to live with that knowledge for the rest of my life. "I'm sorry, baby."

I hold my breath as indecision flickers across her features.

"Okay," she finally says, giving in. "But it's one chance. After that, if I want to walk away, if I want you to leave me alone, you do it. No questions asked."

Even though the thought of that happening is terrifying, it's all I have to work with.

"One chance," I vow, "is all I need."

Chapter Twenty-Four

ALYSSA

I can't believe I'm actually going through with this.

How did I let Colton persuade me into giving him another shot?

Persuade...ha!

If I've come to realize anything, it's that I have no resistance when it comes to the blond, blue-eyed football player. All he has to do is lay his hands on me, and my brain leaks right out of my ear. It's disconcerting.

For the hundredth time today, I pick up my phone and stare at it. I should cancel. That would be the smartest thing to do. Just as I type out a message, there's a knock on the apartment door. My head snaps up as my belly crashes to my toes. I place my palm against my lower abdomen as if that will keep it in place.

It's too late. He's already here.

I straighten my shoulders. Fine, I can do this. It's one date. One single chance. That's all I agreed to. If he fucks it up, I can walk away with a clear conscience. When my heart clenches at the idea of us really being over, I brush it aside and tell myself that it's for the best. Colton isn't the kind of guy I need in my life. He's just the one I'm attracted to.

For a moment, I force myself to relive the way he broke up with me. The text message that popped up out of nowhere. And then waiting outside his locker room when he refused to take my calls. A dull ache fills me as I dredge up the ugliness of his words.

Come on, girl, you had to know this was a long shot when we got together. It was a gamble. You rolled the dice, and it came up snake eyes. You should be giving me props for remaining faithful this long. As much as I've enjoyed your unicorn pussy, this whole exclusivity thing isn't for me. I wouldn't mind keeping you in my back pocket and having a taste of it every once in a while. No strings attached, of course.

It's the rap of knuckles against wood that knocks me out of the painful memory as I force my feet into motion. When I'm standing in front of the door, I inhale a shaky breath before reaching out and twisting the knob. Even though it's not a surprise to find Colton standing on the other side of the threshold, my heart skips a beat.

Instead of his normal jeans or athletic shorts paired with a T-shirt, he's wearing a pale pink polo and chinos that hug his muscular thighs. There's an oversized silver watch wrapped around his left wrist and a sprinkle of dark blond hair covering his bare forearms.

My mouth turns cottony as I take in the sight of him.

Why does he have to be so damn sexy?

I gulp as a fresh burst of nerves explodes inside me. I am in *so* much trouble. This was a mistake. One I never should have agreed to. Already I know there's only one way this will end, and that's badly.

For me.

No matter what happens, I'm going to get hurt. And I'm nowhere near healed from the last time.

The way his gaze skims over me feels very much like a physical caress. "You look beautiful."

Heat seeps into my cheeks as I glance away. It's difficult to hold his stare. The possessiveness that fills his eyes leaves me feeling skittish. "Thanks."

As much as I didn't want to dress with Colton in mind this evening, that's exactly what I found myself doing. Even though it's mid-September, and the weather is seasonable, I know the temperature will drop, and it will become chilly. I decided on a thin, loosely knit, cream-colored sweater with three-quarter length sleeves and a short red skirt with a white tear drop pattern. I've paired silvery sandals with the outfit. It's a little summer and autumn mixed together.

If I was looking for confidence, this outfit gives it to me. Although maybe that approach has backfired because the appreciation in Colton's eyes is clear.

"Let me get my purse, and we can go," I say, needing to break the escalating tension before it reaches a flashpoint.

"Sounds good."

I give myself a silent pep talk as I grab the black bag off the dining room table and return to the entryway.

Nothing is going to happen that I don't want.

That knowledge doesn't provide nearly enough comfort given the fact that I fold like a cheap house of cards every time he lays his hands on me. Fortunately, we'll probably head out to a party. Colton will get swarmed by groupies, and I'll be on my own for the duration of the evening. Then I can tell him he had his chance and blew it. I remember all too well what it was like to go out with him in public. He has an overzealous fan club, and from what I've witnessed since my return, they're as enthusiastic as ever. It's a reassuring thought.

He steps aside as I stride into the hallway and close the door behind me.

A couple of hours, and this will be over.

As I move toward the elevator, he says, "We're not heading that way."

Huh? I grind to a halt before swinging around to face him. "I don't understand."

One side of his mouth hitches at the confusion that must be written across my face. "I made dinner for us at my apartment."

My mouth dries at the idea of spending time alone with him. "Oh." Well, shit. This isn't good. "Um...I thought we were going to hit a party."

Heat fills his eyes, and his voice drops. "I didn't want there to be any distractions."

I gulp down my growing unease.

Yeah, that's exactly what I'd been counting on. Distractions, and plenty of them.

I shift uncomfortably from one foot to the other before blurting, "I'm not going to have sex with you again."

"It's just dinner, Lys." A chuckle escapes from him. "That's all this is."

It won't ever be *just* dinner.

Not with Colton.

Not with the way my heart is hammering under my chest.

And Beck won't be there to run interference either. His parents are having an anniversary celebration this weekend. Both he and Mia returned home, albeit separately. Like they would ever travel together? Ha! Not likely. My bestie wasn't looking forward to it.

Colton holds out his hand for me to take. "Are you ready?"

Nope! Not at all.

Instead of admitting the truth, I jerk my head into a tight nod, tentatively placing my fingers in his. A sizzle of awareness shoots down my spine as his larger ones close around them. Why does it have to be like this between us? After everything that happened, how is he still able to affect me like this?

A horde of butterflies erupts in my belly with every step that brings me closer to his apartment. Any moment, they're going to find an escape hatch and break loose. Once the door is opened, he ushers me inside. I pause in the entryway and glance around. The place is dimly lit, but it smells—I cautiously sniff the air—really good.

Familiar.

When I realize what it is, I spin toward him. "You ordered chicken parmigiana?"

His smile widens. "Nope, I made it with my own two hands."

"What?" Since when does Colton cook?

He chuckles at my surprise. "Trust me, it wasn't easy. I had Jenna on the phone for an hour, walking me through the steps."

I...have no words.

"Why would you do that?" I whisper, trying to wrap my head around this information.

"Because it's your favorite." He shrugs. "At least it used to be." The question is there, lurking in his eyes.

"It still is," I begrudgingly admit. I love Italian to begin with, but chicken parm is my absolute favorite. I've had it at every Italian restaurant I've ever visited. Some have been amazing, while others have just been good.

When I continue to stare in bewilderment, he places his hand on the small of my back and propels me gently inside the apartment. Ten steps bring me into the dining room. The setup is exactly the same as ours. Two bedrooms to the left with a bathroom in the middle and a small living room straight ahead. Outside there's a balcony big enough for a cafe-style table and two chairs. The kitchen is to the right with all the essentials, minus a dishwasher, crammed into the tight space. A breakfast bar surveys the living room/dining room combination. While my apartment is decorated and homey with artwork and photographs, the guy's apartment is bare. More utilitarian in nature. It's a place to drop their bags at the end of the night and crash.

"Would you like a glass of wine?" he asks, interrupting my perusal.

Holy crap. Is he offering me an adult beverage?

Well, he's certainly pulling out all the stops. It's a little frightening. At least, I'm alarmed by it. As much as I shouldn't give in and have a drink, I need something to steady my nerves.

"Go ahead and sit down." He points to the table, which is already set with plates and silverware. "Everything is ready."

On wooden legs, I force myself to the table and awkwardly take a seat on the chair. My fingers fidget restlessly in my lap. Colton returns with two glasses of red wine before offering one to me.

Once mine is in hand, he raises his glass and offers a toast. "To new beginnings."

Another burst of nerves explode inside me. With stiff lips, I echo the sentiment and raise the glass to my mouth before gulping down at least half the contents. If this behavior continues, I will never make it through the evening.

If he's aware of my anxiety, he refrains from commenting. Instead, he returns to the kitchen and brings out a colorful-looking salad filled with lettuce, tomatoes, cucumbers, and croutons before doling out our servings. There's a bottle of Italian dressing already on the table. I pour just enough to give the greens taste. What I've discovered over the years is that there is no way to hide a few extra pounds in a skintight leotard.

As much as I hate to admit it, if the dinner Colton made tastes half as good as it smells, I'll be going back for seconds. I haven't had this dish since I left for London. As delicious as the food was across the pond—hello, fish and chips with malted vinegar—I missed a few favorites.

This was definitely one of them.

Colton keeps the conversation flowing, peppering me with questions about my study abroad program. As I finish off the salad, I lift my glass to take a sip and realize it's empty. He quickly refills it without asking.

While I silently debate a second glass, Colton brings out the main course along with a plate filled with buttery-looking garlic bread. This guy is really trying to kill me. If there's one thing I've learned over the years, it's that carbs and dancing don't mix. Well, they do in that they give you energy which is needed to dance. But processed carbs are a big no-no. That being said, it doesn't stop me from grabbing a slice oozing with butter and herbs and placing it on my plate along with the chicken dish he serves.

I haven't even taken a taste yet, and already my mouth is salivating.

"Be honest, did you really cook all this?" I'm finding this scenario a little difficult to wrap my head around. The Colton I remember never went out of his way for a girl. The truth is that he didn't need to impress the female sex, they chased after him regardless. All he had to do was sit back and soak up the adoration. And yeah, I was right there, in the thick of it, vying for his attention. Even when we dated sophomore year, girls continued to hang on him, propositioning him when my back was turned. And nothing has changed in that regard. So why is he bothering with this?

Why is he bothering with *me*?

"I did." His gaze stays locked on mine from across the table as he takes a sip of his wine.

Unable to hold the intensity of his gaze, mine drops to his lips as arousal explodes in my core where it settles uncomfortably. I shift on my chair, but it does nothing to alleviate the growing tension that simmers between us.

"Lys."

I blink out of the daze and glance at him. What I find smoldering in his blue depths only adds to the growing tension brewing inside me. I've had too much wine and not enough food. That has to be the problem.

As I reach for my fork, he extends his hand across the table, laying it over mine. Awareness crackles in the air between us. "I'm trying to be good here, but when you stare at me like that, it makes me think you want me as much as I want you. I'm trying to take this slow and prove that I'm not the same guy I was before." He pauses. "But you're making that difficult."

All of the saliva in my mouth dries. I tell myself to look away but can't do it. Colton Montgomery is like the sun. And I find myself getting sucked into his gravitational force even though I've done everything in my power to avoid it.

"Is there anything else I can get for you?" he asks. "Maybe a water?"

"Yes, please." My voice comes out sounding more like a croak.

As soon as he disappears into the kitchen, I drag a hand over my face and order myself to pull it together. Barely do I get a chance to huff out a breath before he's returning and handing over a bottle. With trembling fingers, I twist off the cap and guzzle down half of the cold liquid. It does nothing to alleviate the fire burning inside. Any moment, I'll go up in flames, and there's not a damn thing I can do about it.

How can I put Colton in my rearview mirror and move on with my life when he's doing everything possible to drag me back in again? This would be so much easier if he was the same jackass who broke up with me through text. He's trying to chip away at the walls I've erected, and if I'm not careful, he'll smash right through them.

By the time I finish my chicken parmesan and set down my fork, I'm a jittery mess and sliding headfirst into a food coma. I need to get out of here before my resolve softens.

"Thanks for dinner." I wave a hand toward the table and my demolished plate. "This was amazing." Who knew that Colton Montgomery actually had mad culinary skills? If the word got out, he'd be even more of a hot commodity than he already is.

"Thank you for agreeing to come over."

I jerk my head into a nod and rise from my chair. "I, ah, should—"

Go before anything regrettable happens.

"Wait, I have dessert." With stealth-like grace, he pops to his feet. One step is all it takes to close the distance between us.

I shake my head, tempted to make a mad dash for the door. "I couldn't possibly eat anything more. I'm stuffed."

"Fair enough." His fingers swallow mine up as he takes my hand. "How about we watch a movie, and then we can have dessert in a little bit?"

No way. That's a terrible idea.

He sweetens the deal by adding, "I'll even let you pick out the movie."

Say what now?

I hate to admit just how tempting the offer is. When we were together, I had to practically force Colton to sit through a rom-com or anything sappy.

With narrowed eyes, I can't resist testing the waters. "Amy Schumer has a new comedy out."

His jaw ticks as he sucks in a sharp breath before steadily releasing it back into the world. "Amy Schumer?"

My lips tremble at the corners. "That's right. I remember how much you enjoy her as an actress."

Even though he remains silent, I can tell that he's tempted to argue the point. With any luck, he'll turn me down flat, and I can scamper back to my place.

"Okay," he says with a shrug. "We'll watch it."

Well, damn.

I glance at the couch and realize I've made a tactical error in judgment. Unfortunately, it's much too late to back out now. Plus, I've really wanted to watch this movie and haven't had the time. School and dance have kept me busy, which is good. Less time to dwell on Colton. I almost wince at that unchecked thought as it pops into my head.

Reluctantly, I grab my bottle of water and beeline to the overstuffed chair in the corner, while Colton runs the plates to the kitchen. This seems like the safest option. I'll be an island onto myself. As I nestle into the chair, I'm actually feeling fairly proud of my strategic maneuvering. I've beaten him at his own game, and I get to watch a movie I'm interested in. Seems like a win-win to me. I keep my face carefully blank as he saunters into the living room. He'll be forced to sit on the couch all by his lonesome. I'm sure he wasn't expecting that.

Ha!

I'm tempted to crow—*checkmate* but keep my giddiness contained.

Instead of heading to the couch like I expect, Colton stops in front of me. I'm about to ask what he's doing when he leans down, slides his arms around my body, and scoops me up in one smooth movement. A yelp of surprise escapes from me as he settles on the chair before repositioning me so that I'm snuggled against him.

This is definitely *not* what I had in mind.

"Good choice." Humor simmers in his deep voice as he grabs the remote off of the small table beside him. Unsure what to do, I remain stiff as he cues up the movie.

And here I'd thought I had outwitted him. Turns out he's the one who outmaneuvered me.

"Relax," he whispers as the opening credits flash across the screen.

That's easier said than done.

How can I loosen up when his hard body is stretched out beneath mine?

Even though I keep my gaze trained on the television and attempt to focus on the movie, it's impossible. Unable to sit still, I squirm until his hands settle on my shoulders, gently pulling me toward his chest. His legs are stretched out in front of him as mine hang off the side of the chair. The position is entirely too comfortable and, after a while, my muscles turn slack as my head nestles against the hollow of his neck. The woodsy scent of his cologne inundates my senses, lulling me into a strangely contented state.

A sigh of contentment escapes from me as Colton absently strokes his fingers through my hair. Only now do I realize how much I've missed these quiet moments. There were a ton of parties, but it was the nights we spent shuttered away from everyone that were my favorite because I had Colton all to myself. It wasn't necessary for me to share him with his teammates, friends, or other girls. He was all mine.

Midway through the movie, I realize that I have absolutely no idea what's going on. I'm not even sure what the plot is. The only thing I'm capable of focusing on is the way his fingers stroke over me. I'm so tempted to purr and stretch like a cat basking under the warmth of the sun.

Every caress fuels the flame of desire he has carefully kindled to life deep in my core. I have to fight the temptation to turn in his arms and straddle him. I want to pepper kisses along his shadowed jawline. I want to nip his earlobe between my teeth. Part of me wants to sink to my knees and take him in my—

Crap.

As those sneaky thoughts invade my brain like a swarm of locusts, I jolt to awareness before scrambling off his lap. "I need to go." The words come out sounding ridiculously breathy as need bubbles up inside me.

Unaware of the dirty thoughts running rampant through my brain, his brows jerk together as he points to the television. "But the movie isn't over yet."

I wave a hand. "Yeah, I know, but I really should go." Even though I have no idea what time it is, I add, "It's late."

He glances at the silver watch adorning his wrist. The one I'd found so damn sexy when he picked me up earlier. It does nothing to alleviate the arousal crashing around inside me. "It's only ten."

"Yeah, but I'm exhausted." I feign a yawn but stop short of stretching my arms over my head. "It's been a long week."

As I back into the dining room area, Colton rises to his feet. "Do you want dessert before you leave?"

Hell, no.

I shake my head and pat my belly. "I'm still full."

Disappointment flickers in his eyes. "Well, at least let me wrap it up, and you can take it home with you. Maybe have it for breakfast tomorrow morning."

Argh.

He's being entirely too nice. I almost can't take all this sweetness. "You really don't—"

"It's not a problem," he interrupts. "Give me a couple of minutes to get it packed up."

Colton disappears into the kitchen before I can decline the offer for a second time. Shifting restlessly, I wring my hands, only wanting to escape before the images rolling through my head have any chance of coming to fruition. A few minutes later, he returns with a transparent container filled with chicken parmesan and a small white box that I assume holds the dessert.

Relief floods through me as I nip my purse from the counter and hold out my hands for the boxes. "Thanks, you really didn't have to do that."

"I wanted to," he murmurs before nodding toward the door. "Come on, I'll walk you home."

A chuckle bubbles up from my throat. "Don't worry about it. I think it's safe enough for me to walk forty feet."

He cocks his head as his gaze searches mine. "Escorting you to your apartment has nothing to do with safety."

And just like that, my belly hollows out, and my chest constricts. It takes everything I have inside not to melt into a puddle of goo. As tempting as it is to argue, I don't bother. I know a losing battle when I see one. Instead, I scramble out of his apartment, striding down the hallway as fast as humanly possible. The quicker I get to my door, the sooner I can escape from him. No matter how swiftly I move, Colton is right there beside me. His long legs are no match for my shorter ones.

Even though I don't want to be hyperaware of his presence, that's exactly what I am. The warmth that emanates from him. His aftershave as it teases my senses with memories. It's almost too much to bear. Any moment, I'll come undone.

A puff of air breaks free as I find myself standing in front of my door. With a smile plastered across my face, I spin around and thrust out my hand, only wanting to say good night and get this over with. More like get away from the tangle of emotions he rouses inside me. Further inspection isn't necessary to realize that they're dangerous and counterproductive to everything I've been attempting to accomplish since my return to Wesley.

He steps closer, and the distance between us gets swallowed up. I tilt my head in order to maintain eye contact as his warm breath drifts over me. Why does it have to feel so intoxicating? It takes effort not to strain forward and inhale a big breath of him.

I clear my throat and glance away, attempting to break the tentative connection that has formed in the span of a few short hours. "Thanks again for dinner."

My gaze jerks to him as his fingers slip beneath my chin. "I'm glad we could spend a little time together. It was nice."

A shiver slides through me as I press my lips together, reluctant to agree. As much as I hate to admit it, he's right. It was...enjoyable.

When I remain silent, he raises a brow in askance.

"Yes, it was," I admit begrudgingly.

He tilts my chin higher. "Nice enough to do again?"

No way. Being with him is sweet torture, and there's only so much I can take before I eventually break.

When my tongue darts out to moisten parched lips, an answering groan rumbles up from deep in his chest. Just when I expect him to lean in for a kiss, my fingers scramble behind my back, grabbing hold of the handle and twisting. When the door springs open, I realize that I didn't lock it earlier and nearly fall inside the entryway. The motion is enough to break the spell he has effortlessly woven around me. I stumble back a step before he reaches out and grabs my shoulders.

Before he can detain me any longer with his voodoo magic, I snatch the containers from his other hand and take a hasty step in retreat, slamming the door in his face.

"Thanks for dinner," I yell through the barrier that now separates us.

"Anytime," he says in reply, humor dancing in his voice.

I don't care if he's laughing at my awkward attempts to keep him at bay. The only thing that matters is that I was successful. There's a beat of silence as I tiptoe through the entryway and cautiously press my ear against the wood. It's only when I hear his door from down the hall slam shut that I release a breath of relief before swinging around and collapsing against it. Curiosity gets the better of me as I stare at the small white dessert box before breaking down, opening the lid, and peering inside.

What I find has my throat closing up.

Chocolate-covered strawberries.

My favorite.

Damn him.

Chapter Twenty-Five

ALYSSA

For what feels like the hundredth time, I roll onto my back and stare at the ceiling in the darkness that fills the bedroom. Even though I glanced at the clock on the nightstand less than two minutes ago, my gaze flickers in that direction again. It's after midnight. If it were simply a matter of closing my eyes and allowing my mind to wander until sleep took over, I'd already be happily snoring away. Instead, every time I close my eyes, an image of the hot, blond football player materializes in my mind. No matter how much I try, I can't stop thinking about him.

I can't deny that this Colton—the one who prepared dinner for me tonight—is different than the guy I dated a year and a half ago. It's not that I don't think people can grow and change. Of course they can. I'd like to think that I've matured somewhat over the years. But am I necessarily ready to take the risk only to wind up nursing a broken heart?

That's a complicated question with an even more complicated answer. The unnerving part is that it shouldn't be. After the way he treated me sophomore year, I should be immune to his charms. But Colton has always been my weakness. That, unfortunately, has not changed.

A month ago, when I was living in London, life had seemed so much simpler.

Now?

Now I'm a confused mess.

If I had any brains whatsoever, I'd stay as far away from Colton as humanly possible—and even that wouldn't be enough distance. Ever since my return, he's been carefully chipping away at my resistance, and I'm afraid that tonight might have truly weakened me.

Just as I flop over onto my side and squeeze my eyes tight, willing myself to find slumber, my phone chimes with an incoming message. Before glancing at the screen, I already know who it's from. It's like he can sense my vulnerable state even though we're nowhere near each other.

Don't do it!

Don't you dare do it!

Ignore him.

I hold out for roughly ten seconds before rolling over and reaching for my phone.

I had a great time tonight. Hope you realize I won't give up easily.

My breath escapes in a rush as I pour over the message half a dozen times.

His words scare the hell out of me. Deep down, I know they're true. He won't give up. Colton will continue to pursue me until I give in. As tempted as I am to do just that, I'm terrified he'll only hurt me in the end.

The day he dumped me, it felt as if someone had reached into my chest, wrapped their hand around my beating heart, and ripped it free. There's no way I can go through that again.

That boy had meant everything to me. More than I ever imagined possible. Until he threw it all away. Until he threw *me* away. The darkness that had fallen over me after our breakup had been all-encompassing. I'd had to fight my way free, and that had taken time and determination.

To allow Colton back into my life again simply because he says he's changed has the potential to undermine all the painstaking progress I've made. I don't understand what it is about him that draws me in almost against my own will. If I'm being truthful with myself, there's *always* been something about him.

Instead of placing the phone on the nightstand where it belongs, I carefully type out a response.

I had a good time, too.

Instead of addressing the second part of the message, I ignore it.

As soon as I press send, another text from him pops up within seconds.

I meant everything I said, Lys.

I release the pent-up breath from my lungs as everything softens inside me. He knows the nickname pulls at my heartstrings, and he's using it against me.

I need time.

Then that's what I'll give you.

I chew my lower lip and set the phone down before turning my back to it.

Another hour drags by, and I'm still wide awake. Even though I'm exhausted from a long week of classes, dancing, and teaching, I can't turn off the thoughts that churn through my head. I'm unable to stop my body from craving the one guy who forced me to my limits.

I roll over and snatch up the phone. Even though I know it's a mistake, I type out a message and hit send. My heart riots painfully under my breast as I wait for a response. One minute slowly stretches into two, and still, there's no answer. For all I know, he fell asleep and won't get it until the morning. A fresh wave of humiliation crashes over me. I should have held strong and not given in to temptation.

Ugh.

Irritated with myself, I drop the phone on the nightstand and roll over.

It's the light knocking on the apartment door that has my eyes springing open. My heart leaps as I throw off the covers and roll from the bed, padding through the living room before arriving at the entryway. It's only when I reach for the lock that I hesitate and consider the consequences of my actions.

Is this truly what I want?

To allow Colton in again?

Not just the apartment but my heart?

My life?

It takes effort to still the nerves that churn inside my belly. Maybe I'm uncertain if that's the best course of action, but something is urging me to take a cautious step in that direction.

As I twist the lock and open the door, I'm hit with a punch of arousal. "Hi."

The corners of his lips lift as he echoes the sentiment, "Hey."

His blond hair is tousled, and I'm ridiculously tempted to plow my fingers through the thick strands that are cut longer on top and shaved on the sides. A Wesley Wildcats T-shirt stretches across his chest as black athletic shorts hang loosely from lean hips.

When I remain silent, too busy eating him up with my eyes, he asks, "Can I come in?"

I blink out of those thoughts as a punch of heat hits my cheeks. The most I can hope for is that it's too dark inside the apartment for him to witness the effect he has on me. The last thing I want to do is stroke his already inflated ego or give him any more confidence.

Especially where I'm concerned.

In silence, I step aside, allowing him entrance. As he brushes against me, the familiar woodsy scent from earlier this evening wafts around me, cocooning me in the past. In the memories I still hold dear. All I want to do is close my eyes and inhale a big breath of him.

Instead, I lock the apartment door.

If Mia were here, there's no way I would be doing this. My bestie cautioned me about getting together with him the first time. She was afraid that he would hurt me and sadly, she wasn't mistaken.

A groan bubbles up in my throat as I reevaluate the merits of my decision. Let's face it, choices made after midnight are generally questionable by nature. Maybe I haven't been drinking, but this falls neatly into that category.

I've been hesitant to tell Mia what's been going on with Colton. Mostly because I've been too busy denying that I still have feelings for him. If I utter the words out loud, that will make them real. Even now, as he stands inside my apartment at one o'clock in the morning, I'm unsure if I'm ready to take that giant leap.

Whether he realizes it or not, this is the guy who changed everything for me. My life can be broken up into two segments—a *before Colton* and *after Colton*. I'm more cautious than I once was. What this guy taught me is that I'm not as bulletproof as I once suspected.

And yet, that's still not enough to stop me from grabbing his hand when he hesitates in the dining room. A sizzle of awareness shoots through me at the innocuous contact. The energy we always seem to generate is part of the attraction. I'm like a moth to a flickering flame that will ultimately lead to its demise. That knowledge isn't nearly enough to stop the onslaught of emotions from hurtling to the surface.

Once inside my room, I release his hand, allowing mine to fall back to my side.

He grabs the hem of his shirt and drags it partway up his abdomen before pausing. "Is it okay if I take off my shirt and shorts?"

My mouth dries as I jerk my head into a tight nod.

He yanks the soft cottony material over his head before dropping it carelessly to the floor. The shorts get removed next. Once they are added to the small pile, he stands in front of me wearing nothing more than form-fitting boxers. Even in the shadowy darkness of the room, I'm able to make out the hard ridges and contours of his muscular body.

Unable to help myself, I stand rooted in place, simply drinking him in. Football and a rigorous weightlifting regimen have molded his physique into a thing of beauty. Instead of being bulky like a lineman, he's long and lean. His body was built for quickness and speed.

As I shake myself out of those thoughts, I realize that he's studying me with an equal amount of intensity. My muscles tense as air gets trapped in my lungs, making it impossible to breathe.

His gaze is like a physical caress, and my body reacts accordingly. When my nipples tighten, poking through the thin fabric of my tank top, I lift my arms self-consciously to cover them. Before I can fully wrap them around my chest, Colton reaches out, halting the movement. "Don't. I want to look at you." There's a pause as his voice turns rough, sounding as if it's been scraped from the bottom of the ocean. "I've missed this so much."

Hesitantly, I lower my arms and straighten to my full height, allowing him to look his fill. I've never been embarrassed of my body. I've spent my entire life in a leotard. I'm used to scathing remarks from teachers. I've become almost deaf to the criticism.

But this...

I want Colton to like what he sees. The appreciative gleam filling his eyes tells me that he does.

This time, when he extends his hand, it never occurs to me not to take hold of it. With one tug, he pulls me toward the bed. He climbs in first before turning on his side. Once he's settled, I crawl in next to him until our bodies are perfectly aligned. His bigger one curling protectively around my smaller one. His arm bands around me, locking me in place. For the first time in what feels like forever, contentment suffuses every fiber of my being.

Now that Colton is holding me in his arms, I realize this is the reason I couldn't fall asleep. I needed him here with me. Even though I've spent all this time fighting against him, trying to break free of the hold he has on me, it turns out that I've been battling myself as well. It's a relief to drop the pretense.

At least for the night.

Chapter Twenty-Six
COLTON

Harsh sunlight filters through my eyelids, and I wake with a satisfied stretch. It's been a while since I've felt this well-rested. Like I slept for twenty-four hours straight. As soon as I shift, I realize that I'm not alone. There's a warm body snuggled up against me.

It takes a moment for my sluggish brain to sift through the events from last night.

Alyssa.

Dinner at my place.

Unable to sleep and shooting her a text.

I crack open an eye only to find her sprawled across my bare chest. There is nothing better than waking up with this girl in my arms. Even though my feelings for her scared the shit out of me, I regret pushing her away sophomore year. I have no idea if it's possible to get back to a place where she can trust me again, but I'm determined to do everything in my power to make it happen and prove to Alyssa that I can be the man she needs.

All I know is that I've got to slow my roll and not come on too strong. If I push too hard, she'll bolt. And I can't blame her for that. She handed over her heart for safekeeping, and I stomped it to smithereens.

A strange contentment fills me as I watch her sleep. Even though I want this moment to last forever, I know it won't. As soon as she wakes, the protective armor she cloaks herself in will fall back into place, and she'll continue to hold me at arm's length.

Unable to resist touching her, I stroke my fingers over her golden head. Alyssa has beautiful long hair. I love having it swathed across my body. I love wrapping the thick length around my fist and tugging it. I told myself when we were together that it was pure and simple fucking. She'd always been up for anything. Whatever I wanted to do. However I wanted to use her body, she let me do it. She was always willing to push the limits.

But the last time we had sex was different. No longer could I pretend that it was mindless screwing. Her feelings freaked me out, and I pushed her away. I made damn sure to blow up our relationship. Not once did it occur to me that moving on from her would be impossible.

A soft sound escapes from Alyssa as she shifts against me. My fingers still. I'm nowhere near ready for this interlude to be over. For a few more minutes, she drifts in and out of sleep before cracking open an eye and turning her head until our gazes can collide. It takes a moment for her to blink away the sleepiness.

My muscles lock, waiting to see how this scenario will play out.

"Morning," she finally says.

Sometime during the night, her top was shed, leaving her as bare-chested as I am.

I clear my throat along with the thick emotion trapped inside it. "Did you sleep good?"

"Yeah, actually I did."

Ever since I was a freshman in college, I've made it a rule never to spend the night with a chick. Fucking is one thing. Sleeping with someone and having an awkward convo the morning after is quite another.

Alyssa has always been the exception to that rule. She's the only girl I've held in my arms for hours at a time. The only one I've woken up with in the morning. I have no idea if it's the same for her. I've done my best to blot out the nineteen months we spent apart. As much as I want to ask, I'm unable to summon the words. I have no right to delve into her past when I'm the one who forced her away.

"Me, too." Even though I'm afraid to push my luck, the question escapes before I can rein it in. "What are your plans for the day?"

More of her drowsiness falls away as she watches me cautiously. "Homework. Maybe a little grocery shopping in the afternoon."

As we stare at each other, it feels like I'm standing on the edge of a precipice. One careless misstep and I could plummet to my death. The fear of being rejected is terrifying, but I don't allow that to stop me. "Maybe we could spend it together?"

Indecision flickers in her eyes as she gnaws her lower lip and glances away. "I don't know. Is that necessarily a good idea?"

My hands go to her cheeks, forcing her to meet my stare. "I told you that I'm not going to give up on you. Or us. We can take this as slow as you need. Just give me time to prove I'm not the same guy. That's all I'm asking."

My heart jackhammers almost painfully as a heavy silence stretches between us. I've done everything I can think of to change her mind. And maybe...maybe it won't be enough. "Lys?"

She draws in a breath before whispering, "Okay."

Relief rushes through me, leaving me to feel almost giddy. Before I can think better of it, I give in to the impulse rushing through me and lock my fingers around her wrists before flipping her over onto the mattress. A squeak of surprise escapes from her as I drag her arms above her head and pin them to the headboard.

I'm all about taking this slow, but I also want to feed the need she has. And I know exactly what Alyssa craves because it lives deep inside me as well.

"Colton..." A fine tremble works its way through her voice as she shifts restlessly beneath me.

"Yeah, baby?" My lips ghost over hers, never giving in to the baser urges clawing beneath the surface of my flesh. More than anything, I want to rip her panties away and bury myself deep inside her tight heat.

But I refuse to do that. The next time we have sex, there won't be any question as to who she belongs to.

"You said we could take this slow," she whispers.

I press my mouth to hers. "And so we will."

With that, I release her wrists and pull away just enough to stare down at her. She's so fucking beautiful with her wheat-colored hair spread out across the snowy white pillowcase. Her blue eyes are wide and watchful as a deep flush stains her cheeks. A thin scrap of material is all that bars me from her. My cock stiffens as a punch of arousal hits me full force. The urge to plunder her sweetness roars through me. It takes every ounce of restraint to beat back the need I have for her.

Even though I'm no longer holding her captive, her arms remain above her head as she shifts beneath my gaze. Her breasts are high and tight with little pink nipples that beg to be played with. When the temptation becomes too much to withstand, I lean over and capture one perfect bud. A whimper slips free from her as I suck it greedily into my mouth. After a few moments of torture, I allow the hard tip to pop free before drawing its twin between my lips.

Her fingers thread their way through my hair as if to hold me in place. I've missed her gentle touch something fierce. It only makes my dick harder. Any moment, I'm going to explode in my boxers, which hasn't happened since...well, never. It's yet another indicator as to how this girl affects me. The truth of the matter is that she always has. Only now am I coming to terms with it.

Alyssa shifts impatiently, and I know without a shadow of a doubt that if I stripped her bare and mounted her, she wouldn't stop me. No, she'd probably beg for it.

But then I'd be breaking my promise to take this at a gradual pace, and I refuse to do that.

If I've learned anything over the past couple of weeks, it's that Alyssa will go into avoidance mode in the blink of an eye. She attempted to pull a disappearing act after both times we were together. So, I'm not about to give her a reason to turn tail and run from me for a third time. I need to remember that slow and steady wins the race—especially when it comes to this girl.

It's with a shit-ton of regret that I allow her nipple to pop free from my mouth. Both breasts are rosy from all the attention. Unable to help myself, I pluck the tiny buds between my fingers, continuing to toy with them. Her eyelids feather close as she arches her back as if silently offering them up to me.

"I love your breasts." I pluck at the stiff little nipples, pulling and tweaking them in tandem. It's pleasure infused pain at its finest. What I love most is that this turns her on just as much as it does me. With one last playful tug, I release them.

If I don't shift gears now, it'll be too late, and I'll end up spreading her thighs and doing exactly what I know we shouldn't. "How about I run out and grab us some coffee?"

Alyssa blinks a few times as if that's the last thing she expected me to say. *"Coffee?"* Her lips wrap around the word as if it's foreign. *"Now?"*

"Yup." I roll from the bed and stretch.

Her gaze roves over my body before settling at my groin. I glance down to see what has captured her interest and realize that I'm sporting a massive boner. Since there's no shame in my game, I let her look her fill. Propped up on her elbows, she makes a pretty picture lying there all naked and flushed.

I really need to get out of here before I dive headfirst back into bed. I grab my athletic shorts and yank them up my thighs before tugging on my T-shirt. Now that I'm dressed, the situation feels less explosive. It's like I've got a protective shield in place.

Once I've got my slides on, I retreat from the room. "Is a mocha frappe still your preferred drug of choice?"

Her lips tremble at the corners as she relaxes against the mattress. "Yeah, it is."

There's a sliver of comfort in the knowledge that while some things are completely different, others stayed the same.

"Okay. I'll be back in fifteen."

With that, I disappear from the bedroom and out of her apartment. I make a quick pitstop at my place and grab my wallet before heading to my BMW parked in the lot. As I slide behind the wheel and shove the keys into the ignition, the vehicle purrs to life. That's three hundred and thirty-five horses waiting to break free under the hood. I rev the engine before pulling out and heading up the street about half a mile before swinging around the corner. There's a little coffee shop off the beaten path where the locals stop for java. I have no idea if Alyssa has frequented the place, but I know her penchant for coffee, and I'm pretty sure she'll enjoy it.

At this time on a Sunday morning, the shop is fairly quiet, and I'm in and out in a matter of minutes. All I want to do is get back to Alyssa so we can spend the day together. I don't give a crap what we do. I just want to be with her. I want our relationship to feel like it did before I blew everything to shit, even if it's just for a few fleeting moments.

As I park the convertible in the apartment building lot, I grab our containers of coffee along with the fresh-baked almond scone I picked up for Alyssa and head inside the lobby before beelining for the elevator. Normally, I would take the stairwell, but my hands are full. Using my elbow, I hit the button and wait for the car to arrive. Once it does, I hop onto the platform. I almost shake my head when I find myself whistling a little tune.

Whistling, for fuck's sake.

I can't remember the last time I did that. Or felt this happy. And it has everything to do with Alyssa.

"Hold the lift!" someone yells just as the doors slide shut.

Without thinking, I wedge my foot between them. The metal bounces off my shoe before sliding open. A dark-haired guy with a suitcase jumps onboard. He's slightly winded as if he's just run a mile. Although that's doubtful since he's wearing pressed khakis and a crisp, light blue-colored button-down shirt.

"Thanks, mate!"

Hmmm. Interesting.

British accent, if I'm not mistaken.

"No problem. Seems like you're in a hurry," I say, making idle conversation.

Once inside, he glances at the control panel but doesn't press another button, which probably means he's getting off on the third floor. I've lived here since July and haven't seen this guy around before.

He cracks a smile. "I've just come straight from the airport." Before I can ask, he offers, "I'm here to visit a friend."

A prickle of unease blooms in the pit of my gut as I study him more carefully.

"Oh?" I try to keep my tone nonchalant. More than likely, there's nothing for me to worry about. "Your friend lives on the third floor?"

"Yes." Once the doors slide open, he glances at the drinks in my hands before placing a palm across the metal threshold. "After you."

"Thanks." I roll my shoulders, trying to shake off the thick tension that has gathered between them before stepping into the carpeted hallway. The air gets clogged in my throat as I give him a bit of side-eye, waiting to see which direction he'll head in. If he turns to the right, then I don't have—

Fuck.

Not only is he walking in the same direction I am, but he's pulled up along-side me. With every step that brings us closer to Alyssa's apartment, my apprehension ratchets up until I'm practically vibrating with it. While I asked Alyssa questions about her time in London, I painstakingly avoided the topic of people she might have dated. Like I wanted to know all the gory details?

Hard pass.

The British dude glances at the silver numbers alongside each apartment door. Just when I think he'll walk by her place, he stops and checks the address. "Looks like this is it." He flashes me another smile. "Cheers, mate!"

My footsteps falter as he raps his knuckles against the wood and waits. Within seconds, the door swings open, and Alyssa stands on the other side of the threshold. Thank fuck she's wearing more clothing than when I walked out twenty minutes ago. She's pulled on a white T-shirt and red shorts that are so teeny tiny, they do absolutely nothing to cover her long, lean legs. A growl of jealousy rumbles up from deep within my chest.

Alyssa freezes as her eyes widen and her jaw drops open. It takes a moment for her to blink out of the stupor she's fallen into. "Jack?"

Jack?

Why the hell does that name sound so familiar?

Wait a minute. Is this the dude who was texting her?

"Surprise! I was in Chicago for an interview and decided to make a slight detour." He releases the suitcase handle and opens his arms wide.

Every instinct is screaming at me to rip her away from him. Possessiveness bubbles up in my throat until it feels like I might choke on it. My hands tighten around the containers of coffee as she steps into his embrace. I lurch forward before grinding to a halt.

There was a time when Alyssa belonged solely to me, but that's no longer the case.

Her gaze fastens on to mine as he presses his lips against her cheek.

All I know is that I can't continue standing here, watching their happy little reunion without ripping him to shreds with my bare hands. Even though it goes against every instinct, I swing away and force my body into motion. It takes effort to put one foot in front of the other and walk away from the only girl I've ever cared about. As I slip the key into the lock and turn the handle, I steal a reluctant glance down the hallway only to find it empty.

I can't help but feel that I allowed her to slip through my fingers for a second time.

Chapter Twenty-Seven

ALYSSA

My mind continues to somersault as I press my hands to my mouth and stare at Jack. He's settled on the couch across from me. "I still can't believe you're really here," I whisper for what feels like the hundredth time. "Why didn't you tell me that you were planning to visit?"

His smile grows wider until his dark eyes crinkle at the corners. "I wanted it to be a surprise."

Laughter bubbles up in my throat. "Mission accomplished." I'm having a hard time wrapping my head around this new turn of events. When I'd opened the apartment door, I had fully expected to find Colton waiting on the other side.

Instead, I'd found Jack.

And Colton.

My belly twists as I recall the hurt etched across the blond football player's face. All I could do was stare at Jack in shock. At some point, I'll have to deal with the Colton situation.

It takes effort to shake off those thoughts and focus on the guy in front of me. Even though it's only been a couple of weeks since I left him behind at Heathrow Airport, it feels like forever. Now that he's here, I realize how much I've missed our friendship. Facetime and texting are not the same as being in the same room and spending time together.

"How long are you in town for?" I'm hoping that it's at least a few days. Maybe even a week. I'm sure Mia wouldn't mind having an unexpected guest crash on the couch. They met in London when she visited over Christmas break and struck up an instant friendship.

The wattage of his smile dims. "Twenty-four hours."

"What?" My heart sinks. "That's it?"

"I'm afraid so, love." He shrugs. "I need to return by Tuesday. Even though it's a quick turnaround, I couldn't fly to the States without visiting you."

"I'm glad you did. I've missed you so much." As thrilled as I am to see Jack, I'm already filled with sadness that this will be such a brief trip. It'll be over before I know it.

"I've missed you, too. Perhaps I can convince you to return to London for a holiday."

Even though I left behind quite a few friends, I haven't given any consideration to visiting so soon. Sometimes it feels like I'm still trying to acclimate to life at Wesley. Not to mention, I'll be graduating this spring. I need to get my act together and figure out a plan for the future.

And then there's Colton. At every turn, he's there, pushing me, refusing to back off. He's gradually taken over more and more of my headspace.

Jack must see the flicker of emotion as it crosses my face. He gives me a considering look before asking lightly, "The lad from the hall, is he a friend?"

And there it is.

The dreaded question.

Heat suffuses my cheeks.

Jack knows all about Colton. The good, the bad, and the heartbreaking. Perhaps I shouldn't have been quite so truthful with him, but it had been important to work through all the crap in my head, and Jack had been a willing listener. Plus, I'd wanted him to understand that I couldn't move forward with a new relationship when I was hung up on a different one.

I blow out a steady breath, unsure where to begin.

His voice softens as he searches my eyes. "Come on then, is it really that bad?"

Ha! He doesn't have a clue. But that's only because I've been reluctant to divulge the details since I've returned to Wesley. I know Jack is holding out hope that with enough time, there will come a point when I'm ready to move on. And when that happens, it'll be with him.

"Friend might be overstating our relationship," I say lightly. "That was Colton."

His brows arch. "*Ahhh*."

That one-word response says it all.

I snort. "Exactly."

He shifts on the couch as understanding floods his features. "Do you want to talk about it?"

My heart constricts almost painfully as I jerk my shoulders. Of course, that would be Jack's response. There is no sign of anger, jealousy, or even disappointment.

Only concern. It makes me feel even worse about the situation. Why couldn't I have fallen head over heels for this guy?

He really is perfect. Kind and considerate. I've never had to guess where I stood with him. He let me know from the very beginning.

"No matter what happens," he says softly, "I'll always be here for you."

It takes effort to blink the wetness from my eyes. Before I realize it, I'm flying out of the chair and hurtling myself at him. As soon as I land against Jack's chest, he wraps his arms around me and holds me close. I squeeze my eyes tight as the citrusy scent of his aftershave soothes my senses.

When he presses his lips against my hair, I lift my face until our gazes can lock. One hand rises, the blunt tips of his fingers settling under my chin before tilting it upward until our mouths are able to align. The caress is a light sweep, but it's more than enough.

Enough to know that he will never stir the kind of emotion that Colton does. Jack is a safe port in a storm, but he's not the man I long for. He doesn't send my pulse skittering or put my body into overdrive.

He is steady and calm. And I'm probably the biggest idiot in the world for not giving him a real chance and exploring the possibilities.

But I can't. It wouldn't be fair to Jack. He deserves a woman who is head over heels in love with him, and that's not me.

How can it be when I already feel that way about someone else?

Chapter Twenty-Eight

COLTON

"Dude, what the hell is up with you?" Beck mutters, barely glancing away from the seventy-inch television and the campaign he's intent on winning.

"Nothing." I swing around, pacing to the other side of the living room.

He snorts but stays laser-focused on the video game unfolding on the screen. Gunfire erupts from the surround sound in a burst of noise. "Whatever you say, man. Just remember that we have practice today at three."

Fuck.

My head is much too full of Alyssa and the British prick that came out of nowhere for me to concentrate on anything else. I might as well plant my ass on the bench now because it's doubtful I'll see the playing field anytime soon.

Here's the way I see my day unfolding—I'll stew about Alyssa for a couple of hours, head to practice, more than likely fumble a few plays, get my ass chewed out again by coach, and end it all by berating myself for letting go of the one girl I ever cared about.

I drag my fingers through my hair.

It's been more than twenty-four hours since that dude showed up at her door. After dumping the coffee I'd picked up Sunday morning in the trash can, I'd paced a hole in the floor the rest of the day, all the while considering the merits of stalking over and laying claim to her.

Except...she's not really mine.

When it comes down to it, I have no right to question what she does or who she spends time with. I lost that privilege when I broke up with her. For all I know, she had a relationship with this guy while in London. That thought is enough to make me want to slam my fist through the wall.

And do you think I slept one damn wink last night?

Of course I didn't.

All I could think about was the two of them in bed together. His hands on her body. Touching her the way I used to.

"Can you sit your ass down for five minutes? You're really throwing off my game."

I glance out the slider door. The skies are a dark leaden gray. I'm no meteorologist, but my guess is that it'll pour any moment. "I'm going for a walk."

"Excellent idea." He shakes his head. "And they say that *I'm* the one with ADHD."

Not bothering with a response, I swipe my keys off the breakfast bar and stride out of the apartment, slamming the door closed behind me. Emotion continues to pound through my veins. I don't like it. I don't like feeling out of control. Now that I've actually made some headway with Alyssa, it feels so much worse to have it all ripped away.

As I stalk through the narrow hallway, I grind to a halt in front of her closed apartment door. My hands tighten into fists that hang uselessly at my sides.

You know what?

I need answers. Maybe I don't deserve them, and I have no right to them, but that doesn't mean I'm not going to try and figure out what's going on between these two and where that leaves me.

Is this guy a friend?

Or more?

How long is he in town for?

And where the hell did he crash last night?

It damn well better not have been where *I* slept the night before. That's all I got to say. Or we won't have to worry about him. The guy will be dead. With those thoughts crashing through my head, I straighten my shoulders and raise my fist. Before my knuckles can make contact, the door is yanked open, and Alyssa stands on the other side.

"Oh!" she says in surprise, falling back a step. It's difficult to tell who is more taken aback by my unexpected arrival on the scene. Although, I'm thinking that it's probably her. "Colton." Confusion flickers across her face. "What are you doing here?"

That's an excellent question. Since I hadn't gotten that far in my thought process, I'm forced to pull something believable out of my ass. It's not like I can just stomp over and demand answers. Well...maybe I could. But I won't. I don't see that approach playing out well for me in the end. "I was just wondering if you were heading to class."

"No, I'm skipping today and driving Jack to the airport."

Jack—or as I like to call him, the British prick—wheels his suitcase into the entryway and proceeds to stand entirely too close to Alyssa. It's on the tip of my tongue to tell him to back the fuck off.

Before I can snap out the demand, her words replay in my head.

He's leaving.

My brows shoot up as relief rushes through me. "Don't skip class. I've got a couple of hours to kill before practice. I'll drop him off."

Alyssa blinks, clearly bewildered by the offer. It's on the tip of her tongue to argue. "Umm—"

"It's not a problem. You shouldn't be missing a dance class, anyway." I glance at the dude who continues to hover over her. "Right, Jack?"

His expression hardens as his eyes narrow. "Absolutely."

She shoots a cautious look over her shoulder before biting her lower lip. "Are you sure you don't mind? I hate the idea of not seeing you off."

"Don't worry about it." Now that she's no longer looking at me, his lips lift into a smile. I don't like the way his eyes soften when he stares at her. "Your friend is correct. You shouldn't miss class."

"Colton," I say, interrupting their conversation.

Jack's eyes turn steely as they shift to me. "I'm aware of who you are."

Well, all right then. Apparently, my reputation precedes me. That's probably not a good thing. I have a sneaking suspicion Jack and I will be having an uncomfortable convo in the car.

Wariness ignites in Alyssa's gaze as it bounces between the two of us. "Maybe this isn't such a good idea after all. I'll just—"

"It's all good." Refusing to take no for an answer, I grab the handle of Jack's suitcase and wheel it into the hallway. I'll be damned if this guy spends another minute alone with Alyssa. The thought of shoving him on a plane and getting him off US soil sends a massive amount of relief pumping through me.

"All right," Alyssa mutters, still looking unsure. "I need to change before heading to class." She gives me a bit of side-eye before stepping closer to the dark-haired guy.

They ignore me as he takes her into his arms. Everything inside me riots painfully as I stand by and watch them have an intimate moment. My jaw locks as I grind my back teeth together. It takes every ounce of willpower not to rip her from his embrace. He turns his face and presses a kiss against her cheek before murmuring something in her ear that I can't quite make out. I'm on the verge of breaking up this little lovefest when they finally splinter apart.

"I guess this is goodbye," she says, sadness filling her voice.

"For the time being," he adds. "We'll continue to talk. Just remember that I'm only a phone call away."

Not if I can help it.

I clear my throat. Even though I have no idea what time his flight leaves, I say, "We should probably get moving. Wouldn't want you to miss your plane."

Not bothering to wait for a response, I drag the suitcase down the hall to the elevator. The sooner I get this guy away from Alyssa, the better off I'll feel—even if I have to drive him to the airport myself. I'm not looking forward to the next thirty minutes of my life. I have the feeling it's going to suck major ass.

I punch the button and tap my foot, shooting impatient looks down the hall. Once the car arrives, I roll the suitcase inside. The door tries to close four times before he finally gets his British ass into the elevator. The ride to the lobby is made in absolute silence—as is the stroll through the building. The parking lot turns out to be no different. With every step we take, the oppressiveness intensifies until it's enough to choke on. A few raindrops fall from the sky, which seems about right.

When I finally stop in front of my 840i, his expression lightens. "Nice roadster."

"Thanks," I mutter. Under normal circumstances, I'd be more than happy to show off a few of the bells and whistles. In this instance, that's not happening.

In one swift motion, I pop open the trunk and toss his luggage inside before slamming it shut and clicking the locks. We both slide into the vehicle before I start up the engine and pull onto the street, heading toward the metropolitan airport about thirty miles away. Normally, with traffic, it's a forty-minute drive. My plan is to have him there in under twenty-five.

See if I don't.

Not only does it take effort to unlock my fingers from around the leather steering wheel, but I also have to unclench my now aching jaw. I search my brain for something to say. Something that will break the uncomfortable tension that has fallen over us. I glance at him from the corner of my eye. The British prick sits ramrod straight as if someone shoved a two-by-four up his ass.

What the hell does Alyssa see in this guy?

He's dark-haired where I'm blond, and slightly shorter. You bet your damn ass I noticed that right off the bat. Sure, he's broader in the shoulders. Beefier. His physique is more suited to a brawler where I was built for speed on the football field.

I clear my throat. "Short trip, huh?"

That's the best I've got. Even though I've separated him from Alyssa, jealousy continues to gnaw away at my insides. I hate that he holds a special place in her heart. More than that, I hate that he's trying to oust me from hers. I can see it in his eyes. That's *exactly* what he's attempting to do. And I'll be damned if I allow it to happen.

His gaze flickers toward me. "Unfortunately, work prevented me from tacking on a few more days and making a proper holiday of it."

Unfortunate for who?

Certainly not me.

His eyes narrow as if I spoke the words out loud. He shifts on the leather seat and says in a clipped tone, "I know all about you."

My brows shoot up. "Excuse me?"

"You're the wanker Alyssa dated before her study abroad in London."

I press my lips together. I might not be familiar with the term *wanker,* but I'm pretty sure it's not a compliment. By the icy contempt marring his face, I can imagine that Alyssa revealed all the gory details of our relationship. What sucks is that there's nothing I can say to defend myself.

It's all true.

I'm a *wanker.*

My fingers tighten around the wheel until the knuckles turn bone white. "I'm not the same guy that I was a year and a half ago. I've changed." More than anything, I want that to be true. I'm fighting not to be the guy who was frightened away by three little words strung together.

His upper lip curls as he snorts, "Well, I should certainly hope so." Even though we're roughly the same height while seated next to one another, he's mastered the way of peering down his nose at me so that I feel like a piece of gum he scraped from the bottom of his wingtip. I don't like it. And I sure as shit don't like *him.* "Did she mention that we had a go at it?"

Had a go at it?

Much like *wanker,* I can pretty much guess what he's trying to say.

Dated.

The acidic taste of bile rises in my throat as I stare straight ahead. I can't even look at him. I don't want to see the smug expression on his face. I'm afraid that if I do, I'll jerk the car over to the side of the freeway and beat the piss out of him for daring to lay hands on her.

"You realize she's perfect, right?" he continues.

Does he think I'm a complete dumbass? Of course, I do!

When I press my lips together, stewing in silence, he adds, "She's the kind of girl who makes a man think long term."

I want to slam my fist through the windshield.

Why the fuck is he telling me this? To rub my face in the fact that I had the one girl worth having, and I let her slip away?

"As soon as we met, I knew there was something special about her."

My foot slams down on the accelerator, and the engine revs as we shoot through traffic. I'm going at least twenty miles per hour over the speed limit as raindrops hit the windshield.

"Unfortunately, she couldn't move on from the likes of you," he goes on to say.

That piece of unsolicited information is probably what saves his damn ass from becoming a statistic.

"It wasn't until the last month that we became romantically involved. Although, she never gave it a real chance to deepen. When the time came for her to leave, we decided a long-distance relationship wouldn't work. Too many unknowns in regard to the future. But I'll let you in on a little secret."

I have to steel myself for what he'll say next.

"I would have been more than willing to give it a try. Alyssa is worth it."

Barely am I able to suck in air through the thick lump wedged in the middle of my throat. Why had I thought taking him to the airport was a good idea? I'm tempted to pull over and dump his ass along the side of the road. But then he'd still be here, and I can't have that.

"Care to speculate as to why I didn't put up more of a fight?"

Goddamn it! I just need him to shut the fuck up and let me drive. I glance at the speedometer. It's hovering around ninety.

"Deep down, I realized that she was still in love with you. A man who in no way deserves her."

My head whips in his direction.

"Quite honestly, I'd hoped Alyssa would return home and realize she was over you. Then we could pick up where we left off, albeit from a distance." His eyes darken as he shakes his head. "But she still fancies herself in love with a wanker."

I hit the turn signal and crank the wheel, zipping off the exit ramp.

Everything he's just confessed churns inside my head as I enter the airport grounds and turn toward international departures. Once the terminal has been located, I pull to the curb and cut the engine. For a long moment, I stare at the steering wheel. I have no idea what to say to the guy sitting next to me—the one who has been unflinchingly blunt regarding his interest in Alyssa.

The thing is...I can't blame him for it. And I sure as shit can't fault him for attempting to win her over. Or back. Or whatever the hell they had going on. I would do the same if I were in his position.

The way I see it, there are two options here. I can tell him to get fucked or—

I swivel in my seat until our gazes can lock. "I hurt her."

A steely-edged light fills his eyes. Apparently, I'm not telling him anything he doesn't already know. "Damn right you did."

"But I'm not the same guy that I was before. And I'm doing everything in my power to prove that to her."

"Maybe so," he bites out, "but what's to stop you from hurting her again?"

Because...*I love her.*

I always have.

That being said, I'm not about to reveal my true feelings to him. Especially since I haven't delved that deep with Alyssa. If anyone deserves to hear them first, it's her.

My jaw clenches. "I guess you'll just have to take my word for it."

"Not good enough, mate."

I shrug. "For the time being, it'll have to be."

Jack presses his lips into a tight line. It's obvious that if he didn't have a flight to catch, he'd gladly take the time to kick my ass. And part of me feels like I deserve it. All right, fine...I totally deserve it. The way I handled myself sophomore year was childish and immature. I in no way deny it. I made a mistake. And now I'm trying my damnedest to rectify it. Whether I'm able to do that remains to be seen.

"You hurt her again, and I'll be on the first flight back to kick your arse."

"You have my word that it won't happen."

"Better not," he grumbles before exiting the BMW.

I pop the trunk so he can grab his luggage before unfolding myself from the vehicle. As I slam the door closed, I stuff my hands into the pockets of my jeans before grinding to an awkward halt where he waits.

"I wish I could say that it's been a pleasure," he says stiffly, "but it hasn't."

I almost snort. "I suppose that's one thing we can agree on."

The corners of his lips quirk slightly before he clears his throat. "I'd better go."

"Yup." I jerk my head into a nod. The sooner, the better, as far as I'm concerned. I can't get him out of here fast enough.

"I'm sure this won't be the last time we see each other." He wheels his suitcase onto the sidewalk near the entrance.

My brows lower. If I can help it, it sure as hell will be.

When I remain silent, a genuine smile curves his lips. It's as if he can read my thoughts without me having to verbalize them. "Don't worry, mate, I'm not going anywhere."

With that last parting shot, he leaves me standing near the trunk of my car.

Fucker.

Chapter Twenty-Nine

ALYSSA

Zoe wraps her arm around me as we push through the glass doors of the fine arts building. "Have I told you how much I missed your ass?"

"Only about a dozen times, but I'm all ears if you want to tell me again."

"Well, I did. Who else can I be catty with, if not you?"

A gurgle of laughter bubbles up from my lips. Zoe enjoys ripping the other dancers to shreds. She always has the lowdown on everyone. She knows who's sleeping with who and who's cheating on each other. Dancers, as a rule, are a cutthroat bunch. And the ones at Wesley are no exception. They'd stab a bitch in the back without blinking an eye.

And a couple of times, I've been that bitch.

Zoe is actually one of the few girls I've found who has my back. And I have hers. Next to Mia, she's the person at Wesley I'm closest to.

I glance at the sky, surprised to find the sun peeking through the clouds. Earlier this afternoon, it had looked like it would be dark and gloomy for the rest of the day. Luckily, that hasn't turned out to be the case. I'm tempted to close my eyes and let the sun's warmth stroke over my face.

"Hmmm," Zoe says, as we jog down the wide stone steps, "isn't that

Colton Montgomery over there?" Her voice turns speculative. "I wonder what he's doing hanging out on this side of campus."

Those words jolt me out of my lazy thoughts, and my head whips around as I search the crowd for his blond head. It doesn't take long to find him. He's standing off to the side, near a large stone fountain. I've always found the gurgle of water soothing, although it does nothing to calm my nerves at the moment. The fine arts hall is situated directly across campus from the athletic buildings. The artsy students usually hang out at this end of the university. Colton sticks out like a sore thumb. Even when he's clearly out of his element, people still recognize and swarm him.

Unconsciously my feet ground to a halt. I'm not aware that I've stopped moving until Colton's gaze locks on mine. That one look has electricity sizzling in the air between us.

"Damn, girl," Zoe whispers from alongside me where she, too, has stopped, "I could get off on the hungry look in his eyes and little else."

She's not wrong. I feel the heat emanating from him like a physical caress straight down to my toes. As much as I've attempted to stomp out the budding emotions that have taken root inside me where Colton is concerned, it hasn't done me a damn bit of good. They're still there, alive and well.

"Wait just a minute," she hisses, "you two aren't together, are you?"

I shake my head. "No."

"Are you sure? 'Cuz that sexy look in his eyes is all sorts of possessive."

Nope. Not at all.

A shiver scampers down my spine. As much as I don't want that knowledge to thrill me, there's no denying it does.

The outrage in her voice vanishes, and a soft sigh escapes from between her parted lips. "Aw, hell. Who could blame you? Every girl could use a little bit of that in her life."

When I stay rooted in place, unable to budge from the spot on the sidewalk, Colton breaks free from the group he's been mobbed by before swallowing up the distance between us with long-legged strides. Not once does he break eye contact.

Only when he's about five feet away does his footsteps grind to a halt. Uncertainty flickers across his face. It's an unusual expression for him. The Colton I know has always been full of confidence. It practically oozes from his pores—both on the football field and with the ladies.

I can't deny that the last couple of days have been odd. Colton cooked me an amazing dinner Saturday evening. As much as I fought against it, the night ended up with him in my bed. He ran out for coffee Sunday morning and, unbeknownst to him, came back with Jack in tow. We haven't had a chance to talk or sort out where we stand with one another.

I'll be honest, the unexpected visit from my friend has me rethinking my decision to allow Colton back into my life again. I've told myself since returning to Wesley that I would steer clear of my ex, and yet, how many times have I ended up in his arms? Even though my feelings for Jack aren't necessarily romantic in nature, he made me realize that I need to slow down and get some perspective instead of leaping headfirst into a situation that has the potential to leave me brokenhearted.

Colton shifts his weight before shoving his hands into the front pockets of his denim. "Hey."

"Hi." The only reason I can imagine that he would show up here is if there was an issue with Jack. I'm almost afraid to ask. "Were there any problems getting to the airport?"

"Nope." Something flickers in his eyes before vanishing. "None at all."

I cock my head and scour his expression for the truth. I can only imagine what the atmosphere was like in the car. The thought of them alone together—or worse—having words, makes me nauseous. When he remains silent, the question bursts free. "What are you doing here?"

The determined expression that I've become so used to returns full force. "I needed to see you."

His words send a reluctant thrill shooting through me. As much as I don't want to be affected by him, I am. The truth of the matter is that I always have been. "Oh."

Zoe clears her throat, and I blink out of the trance that has fallen over me before shaking my head. It takes a moment to collect my scattered thoughts. But that's nothing new when it comes to the blond football player. I should be used to it by now. "Colton, this is my friend, Zoe."

He glances at the tall brunette. "Yeah, I remember. You're in the dance program with Alyssa."

She straightens. Even though Zoe is a few inches taller than I am, he still dwarfs her in height. "That's right."

They met dozens of times when we were together, but I didn't expect him to realize it.

"I hope you don't plan on jacking around with my girl again," she says in a no-nonsense tone of voice.

Surprised by the comment, my mouth falls open, and I gasp, "Zoe!" She can be blunt to a fault. Most of the time it's a good thing. Every once in a while...not so much.

"What?" She glances at me as a fierce look grows in her eyes. "He'll answer to me if he does." For one brief moment, she channels Xena: Warrior Princess. Trust me, she can be just as fearsome. It's a relief that she's on my side.

"I'm afraid you'll have to get in line," Colton mutters under his breath as his expression darkens.

"What?" My brows draw together, not understanding why he would throw out such a strange comment.

"Nothing." His gaze returns to Zoe. "I have no intention of hurting Alyssa, if that's your concern."

Pleasure slides through me. I couldn't stop it from happening if I tried. And there's definitely part of me that doesn't want to try. At every turn, he's knocking down my walls.

She presses her lips together, all the while giving him the stink eye. "That's *exactly* what I'm worried about. You did a real number on her when you walked away sophomore year. I don't want to see that happen again."

Before I can utter a squeak of mortification that they're talking about me as if I'm not standing here, Zoe pulls me in for a quick hug and kiss. "I gotta run, but I'll see you tomorrow in class." She gives him one last steely look that would have lesser men glancing away. Maybe even tucking their tails between their legs.

Silence descends as Zoe disappears into the crowd of student traffic. I wrack my brain for something that will break the strange tension that fills the air between us. I have no idea where we go from here.

"Why did you want to see me?" I glance away as those thoughts pound through me. Only when I've wrangled all these out-of-control emotions into submission do I force my stare to his.

"We're celebrating my stepmother's birthday tonight, and I was hoping you'd come with me."

I blink, thrown off guard by the invitation. Not once during the time we dated did Colton offer to take me home to meet his family. Even when his parents attended Wesley football games, he was careful to keep us separated. I brushed away the hurt, telling myself that it would take time to earn his trust. In hindsight, it was yet another red flag that went unheeded on my part.

"Lys?" The way my name sounds sliding from his lips is rough and gravelly. It has me blinking back to the present.

"Why?" *Why is he doing this now?*

"I want you to meet my parents." He closes the distance between us before reaching out to tuck a stray lock of hair behind my ear. "It's something I should have done a long time ago."

I hate that he's saying all the right things. Everything I wish he would have told me nineteen months ago. "What's the point? We're not together." I force out the rest. "When it comes down to it, we're not even friends."

"Aren't we?" When I remain stoically silent, he adds, "Friends, at the very least?"

"I don't know." I glance away before I can get lost in his blue depths. They've always had the ability to draw me in, making me a little stupid in the head.

"Maybe being friends is a good place to start. What do you think?" He picks up my hand, loosely entwining our fingers together. I can't help but stare at them and remember how good it felt to wake up in bed with him Sunday morning. "I want more than that, but I'm willing to take this slow and build your trust over time."

Am I a total idiot for faltering? For believing him? For wanting to take a chance that he's matured, and won't push me away at the first opportunity when real emotions come into play?

Probably.

If I have one weakness, it's for Colton Montgomery. Sadly, I don't think that will ever change.

I release a puff of air from between my lips, afraid to take this leap. Afraid of what it'll mean.

"Alyssa?" He squeezes my fingers, effectively pulling my attention back to him.

"Okay," I blurt. "I'll come with you."

My heart pounds a painful staccato as a hesitant smile spreads across his face, as if he, too, is surprised by my easy capitulation. "Really?"

"Yeah."

"Awesome." He lifts my hand to his lips before brushing a kiss across the knuckles. "I promise, you won't regret it."

I hope Colton's right about that, and I'm not setting myself up for more heartache where he's concerned.

Chapter Thirty

ALYSSA

Three hours and a shower later, I'm settled in the front seat of Colton's BMW. The top is up, and we're headed north toward the place we both grew up. Although, admittedly, Colton's upbringing was vastly different than mine. He was raised in a wealthy neighborhood near Beck and Mia, while I was on the other side of town, in a more middle-class area.

I can't resist glancing at him from the corner of my eye as I sit in the passenger seat.

Was this a mistake?

If so, it's too late to back out now. This is happening. There's no getting out of it. After a couple of miles, the familiar exit comes into view, and we leave the highway before turning onto a country road surrounded by farmland. I roll down the window and inhale a deep breath of fresh air. There's something comforting about the wide-open spaces that settle the nerves fighting to break free at the bottom of my belly. I need that right now more than anything. Once on the outskirts of town, Colton turns into the drive of a gated subdivision before stopping outside an enormous iron entrance. He rolls down his window and taps a code into the control panel. After the gate slides open, we drive on through.

"Fancy," I murmur from the side of my mouth. Even being here makes me sit up a little straighter in my seat.

He snorts, gaze pinned to the landscape beyond the windshield.

As much as I want to remain lowkey about the situation, I'm curious to see where Colton grew up and meet his parents. I'm hoping it will shed a little insight into who he is. Lord knows I need it. Even though we were together for six months, he's still a mystery to me.

Each house we pass—if that's what you want to call these monstrosities—grows in square footage. All have intricate stone masonry and thick wrought iron embellishments. Unable to help myself, I press closer to the passenger side window. Each residence has perfectly manicured lawns and flowerbeds that riot with intense color. Trees and shrubs have been pruned to an inch within their lives.

When I was younger, I'd look at the people who lived in these mega-mansions and imagine their existences were picture-perfect. I mean, how could they not be? Gorgeous houses, fancy cars parked in the drive, trips to warm locales, and the best of everything.

Only now do I know better.

Money doesn't necessarily equate to happiness. Although, let's face it, it sure as hell makes life easier. I'm not naive enough to believe that it doesn't. My parents are comfortable, but they've worked hard to attain that level of financial independence. While we've never had an excess of money, I'm lucky they could afford for me to dance. It's not a cheap activity by any means. Between the classes, clinics, costumes, travel, and competition fees, it all adds up. It's one of the reasons I've taught in my spare time.

I blink out of those thoughts as Colton turns into a long winding driveway. Trees that are in the process of losing their leaves dot the front lawn as a majestic stone structure comes into view. It has to be easily twenty thousand square feet in size. I knew he came from money, but I never imagined that it was this kind of wealth.

Colton pulls up to the front door before cutting the engine. For a long moment, he stares at the house as it looms in front of us. I do the same before tentatively glancing at him. A pit forms at the bottom of my belly.

The words shoot out of my mouth before I can stop them. "Are you sorry that you brought me with?" Truth be told, I wish I'd had the foresight to turn down the invitation.

What am I doing here with Colton?

From all outward appearances, he's different than the guy I left behind a year and a half ago, but is it enough? Or am I just setting myself up for a world of hurt?

I wish there were an answer.

Surprise fills his gaze as it snaps to mine. "Of course not. I wouldn't have asked you to come with me if I had any doubts." In no rush to leave the car, he angles his body toward mine. "And I wouldn't have put you in a situation that was uncomfortable either."

Some of the nerves prickling along my flesh evaporate as his fingers drift across the curve of my jaw. It's so tempting to close my eyes and sink into his touch, but something holds me back.

"Do they know I'm coming with you?" If not, that could make for an awkward situation.

"I checked with Jenna this afternoon before I extended the invite."

Why does this suddenly feel like such a big deal? "What did you tell them about our relationship?" Or lack thereof.

One side of his mouth hitches. "Are you asking if I told them you were my girlfriend?"

A shiver dances down my spine as I jerk my head into a nod. Two years ago, I would have been thrilled to be introduced to his family as such. Now...

That's no longer the case.

A soft puff of air escapes from his lips. "I told them you were an old friend from high school. Can't go wrong with the truth, right?"

I suppose not.

His hand drifts from my face to my fingers which lay twisted together in my lap. He squeezes them as if to reassure me that everything will be okay. I'm trying really hard to believe that it will. "You ready to do this?"

Nope.

"I think so."

"It'll be fine. Just a couple hours, and then we'll head back to campus."

With that, Colton reaches into the back seat and grabs hold of a large bouquet of wildflowers he picked up from the florist, and then we exit the vehicle. As Colton rounds the hood, he extends his hand for me to take hold of. I hesitate for a heartbeat, unsure what to do. This feels like so much more than what he's claiming it is. As much as I want to keep my heart protected against him, it's becoming increasingly more difficult.

When I don't immediately place my fingers in his, a patient look fills his eyes. It's as if he knows all of the thoughts running rampant through my brain. A tentative connection forms between us in the driveway—one that is undeniable. Against my better judgment, I find myself cautiously placing my hand in his. It feels as if we've arrived at a decision—an unspoken promise of sorts.

Together, we climb the stone stairs that lead to the front porch. It's wide and sweeping—a grand entrance. The massive mahogany door stretches twenty feet in height. Colton grabs the ornate handle and pushes it open. My feet stutter as I take in the two-story foyer. There is an ocean of white marble as far as the eye can see. An elegant crystal chandelier hangs suspended from high above. It sends glittering patterns of light dancing across the polished-to-a-high-shine floor. A sweeping staircase with an elaborate wrought iron banister leads to a second-floor gallery. Everything is open, airy, and reeks of wealth.

Sheesh.

When I turn wide, questioning eyes to Colton, he shrugs. Before I can fire off one of the many questions that sit perched on the tip of my tongue, he raises his voice and calls out, "Hello? Jenna?" He pauses as we listen for any signs of life coming from within this castle-like home. "Dad?"

There's the soft padding of feet before a small blond woman with dark eyes walks into the entryway. A warm smile lights up her face as she pulls Colton in for a hug.

For a moment, I'm able to stand back and observe their interaction. She's so petite in size that Colton nearly swallows her up in his arms. There's something sweet about their reunion. About the tenderness that flits across his face. Once they break apart, he hands over the bouquet. Her face lights up as she buries her nose in the fresh blooms.

"They're beautiful! You didn't have to do that!"

He shrugs. "I wanted to. Happy birthday!"

"Thank you!"

And then she's turning bright eyes to me. Her expression is so warm and welcoming that I'm instantly put at ease. "You must be Alyssa." She takes me into her arms as if we are old friends instead of strangers greeting one another for the first time. "It's lovely to meet you," she says before drawing away.

"You, too. Happy birthday!"

"Thank you." A smile curves her lips. "I'm delighted you could join us. The more, the merrier."

"Thanks for having me."

Colton glances around the foyer. "Where's Dad? Is he still at work?"

"Nope, he ran out to pick up dinner." She rolls her eyes. "I told him that I was more than happy to throw something together for us, but he insisted on grabbing carryout from Marco's."

"I love that restaurant," I say. It's one we often frequented as a family when I was a kid. Their chicken parm is to die for. Although, a new bar has been set with Colton's dish. I glance at him, still blown away that he went through all the trouble of preparing dinner for me.

"It's one of my favorites, too." She reaches out and takes hold of Colton's hand. "I hope you realize that you didn't have to make such a long trip just for dinner."

"It wasn't a problem. I wanted to be here to help celebrate." His gaze flickers to mine. "Sometimes it's nice to get away from campus, even if it's just for a couple of hours."

"Well, I'm glad you're here." Her gaze touches upon me. "Both of you." She releases his hand before waving us to the back of the house. "Why don't we move this to the kitchen while we wait for your father to return?"

With that decision made, we travel through the immense foyer before entering an arched gallery. Artwork hangs on the walls. Small brass lights illuminate the paintings. This place resembles a museum rather than someone's personal home. As tempted as I am to stop and admire some of the art, I keep it moving. My gaze flickers to a sprawling living room that lies beyond the gallery. A bank of floor-to-ceiling windows line the far wall, showcasing an expansive backyard. The furniture is a mix of antique collectibles and modern pieces. There are thick colorful rugs that add texture and warmth to the space.

Twenty seconds later, we arrive at the kitchen. Like the other rooms I've glimpsed, it's spacious. There are long stretches of white marble, stainless steel appliances, and gorgeous crystal lighting. Bowls of fruit and small potted topiaries are strategically placed on the countertops. It looks like something you would find in a glossy magazine spread.

"What can I get for you to drink?" Jenna asks, interrupting the whirl of my thoughts.

"Water is fine. Thank you."

"Are you sure?" She pauses at the massive island in the middle of the room. "You're more than welcome to have a glass of wine. We have a well-stocked cellar downstairs."

I shake my head. Something tells me that it would be prudent to keep my wits about me this evening. Already, I feel myself falling hard, and it's a scary prospect. All I want to do is pump the brakes. Colton has promised that we would take this relationship slowly. But I'm no longer sure that's possible, everything seems to be happening at lightning speed.

"I'll have a water, as well," Colton says.

Jenna moves to the mini-fridge built into the side of the island and pulls out two bottles of water. I grab the one that is set in front of me before twisting off the cap and taking a sip. Again, I'm afforded another opportunity to observe Colton's interaction with his stepmother. There's an easy banter between them. It's obvious they have a strong connection as she teases him with sparkling eyes. I've known Colton for more than a decade, and this is probably the first time I've seen him this relaxed. It only makes me realize that even though we spent six months together, he never fully lowered his guard. A pang of sadness blooms inside me at that knowledge.

I'm yanked from those thoughts by the sound of the backdoor opening from down the hall before an older man walks into the kitchen carrying two white bags with the Marco's logo stamped across them. He sets the containers on the counter and immediately leans over to kiss Jenna. "Happy birthday, sweetheart."

With a smile, he greets Colton before pulling him in for a hug. It's one of those manly types where they clap each other on the back before quickly stepping away. His friendly gaze falls to me. Before I can stretch out my hand for him to shake, he swallows me up in a giant bear hug. Warren Montgomery is a big, burly man. He and his son are similar in height, but Warren is broader in the chest and shoulders. Kind of like a bull. His dark hair and beard have silvered over the years. His eyes, much like his wife's, twinkle with kindness.

"Hello, Alyssa. It's nice to meet you. Jenna and I are glad you could join us tonight."

"Thank you for extending an invitation," I tell him.

The older man's eyes flicker to Colton. "It's not often my son brings home friends from college."

"Dad," Colton grumbles as if embarrassed.

Unbothered by the rebuke, he continues, "I heard that you grew up around here, and the two of you attended high school together." He unpacks a few of the covered containers before spreading them out on the massive island.

"Yes, we did," I say with a nod.

"I've already set the table in the dining room, Warren. Let's take everything in there," Jenna cuts in before the remaining food can be unloaded.

We each grab a couple of containers and follow her into the two-story dining room off the kitchen. When all of the dishes have been laid out, we settle on our respective chairs. The table is sleek and black, stretching at least thirty feet in length. There is enough seating for twenty people. Since it's just the four of us, delicate ivory and cerulean-colored China has been set at one end. Warren takes his place at the head of the table. Jenna settles on one side as Colton and I move opposite of her. Everything is family-style, and we all dig in, helping ourselves to the entrees.

His parents pepper me with surface-level questions throughout the meal. They tease Colton every chance they get. They talk about the upcoming game next weekend, and how they're both looking forward to cheering him on. If I weren't so attuned to Colton's presence, I would have missed the barely perceptible tightening of his jaw.

Jenna turns to me and says, "Hopefully, we'll see you there."

I've avoided attending football games this season. I've been trying to break free from the hold Colton has over me, and sitting in the stands for three hours, watching him on the field, certainly won't help reach that objective.

"Maybe," I say lightly.

"You know," Colton clears his throat before shifting on his seat, "if you guys are busy, there's no need for you to make the trip. It's cool."

Jenna's brows draw together as she scoffs, "Are you kidding? We haven't been able to attend any this season." She glances at her husband. "We've missed watching you play. Now that your father isn't traveling so much, we'll be able to make the rest of your home games."

A look of dismay flashes across his expression. It's there and gone before I can decipher exactly what it means. Even though I get the feeling Colton wants to argue, he jerks his head into a tight nod. "Great."

As the conversation turns to other topics, I'm aware of the thick tension radiating off Colton. I can't help but wonder what's going on with him. Since I've returned from my study abroad program, I've tried so hard to keep my distance. If people are talking about Wildcats football or the blond wide receiver, I promptly tune them out. Only now do I wonder if there's a problem.

I don't realize that I've reached under the table until my fingers wrap around his, and he turns his head, gaze locking on mine. As much as I don't want to feel the connection strengthen between us, that's exactly what happens. I'm powerless to stop it from occurring. And maybe there's a part of me that is weary of fighting against something that feels inevitable.

After dinner, I help clear the table and wash the dishes. Jenna chats about her job as an elementary school teacher and the upcoming trip they have planned after Christmas.

"So, you and Colton? She watches me from beneath a thick fringe of lashes before picking up a plate and drying it. "You've known each other for a while?"

It's a question...but then again, not really.

"Yes." I'm unsure what to say or how much of our past to reveal. That's up to Colton. And I don't want to lead her in the wrong direction. Or myself, for that matter. Although part of me wonders if it's much too late for that.

With a thoughtful expression, she nods. "Colton doesn't bring many people home. In fact," she falls silent, almost as if she's searching her brain, "you're the first since high school."

That doesn't surprise me. Even though Colton has a lot of friends and girls are constantly buzzing around him like drunken bees, they're all surface-level acquaintances. None, with the exception of Beck, have managed to drill beneath the surface.

When I remain silent, she continues, "He doesn't allow a lot of people into his life." Her lips quirk at the corners. "You must be special."

I shake my head, unwilling to let that little seed get planted in my psyche. "We're just friends." I force the words from my lips not only for her benefit but mine as well. Allowing myself to get caught up in the moment would be a mistake. I've been burned before. I'm unwilling to chance it again.

"Hmm. That's too bad. I think you would be perfect for him."

Once upon a time, I'd thought the same thing.

Now I know better.

As I finish up with the last dish, someone clears their throat from the arched entryway. I nearly bobble the plate before setting it carefully on the drying rack as my gaze slams into Colton's blue one.

His arms are crossed over his chest as he leans casually against the doorframe. "Do you mind if I steal Alyssa away?"

Jenna picks up the delicate China from the wooden drying rack. "Of course not. We'll have dessert in about thirty minutes. Sound good?"

"Yup." This time, when he stretches out his hand, I don't bother to fight it. There are so many emotions warring inside me. I gravitate across the kitchen before taking hold of his larger one. As I do, a spark of energy tingles through my fingertips. The chemistry between us is like a living, breathing entity. It always has been. As much as I've tried to fight it, it's not a battle I will ever win.

With a gentle tug, he pulls me through the gallery and foyer before we climb the sweeping staircase to the second floor. My mind buzzes on sensation overload. Without trying, Colton rouses all the dormant emotions locked inside of me. As much as I want to keep him at a safe distance, it's impossible to remain indifferent.

Once on the second-floor landing, I'm given a bird's eye view of the entryway. "Your house is beautiful."

"Thanks. My dad built it after he and Jenna got married."

"How long have they been together?" I ask, genuinely curious about Colton's family.

His brow furrows in contemplation. "Let's see, they got married when I was seven years old. So, they've been together for fourteen years. The trip they're taking at Christmas is to celebrate their fifteenth wedding anniversary."

I nod, processing that tidbit of information. "She's really nice." It's obvious that Colton and his stepmother have a genuinely close relationship.

"Jenna is amazing."

Our shoes click against the glossy hardwood that stretches throughout the hallway. Family photographs dot the walls. I'm tempted to stop and study them. This is the first time that I feel like I've been given a rare peek into who the real Colton Montgomery is. I'm loath to push too hard or do anything that will shut down his inclination to share more of himself with me.

When he opens the last door on the right, I realize with a glance that he's taken me to his bedroom. The walls are painted navy, and there is a king-size bed dominating the space. A sleek dresser and desk match the dark wood of the bed frame. A plush velvet sofa is arranged on the opposite side of the room, along with a matching chair and antique coffee table, making an intimate spot to relax and chat. Next to the sitting area is a wall of built-in cabinetry. A mini-fridge is tucked beneath the counter and a fancy stainless steel coffee maker takes precedence on the sleek marble countertop.

Across the room are two arched doorways. I imagine one is a walk-in closet, and the other is a private en suite. The place resembles a tiny apartment. The walls are dotted with football memorabilia and more framed photographs. Some are in color, while others are in black and white. If Colton weren't standing next to me, tracking my every movement, I'd take my time and stroll around the space, studying it with more care.

Unsure what to do, I separate myself from him and settle on the comfy couch. Instead of following me to the sitting area, he wanders to the desk before lounging against it. His easy stance belies the tension that crackles in the air between us.

I shift, unnervingly aware that his gaze is fastened on me. "Your parents are nice. I like them."

"The feeling is mutual." There's a pause as remorse flickers across his expression. "I should have introduced you sooner."

When I shrug, unwilling to dwell on our past, he shoves away from the desk, closing the distance between us before settling on the sofa. I gulp. It felt so much safer when he was standing on the other side of the room. He swivels his body toward me as one muscular arm stretches across the back of the cushion. His proximity has the tempo of my heart picking up speed. When I remain still, his fingers strum the gentle slope of my shoulder. Even though I'm wearing a light sweater, I feel the caress down to the tips of my toes. The heat of them singes my flesh, and a bevy of tingles erupt inside me before careening down my spine. No matter what has transpired between us, I can't imagine there ever being a time when my body doesn't react to him in such a manner. I might not want it, but that doesn't matter. It's not something that can be controlled.

My tongue darts out to moisten my parched lips as I search my mind for something to say. Something that will get us back on even terrain. The question is out of my mouth before I can stop it. "Earlier at dinner, when Jenna mentioned attending your game, you didn't seem happy about it."

The sexual energy that had been ratcheting up between us dissipates, and for that, I'm grateful. His muscles stiffen. Even though he glances away, his fingers stay connected to my shoulder. I can't deny that part of me is thankful for killing the mood. I'm not ready for this to progress into something more.

When he remains silent, I begin to wonder if he'll bother with a response. Maybe it's better that way. If Colton can't open up and talk to me about his feelings, then what's the point of us going down this road again?

I didn't intentionally set this up to be a test, but that's what it's turned out to be.

As I open my mouth to suggest we head downstairs, he drags his other hand through his blond hair as his gaze returns to mine. "I don't want them attending because Coach benched me."

No matter what I thought he might say, that wasn't it. I've watched Colton on the football field all through high school and the first two years of college. He's amazing. Solid. He could play in the NFL if that's what he wanted.

All of the emotion swirling through me dissolves as I turn toward him, my hand settling on his thigh. "What happened? Were you injured?"

It's obvious from the pinched expression that settles on his face that he's reluctant to discuss the situation.

"No, it's nothing like that. To be honest, I'm not sure what the problem is," he mutters. "No matter what I do, I can't seem to pull it together. And I really don't want Jenna and my dad to make the trip to Wesley when it's doubtful I'll see much of the field. They'll ask questions. And at the moment, I don't have any answers."

Sympathy floods through me as I squeeze his thigh. "I'm sorry." Even though football and dance aren't the same, I know what it's like not to perform to the best of your ability. To know you can do better but, for whatever reason, aren't able to tease it out. It's both frustrating and scary because you don't know if it's a phase that will pass with enough time, or you've actually lost your edge. Once you meander down the road of self-doubt, it can be a real mindfuck. "Is there anything I can do to help?"

"I don't think so." He shakes his head as his gaze darts to mine. "It's something I need to figure out for myself."

When I've struggled in the past, I was lucky enough to have Mia by my side. Does Colton have anyone to unload on? Somehow, I can't imagine him and Beck sitting around the apartment, doing a deep delve into their feelings. I find myself saying, "If you ever want to talk, I'm here."

"Thanks, I appreciate the offer. It means more than you know." There's a pause before he releases a breath. "I keep telling myself that it's a slump and it'll pass, but so far, that hasn't turned out to be the case."

As I rub his thigh with long comforting strokes, his gaze drops to my hand. Our muscles tense before I hesitantly remove it and clear my throat, shifting away and fiddling with the hem of my shorts. My gaze bounces around the room, looking everywhere but at him. I notice a couple of photos with Colton, Jenna, and Warren. One where they're skiing in Colorado. Another with them posing in swimsuits on a tropical beach. My gaze settles on a framed picture from high school graduation before shifting to an eight-by-ten taken with Beck. The two boys are wearing their high school football uniforms. Their arms are thrown around each other's shoulders as they beam at the camera.

He talks about Warren and Jenna, but he's never mentioned his mother. I've heard the whispered rumors that swirled through the hallways of our high school, but I have no idea where the truth lies. When we were together, I was too afraid to bring her up. As curious as I am, the question sits perched on my tongue, but still...I'm unable to release it into the atmosphere.

"What are you thinking?" he asks.

My teeth sink into my lower lip as I shrug. The words are so close to bursting free, but I'm afraid to push for more information. I'm fearful that he'll shut down, and this little bit of intimacy we're sharing will vanish in the blink of an eye, never to reappear again.

With a slight tilt to his head, he narrows his eyes. "Come on, I can tell there's something on your mind. Out with it already."

Even though we're not together and haven't been for a while, Colton is still able to easily read me. It's both disconcerting and reassuring at the same time.

"There are pictures of Jenna and Warren, but none of your mother." Hastily, I tack on, "You never talk about her."

My breath gets clogged in my throat when his expression darkens. Too late do I realize that my question has crossed an invisible line.

"No," he mumbles, "I don't." His lips curve into a frown as his forehead creases.

The moment stretches uncomfortably between us as he remains mute.

"I'm sorry," I whisper. "I shouldn't have brought it up."

"Don't be."

In one swift motion, he reaches over and plucks me off the couch before depositing me on his lap so that I'm straddling his thighs.

Searching his gaze, I recognize the naked vulnerability that ricochets within the blue depths. "Forget I asked. We can talk about something else." Or nothing at all.

His hands wrap around my waist to hold me firmly in place. The heat of his flesh burns through my clothes to the skin below. It's like a tattoo that will always be there, branding me as his. Even if no one else is able to see it, I'll know.

"It's all right. You can ask me anything." There's a pause. "It might not seem like it, but I'm really trying to open up." He shrugs. "Just be patient with me. I'm not used to discussing my feelings. Or her."

That's all it takes for my heart to shatter into a million broken pieces. The need to touch him pounds through me, and my hand drifts up to cup his shadowed cheek.

Without further prompting, he says, "My parents met when they were young. My father was attending college, and Candace—that's my mother's name—was in art school. The way dad tells it, they met at a party and fell instantly in love. A couple of weeks later, they hopped on a plane and flew to Vegas to tie the knot."

Wow. That's actually a super romantic story.

Before I can pummel him with questions, he continues, "For the most part, they were happy. Dad finished school and found a job working in finance. Candace rented a studio space so she could paint. Two years later, I was born. That's when their marriage turned rocky. She resented anything that took her away from her work. Dad hired a nanny to take care of me, hoping that would help. Days would slip by, and we wouldn't see her. It was like she'd get lost in her art and lose all track of time." His voice trails off as his eyes take on a faraway quality.

When Colton remains silent, I ask, "What happened then?"

It takes a moment for him to blink back to the present. "When I was five, she decided it wasn't possible to be both an artist and a mother."

My heart clenches painfully as I realize how the rest of the story will unfold.

Any emotion filling his voice disappears even though I see hints of it in his eyes. "She packed her bags and left."

"I'm so sorry." My hand rises so that I can hold both cheeks in the palm of my hands. "Do you ever see her? Talk to her?"

"In the beginning, she would send a card or two a year, but then the contact tapered off." His brow furrows. "Honestly, I can't remember the last time I heard from her. It has to be more than a decade." He shakes his head as if even he can't believe it.

My chest constricts until it becomes difficult to breathe. I can't imagine what it would be like to have one of my parents walk away. I feel terrible for poking my nose where it didn't belong and forcing him to talk about something that has dredged up so many painful memories.

Colton's hand rises to my face before his thumb carefully feathers over the delicate skin beneath my eye. Only when it comes away with wetness, do I realize that tears are streaming down my cheeks.

"Don't cry," he whispers.

"I'm sorry," I repeat. Not only for his mother walking away but also for forcing him to share something so painful.

"Don't be. You can't miss what you never had."

He swipes at my other cheek before locking his hands around the sides of my head and pulling me close until our foreheads are able to touch. Our gazes stay fastened as the fragile connection we share continues to flourish.

"I'm really glad you came home with me."

"Me, too." It means more than he can possibly know. More than I'm afraid to acknowledge, even privately to myself. "Thanks again for the invite."

For a moment, the only audible sound that fills the room is our breathing.

"I'm going to kiss you, Lys."

"Okay."

As soon as the word is released, he tilts his head until his lips are able to slant across mine. Unlike the kiss in Bang Bang's parking lot, this one unfolds gradually as if we have all the time in the world to explore each other. When his tongue sweeps across the seam of my lips, I immediately open, allowing him entrance. That's all it takes for the world to fall away. And then it's just the two of us.

The Colton I've unearthed this evening has managed to do the impossible. He's ripped down the walls I carefully erected between us, one brick at a time. It's exactly what I was afraid would happen. Even though I'm scared of being hurt again, that knowledge isn't enough to stop me from tumbling head over heels in love with him for a second time.

Or maybe I never fell out of it to begin with.

Chapter Thirty-One

COLTON

I stare at the ceiling with my arms folded behind my head as everything from earlier this evening crashes around inside my brain. If there's one thing I hate, it's dwelling on Candace. She's like Beetlejuice. Say her name three times, and she magically appears inside my head, taking up residence like an unwanted squatter.

And that, on top of everything else I'm going through, is the last thing I need. The woman abandoned me, walked away without so much as a second glance. And now there's a giant void in the place that once belonged to her. It's one that Jenna has diligently tried to fill over the years.

Everything within me softens as I think about my stepmother. Truth be told, she's so much more than that. The title doesn't do her justice. She's the mother Candace never could be—or, more to the point, wanted to be.

I'm not embarrassed to admit that I love Jenna. I appreciate everything she's done for me over the years. She drove my ass around town before I had a license and helped with homework when I didn't understand a concept. She wrapped her arms around me in the middle of the night when I would cry, missing Candace. Instead of badmouthing my mother, Jenna tried to explain that sometimes people weren't able to be what we needed. And that was neither of our faults.

The few times Candace allowed me to tag along with her to the studio stick out vividly in my head. Probably because they were such a rarity. She would set me in the corner with a few toys while she became absorbed in her artwork. Hours would pass by, and I would try to be as quiet as I could. Even then, at age four, I realized my silence was the only thing that could win her over. In the end, it wasn't enough. No matter how quiet or how good I was, she still chose to leave.

Even though Jenna and I have become close over the years, and she has done her best to make up for Candace's lack of interest, my biological mother's rejection is still there, eating away at me.

It's fucked up.

Why isn't it possible to forget about her and move on? I want to bury all of the painful memories so deep down in my subconscious that I forget she was ever part of my life.

Another thirty minutes pass as I toss and turn before finally throwing off the covers and rolling from the bed. Unable to sleep, I pace the dark room. It's as if there is an itch deep beneath my skin that is impossible to scratch.

The one person I long to see, the only one who can make it better, is asleep in her own bed in the apartment next to mine. She's so close and yet a million miles away. We left my parent's house around nine o'clock and arrived back at campus around eleven. The return trip to Wesley had been made in silence. It's as if we'd both been lost in the whirl of our own thoughts.

Once we had reached her apartment door, I'd cupped her cheeks in my hands and pressed my lips against hers before quickly stepping away. It would have been all too easy to pick Alyssa up and carry her back to my place. The need to be buried in her tight heat had throbbed almost insistently through me. If there's anything that could help soothe the painful memories circling through my brain, it was her. Instead, I'd restrained myself, knowing that Alyssa needed me to prove I wasn't the same guy who walked away from her sophomore year.

Jenna texted on the ride home and told me how much she and Dad enjoyed meeting Alyssa. How they hope to see her soon.

Hint, hint.

Little do they know that the decision for our future rests solely in Alyssa's hands.

As I swing around, ready to pace the length of the room, my phone lights up with an incoming message. I move closer before glancing at it.

Alyssa.

You awake?

That's all it takes for me to pounce on the slim device.

Yeah. Can't sleep.

Me, neither.

Want to come over?

Be there in a minute.

I toss down the phone and go to the apartment door, cracking it open and peering outside. Alyssa is already in the hallway, jogging toward me.

"Hi." A hesitant smile quirks the edges of her lips.

I return the quiet greeting before opening the door fully and stepping aside. Once she's in the entryway, I close it and nab her fingers with my own, towing her to my room. When the lock is secured, I lean against the door. The temptation to take her into my arms is so powerful that I clench my fingers in an effort to stifle the urge. Instead, I hold back, waiting for her to make the first move.

"Why weren't you able to sleep?" I ask.

She jerks her shoulders, restless energy vibrating off her in heavy waves. "There's a lot going through my head at the moment."

"Mine, too." Even though opening up isn't easy, I know it's what Alyssa needs, and so I force myself to add, "Most of the time, I'm able to forget Candace was ever part of my life but tonight brought up a lot of emotions. More than I realized." More than I'm comfortable with.

Concern flickers across her expression as she closes the distance between us, stopping a foot from where I stand. "I'm sorry about that. I shouldn't have asked about her."

Unable to control myself, I give in to the temptation and reach out, tugging her to me. Alyssa's palms settle on my chest, but she doesn't push me away. "No, I want you to ask questions. I'm trying hard to let you in, Lys. It's not easy. I'm not used to it. I've kept everything buried inside for so long." I pause for a moment as an ugly thought forces its way into my head. "For all I know, it's too late for us."

A puff of air escapes from between her lips. "I wouldn't be here if I felt that way."

The tension gathered in my muscles drains away, leaving me limp with relief. I didn't realize how much I needed her to say that until she did. It gives me some much-needed hope where I wasn't sure there was any. My arms band around her, drawing her closer until we're pressed together. Her arms slip around my neck as she lays her head against my chest. The top of it fits perfectly beneath my chin.

Even though the words are scary to admit, especially out loud, I want to share them with her. "Sometimes I wonder where she is," I whisper into the darkness that blankets us. "What she's doing."

Alyssa lifts her head and searches my face. "Have you ever tried to find her?"

Find her?

Hell, no.

Even the thought is enough to make my palms sweaty. I shake my head. Part of me is deathly afraid of what I'd find. In a way, it would be like opening a Pandora's box. Once you do that, there is no shoving everything back inside.

"Is that something you're interested in doing?" she asks, breaking into the chaotic whirl of my thoughts. "Looking for her?"

I suck my lower lip between my teeth and chew it thoughtfully.

I don't know...am I?

I'll admit that part of me is curious. It's been more than sixteen years since I last saw her. And for most of that time, there has been nothing but silence. For all I know, she could be dead. I allow that notion to settle inside me before examining it more closely.

It would probably be easy to figure out. Hell, I could Google her and more than likely come away with enough information to satisfy the interest growing inside me.

Then again, maybe the best thing I can do is leave the past where it belongs.

In the past.

Why does this have to be so damn difficult?

"We could do a quick Facebook search and see if anything pops up," Alyssa offers.

I suppose we could do that. Except the suggestion sends my belly into free fall. It's a terrifying thought. I'm not used to feeling that kind of emotion pump through me. Everything inside screams to shut it down, so I don't have to experience it.

"Colton?"

I blink and refocus on Alyssa's concerned features. "Okay."

Holy shit. Did I just say that?

I'm almost desperate to snatch the word out of the air. Instead, I remain silent, muscles coiled tight.

"Really?" Her brows rise as she carefully searches my expression as if she doesn't quite believe me.

At the moment, I'm not sure if *I* believe me.

"Yeah," I confirm with a grunt as a ball of nausea grows in the pit of my belly. Just because something turns up doesn't mean I have to do anything about it. Best case scenario, what I find is enough to put all these unpleasant emotions scratching beneath the surface to rest once and for all. I want to move on with my life and stop allowing this woman to control my thoughts and feelings. Whether I want to admit it or not, that's exactly what she's done.

"You don't have to do this," she murmurs.

True. But I've come this far. Do I really want to back down now? Will I ever find the courage to do it again?

"I know." It's not like I *want* to, but part of me feels like I *have* to. In order to slay your dragons, don't you have to face them head-on? And Candace is definitely a dragon that needs slaying. It's the only way to free myself from her.

"Should we wait until tomorrow?" Alyssa asks, concern flaring in her eyes.

If I do that, I'll probably find a reason not to go through with it. Scratch that, I'll *definitely* find a reason.

Can you say—bauk, bauk, chicken?

As far as I'm concerned, it's now or never. "Let's just get it over with."

Her hands slide from around my neck to my cheeks as she rises to her tiptoes before pressing her lips gently against mine. The moment I sink into the caress, she pulls back. "I'll be right here with you, Colton. I'm not going anywhere."

I jerk my head into a nod as she steps away. She has no idea how much comfort those words give me.

On legs that feel wooden, I walk across the room and grab my laptop from my backpack before settling on the queen-size mattress. Alyssa sits close enough for our shoulders and thighs to touch. Since her return from London, this is the first time she's taken the initiative to be near me. Almost as if to punctuate that thought, her fingers settle on my thigh.

With a pounding heart, I fire up the computer. It takes a moment for the screen to come alive, and then I'm clicking on the internet icon. When my home screen pops up, my fingers hover over the keys before I force myself to type her full name into the search engine.

"Candace Radcliffe?"

"She never took my father's name," I mumble in response.

I stare at the letters until they blur in front of my eyes. My finger hovers over the Enter button. I don't realize that air has become trapped in my lungs until they begin to burn. It's only when little spots dance across my vision that I force it out again and stab the plastic key before I can talk myself out of it. A second later, a full page of information materializes on the screen.

My heart skips a beat when a colorful photograph pops up.

Alyssa's fingers curl, biting into the flesh of my leg. I don't think she's aware of the grip she has on me. Her gaze stays fixated on the screen. But I'm grateful for it. The pain is the only thing that grounds me in the moment. Otherwise, I would float off into the atmosphere. It's a disturbing thought. "Is that her?"

I scrutinize the picture in silence, absorbing every little detail. The blond hair that falls in soft waves around her shoulders. The delicate lines that bracket both her eyes and mouth. Even though sixteen years have slipped by, it's strange to have this foreign photo replace the image of a younger-looking Candace in my mind. The one I've been carrying around with me since she walked out of my life.

I flinch when Alyssa clicks on the image and it takes up the entire screen.

"She's pretty."

There's a faraway quality filling Alyssa's voice. As if she's talking to me from beneath the water. Then again, everything around me feels murky, so maybe I'm the one who has been shoved under the surface.

I focus on Candace's profile, attempting to dissect it almost objectively.

When I was little, I remember thinking that my mother was the most beautiful woman in the world. Even wearing paint-splattered shirts and jeans with her hair tied up in a blue bandana to keep it away from her face, she was still beautiful. The handful of times I was allowed to watch her work, I remember a look of utter concentration steeling over her face. Maybe the shell of her body was there with me, but Candace was off someplace else. There was always an air of remoteness to her. As if she was nothing more than whisps of smoke that my fingers could slide through. That feeling always made me want to wrap my arms around her and hold tight. I was so frightened that she would simply vanish.

And then she did.

"It says that she owns a gallery where her work is exclusively displayed," Alyssa murmurs.

The words are like a gunshot in the stillness of the room. When I remain silent, trapped in the past, she clicks on the blurb, pulling up another full page of information. A heaviness fills my chest as I skim over the paragraphs. A few likenesses of her paintings and the gallery are showcased. It's the last picture that has me wheezing out an agonizing breath.

"*Oh.*" Alyssa shifts on the bed as her hand moves from my thigh to squeeze my fingers.

It's one of a happy family.

Candace is seated alongside an older man. Each of them holds a child in their arms. One is a boy, and the other is a girl. Both are blond with dark eyes that resemble Candace's. They are the spitting image of her. Heads bent together, all four beam at the camera.

"Colton?" Alyssa clenches my hand when I remain mute. "Are you all right?"

There's that faraway quality again. It makes the edges of my vision blur, and her voice sound as if it's traveling over a great distance. It's funny, I didn't think it was possible for this woman to inflict any more pain than she already has, but I was wrong. My chest constricts, making it difficult to breathe.

"Colton?" Concern floods through her voice. "Please talk to me."

A ragged sound escapes from between my lips.

It's carefully that Alyssa pulls the computer from my hands before setting it on the desk at the far side of the room and returning to the bed where I sit frozen in place. She maneuvers her way between my legs before threading her arms around my neck. With her standing so close, I have no other choice but to tilt my chin in order to meet her worried gaze.

My first instinct is to shut down so the pain-riddled emotion rampaging through me is stopped dead in its tracks before it can inflict further damage. If I do that, I'll close myself off from Alyssa, and that will only push her further away when all I want to do is hold her close.

It doesn't escape me that this situation is completely self-induced. If I hadn't gone looking for Candace, I would still be unaware of her new family. I shutter my eyes and allow the grief to crash over me like a tsunami.

Her hands grip my face, forcing me to acknowledge that I'm not alone in this moment. I take a breath and force out the words. "I'm all right."

That's a lie.

Her lips feather across mine before she whispers, "I'm so sorry."

"Yeah, me too."

"Should I leave? Would you rather be alone?"

The thought of being left to my own devices with all this foreign emotion crashing around inside me is a frightening one. "No, I want you to stay."

"Okay."

We stare at each other for a long heartbeat. Instead of dwelling on Candace, I focus on each steady inhalation as it fills my lungs. One breath. Then another. My gaze stays pinned to Alyssa. She's the only thing grounding me in the here and now.

My head falls forward, resting between the gentle swells of her breasts. Her hands rise, fingers tunneling through the strands, holding me close. There is something so comforting in the way she touches me.

Before I can fully sink into her embrace, she steps away. I open my mouth to protest the distance when Alyssa's fingers settle on the hem of her T-shirt. For a moment, they hesitate. And then she's dragging the soft cotton up her body and over her head. My gaze skims across bare breasts as she shimmies out of the sleep shorts. The material slides down her thighs before revealing her slim form. Not giving me time to soak in the sight, she grabs my hand and pulls me to my feet. With quick fingers, she strips off my clothing until I'm standing before her, as naked as she is.

Somehow Alyssa manages to accomplish the impossible, and all thoughts of Candace and the hurt pounding through me vanish. Maybe it'll be short-lived, and in an hour, the pain will come rushing back, filling me to the brim, but I'll take it.

I'll take whatever she's willing to give.

Chapter Thirty-Two

ALYSSA

This night has swerved in a direction I could have never predicted when I found Colton waiting outside the fine arts building earlier this afternoon. Even though I've done everything possible to keep him at arm's length in an effort to avoid developing further feelings, it's been a losing battle from the beginning. If I hadn't realized it when we talked in his bedroom earlier this evening, I certainly do now.

There has always been something undeniable between us, and I'm tired of fighting the feelings that continue to simmer beneath the surface. I'm tired of denying they exist in a feeble attempt to move on. I can't do it anymore. I have no idea what will happen between us or how it will end. If it's anything like last time, it'll be badly. What I do know is that there is relief to be found in finally coming to terms with the situation.

I place my palms on his chest before slowly sliding them upward, needing to feel the sinewy strength that lies beneath. I rise to my tiptoes until my lips can brush across his. My hands drift from his chest to the rock-solid definition of his abdominals before dropping lower and brushing over his hard length. He stiffens beneath my touch. With one final kiss, I sink to my knees and angle my head to hold his gaze.

"You don't have to do that," he rasps, carefully sweeping the hair away from my face. "It's not the reason I asked you here."

"I know." My lips feather over the blunt tip of his erection. "I want to." As the response bursts free, I realize just how true it is. I love Colton's cock. I love the way it feels in my mouth. I love breaking him down and the way he loses control. Especially now that I know how tightly leashed he keeps his emotions.

As if to prove the words, my tongue darts out to lick the crown. When he groans, I draw him into my mouth. My gaze stays trained on him as his fingers tangle in my hair, holding me loosely in place.

"Fuck, baby. You have no idea how much I missed this," he growls.

The feel of him turning to steel as he slides against the muscles of my throat is its own reward. It only proves what I've been so intent on denying—not only to him but to myself. Sex with Colton has always been explosive. Addictive. All-consuming. Whether I realized it or not, Colton has been the measuring stick I used against every guy I've been with. And they've always come up sadly lacking.

At this very moment, with all these emotions careening around inside me, it seems foolish that I ever thought I could move on from him so easily. Or that I could somehow will it with my mind.

His fingers tighten around the sides of my skull as I draw him in so deep that he nudges the back of my throat. The lines of tension filling his face ease, leaving behind pure bliss in its place.

Me.

I'm the one capable of making him forget. I'm the one who is able to wipe away all the anguish that plagues him.

Instead of feathering his eyes closed and tilting his head back, so he can savor the pleasure, his gaze stays pinned to mine as if he doesn't want to miss a single moment. As if he's singeing this experience into his memory for all eternity.

"I love the way you suck my cock. There's nothing hotter than watching it disappear between your lips."

A punch of arousal slams into me full force, and my panties flood with heat. No one has ever turned me on like he does. His erection grows unbearably hard. When his muscles tighten and his fingers dig into my scalp, I know he's hovering at the edge of his release.

"I'm going to cum," he groans.

The admission only spurs on my movements. My mouth turns voracious as I draw him deeper until the crown of his cock hits the back of my throat. Until I'm able to reach the root of him. It takes every bit of concentration not to gag.

"Fuck."

And then he's exploding. I drink down the hot spurts, milking him until his body loosens, and his thick length turns slack in my mouth. It's only then that I release him and nuzzle the velvety tip with my lips. His hands loosen, sliding from my hair to beneath my arms as he drags me off my knees and to my feet. His lips descend in a hungry kiss that is both possessive and consuming before he spins us around and walks us backward. Before I realize what's happening, my back hits the bed, and he's falling on top of me, pinning me to the mattress.

"Do you have any idea how much I want you?" His mouth roves from my lips to my chin before descending. "I always have. Even when I forced you away, I wanted you. You're the only girl who has ever scared me."

His words circle viciously through my head as I open my eyes and stare at the ceiling. Knowing everything I do, the confession now makes perfect sense. More than a year and a half ago, I admitted my feelings for him, and he shoved me away, terrified of being hurt again.

Colton spreads my thighs wide before settling between them and peppering soft caresses against me as he continues to mutter. I'm not sure if he realizes the secrets he's so intent on spilling.

"I have no idea what you see in me, baby. I really don't."

When his tongue darts inside my heat, I suck in a shuddering breath.

"I never wanted you to get so close. I never wanted you to matter. I fought against it for as long as I could."

He spreads my lower lips with his thumbs. Cool air hits my core as the velvety softness of his tongue swirls intently around my clit. This man knows exactly how to touch me. It's only been a handful of moments, and already I'm perched at the precipice. Every stroke is deliberate. He understands what will shatter me into a million broken pieces.

"It doesn't make any sense," he whispers. My ears prick, trying to catch the words as pleasure continues to wash over me. "How could you love me when my own mother wasn't able to?"

Heartache spears through the pleasure unfolding inside me, jerking me back from the ledge. It's almost as if Colton realizes that his words are counterproductive to what he's trying to achieve. With renewed efforts, he attacks my flesh, pushing me relentlessly when I'd prefer to stop and hold him close, soothing the pain that resides deep inside him. Grief he barely acknowledges to himself and never to me. But he refuses to do that. Instead, his tongue spears inside my body before lapping at my shuddering softness, driving me relentlessly toward orgasm until I have no choice but to dive headfirst off the cliff.

I scream out my release, pressing a hand over my mouth and squeezing my eyelids tightly closed as waves of pleasure crash over me. There's a ruthless determination to his movements as his tongue relentlessly circles my throbbing clit. When I squirm, attempting to lessen the intensity, his grip tightens on my thighs, not allowing me a second of respite.

When my muscles turn lax, he raises his head. My eyes crack open to meet his glowing stare. He crawls up my body and settles between my legs before driving his hard cock inside me with one swift motion. It's only when he's buried to the hilt, and we're locked together, am I able to breathe. There is a rightness to our joining. As if this is exactly where he belongs. In my arms.

When his gaze fastens on to mine, the world around us falls away.

I expect him to take me in the same abrupt manner he did moments ago. Instead, there's a tenderness to his movements as his body rocks gently against mine. Almost as if he's making love to me. The need to ground myself in this act floods through me, and I lift my hands until they can cup his cheeks. Even though I've just cum, another orgasm brews inside me.

"Don't ever leave me, Alyssa," he whispers into the darkness. "Don't leave me the way she did."

Instead of my body splintering apart into a million jagged pieces, it's my heart that does so.

Chapter Thirty-Three

COLTON

Just as I'm adding the finishing touches to a paper, an email pops up in the corner of my computer screen. Everything inside me freezes as I stare at the name. It's as if I'm dangling at the tippy top of a sky-high rollercoaster, perched for descent.

C. Radcliffe.

In what universe did I think reaching out to my mother was a good idea? Why did I assume it would give me the closure I needed to move on with my life?

At the moment, it seems like the worst idea imaginable. A heavy wave of nausea crashes over me, and bile rises in my throat.

Instead of opening up the message and reading it, I slam the laptop closed and shove away from the table I've been working at. The more distance I put between myself and the computer, the better off I am. My chest grows heavy. Tight. As if there is a thousand-pound elephant sitting on it, making it impossible to breathe.

A cold sweat breaks out across my brow as I grab my keys and wallet and head out of the apartment. Twenty strides later, and I find myself at Alyssa's door. I rap my knuckles against the heavy wood and shift impatiently from one foot to another. When half a dozen seconds tick by, I plow a hand through my hair.

Where the hell is she?

I'm about to raise my fist and knock for a second time when the door swings open, and I find Alyssa on the other side of the threshold. Her eyes widen as she takes me in before throwing a cautious glance over her shoulder. "Hi." Barely does her voice hover above a whisper.

My gaze shifts, and I realize we're not alone. Mia straightens on the couch in the living room, watching our interaction with interest. When Alyssa's attention returns to mine, it only takes a moment before her expression morphs into one of concern. It's like she realizes without me having to spell it out that something is wrong.

"Hey." My voice drops, matching hers in tone. "Do you have time to talk?"

"Yeah." She continues to search my face for answers to questions she has yet to pose. "Are you all right?"

I jerk my shoulders. Not really, but there's no way I can get into it here with her roommate looking on in fascination.

With a jerk of her head, Alyssa shoots another tentative look into the apartment before clearing her throat and raising her voice. "So... we're going to grab something to eat."

"Really?" Mia points to the empty food container on the coffee table. "You just inhaled an entire enchilada."

Alyssa's eyes narrow. "I have a big appetite. Are you trying to food shame me?"

Her roommate's lips twitch as her shoulders shake with silent laughter. "Not at all."

When color seeps into Alyssa's cheeks, it occurs to me that she hasn't told Mia what's going on between us. After the way I broke up with her, I can't blame her for wanting to be cautious. I just need to keep proving that I'm worth taking a chance on.

Not bothering with any further explanations, Alyssa mutters, "I'll see you later." Then she swipes her purse off the credenza in the tiny entryway.

"Yes, we'll definitely talk—"

The sentence dies an abrupt death as Alyssa yanks the apartment door closed. With a huff of breath, she drags a hand down her face before it settles against her lips. The words come out sounding muffled. "I'll have a lot to answer for when I return."

"Sorry. I'm not trying to complicate matters for you. It's just..." my voice trails off.

Her fingers drift from her mouth before settling on my hand. I stare at them and focus on the connection between us. Some of the fear and anxiety bubbling up inside me gradually recedes. Now that I'm with her, my chest doesn't feel quite so heavy.

"It's all right." She gives me a tentative smile. "I should really come clean and tell Mia what's going on."

For one glorious moment, I forget all about Candace as I step closer and take Alyssa into my arms. "Hmmm. Is there something going on between us?" Why does everything feel so much better when I'm holding her close?

Her expression softens. "I really hope so."

My lips descend, sliding over hers. Just as I sink into the kiss, needing her sweetness to soothe my soul, her palms press against my chest, creating unwanted space between us.

"Tell me what happened."

That's all it takes for everything to come crashing down on me again. And then I'm buried beneath an avalanche of suffocating emotion. "Let's go somewhere else and talk about it. Are you hungry? Did you want to grab something to eat?"

An impish smile curves Alyssa's lips as she shakes her head and pats her belly. "Mia was right, I just inhaled an enchilada. I'm stuffed. How about a walk?"

"Sure, that works." Maybe I can burn off some of this excess energy simmering beneath my skin. Any moment, it's going to burst free.

With our hands threaded together, we move down the hallway. As I push through the stairwell door, the elevator dings, and the metal gate opens. A man steps off, and Alyssa falters.

"Oh, boy," she mutters under her breath.

I quirk a brow as my gaze slides over the older man. "Do you know him?"

"Yup." She quickly ducks into the stairwell as he stops and glances in the other direction. "That's Mia's father." She digs through her pocket before pulling out her phone. "I need to warn her."

Warn her?

About her own father?

Looks like I'm not the only one with parental problems.

Alyssa fires off a text before slipping her cell back into her pocket. It only takes a couple of minutes before we're walking out of the building and heading up the block. Everything that I've been desperately trying to push to the outer recesses of my mind slams back into me again. I'm so lost in those thoughts that I don't realize we're on campus until Alyssa points to a park bench off the beaten path on a grassy knoll. "Want to sit over there?"

Dread pools in my belly. As much as I don't want to delve headfirst into this conversation, it needs to be purged from my body before it can fester any more than it already has. Maybe the smartest thing to do would be to delete the email and pretend I never saw it.

"Yeah." My fingers stay clasped around hers. She's like a lifeline. One I never realized I needed. Or wanted.

After settling on the bench, she turns her body until we're able to face one another. When I remain silent, she says, "Tell me what happened."

A burst of air escapes from my lungs as I slide the phone from my pocket. My fingers tremble as I pull up the email. It's so much easier to show her than say the words out loud. Alyssa leans closer as we read the message together in silence.

Shock washes over her features as her widened gaze darts to mine. "When did you reach out to her?"

"The day after we found her online." I jerk my shoulders self-consciously. "I'm not sure what I was expecting."

That's not *altogether* true. I haven't heard from the woman in more than a decade. I figured there was no way she'd bother to reply, and I could put to rest all these uncomfortable and turbulent emotions inside me. Instead, she responded.

Alyssa's gaze returns to the phone I'm clenching in my hand. "She wants to meet with you."

A pit of nausea forms in my gut. I have no idea if I'm ready to come face-to-face with Candace. Quite honestly, I can't imagine ever being prepared for that scenario. What would I say?

Hey, how are you?

How's the fam?

Why did you throw me away like a piece of garbage and start fresh?

I wince at the last thought.

When I remain silent, she asks, "This is what you wanted, isn't it?"

I plow a hand through my hair and focus on the trees that dot the landscape surrounding us. The picturesque setting with all its greenery, red-brick buildings, and thick ivy that clings to the walls isn't enough to distract me. Already leaves are falling to the ground, creating a carpet of gold and red. "I don't know." I hesitate before adding, "Part of me is sorry that I ever looked her up."

Alyssa takes a moment to digest that bit of information before whispering, "You don't have to take this any further. You can change your mind." Her fingers tighten around mine. "You don't owe this woman anything."

How sad is that? The woman we're talking about happens to be my mother. Biologically speaking, anyway.

All this has done is dredge up even more turmoil. The hurt and pain of her abandonment is like a living, breathing entity that has taken up residence inside my body. It's yet another realization that the memories and damage she inflicted have held me captive for way too long. Candace might have walked out of my life more than sixteen years ago, but she's still controlling it as if she were here beside me, and I'm tired of it.

Tired of her holding all that power over my life.

There has to be a way to exorcise these demons. What scares me most is that I might not be able to put the past behind me and move forward. Maybe it's too late. Maybe these feelings are too entrenched. I never dealt with the havoc Candace wreaked inside me. Honestly, I thought if I crammed it down deep enough, I would eventually forget about it. Guess the jokes on me—that never occurred. And I've been paying the consequences ever since.

When I was younger, Jenna would broach the subject of counseling every so often, and I'd scoff at not only her, but the idea of crying on some random stranger's shoulder about the bullshit in my past. I couldn't see how my mother walking out on me when I was a kid could have long-term effects on my future or happiness.

Turns out that it has.

I have no idea if counseling could have saved me from some of the heartache I've inflicted on to myself by not dealing with these issues, but it sure as hell couldn't have hurt.

"You're right, I don't owe her anything, but maybe I owe it to myself," I grudgingly admit.

"Whatever you decide," Alyssa says, leaning against my shoulder and holding me tight, "I'll be here for you."

Little does she realize that those words feel like a lifeline right now. In order to move forward and have a fighting chance at a relationship with Alyssa, I need to break free from my past.

And meeting with Candace is the only way to achieve that.

Chapter Thirty-Four

COLTON

Why couldn't I have left well enough alone?

I was perfectly content living my life.

All right, so maybe *perfectly content* is something of an overstatement, but it was all good.

I sit behind the wheel of my BMW in a parking space in front of the coffee shop somewhere in the middle of where we both live. The only person who knows I'm here is Alyssa. I couldn't bring myself to tell Dad or Jenna. They probably would have tried to talk me out of it. Well, maybe not Jenna. I think she would have understood. But Dad?

Definitely not. Even though he loves his wife more than anything, he's still salty about the way Candace walked out of our lives without ever looking back.

As I stare at the weathered cream-colored brick building with a worn wooden sign hanging over the door, I'm kind of wishing I would have given them the opportunity to change my mind. This is the last place I want to be. And yet, I can't bring myself to turn the key in the ignition and drive away. I'm stuck.

Frozen in place.

Instead of exiting the vehicle, I grab my cell from the seat next to me and hit the contact at the top of my list. A few seconds later, the phone rings.

And rings.

Just as I'm about to hit disconnect, a breathless voice comes over the line. "Hello?"

I clear all of the emotion that has welled up in my throat and try to keep my tone deceivingly light. "Hey."

"Hi, sweetie." Her voice warms as if she's pleased that I called. "How are you?"

"Good." That's a lie, but I can't bring myself to tell Jenna the truth even though it sits perched at the tip of my tongue, waiting to burst free.

There's a pause. I can almost hear the wheels turning in her head. That little frown she gets when she's attempting to figure out the truth. Looks like calling her was just as lousy of an idea as agreeing to meet up with Candace. I'm on a real roll today.

"Are you sure?" she questions carefully. "You sound strange. Like there's something on your mind you want to talk about."

That's the thing about Jenna, she's always been perceptive—especially where I'm concerned. I might not be her own flesh and blood, but she's highly attuned to my feelings and moods. Sometimes more than what I'm comfortable with.

Instead of coming clean, I force out a chuckle. "Nah, it's all good. I had a little time to kill between classes and thought I'd check-in and see how everything's going. It's been a couple of days since we've talked."

"You're so sweet." Some of her concern falls away. "You're lucky that you caught me when the kids are at music."

Right. I forgot that she's in the middle of her workday.

"Oh, sorry. Should I let you go?" Jenna is probably knee-deep grading papers and doesn't have time for my bullshit.

"Of course not," she says with a laugh. It's a soft, tinkling sound that washes over me, immediately settling something deep inside. "You know that I love talking to you—even if it's only for a few minutes. I know you don't live far, but I'm looking forward to you moving back and working for your father. Then you can pop home any time you want. Or we can grab lunch."

That does sound nice. I've enjoyed my years at Wesley, but it's getting old if you can believe that. I'm ready to graduate and move on. I know some people don't feel that way. They want to cling to the party lifestyle. A few of my teammates actually toyed with the idea of coming back for a fifth year. Until their parents put the kibosh on that.

"So, what do you have going on for the rest of the day?"

I blink back to the present and stare at the coffee house in front of me. "Oh, you know. Class. Practice." I gulp. "I'll probably hit the library later and study for a test."

"Sounds like college," she says with a laugh.

Yup.

When I remain silent, she asks, "Are you sure nothing is bothering you?"

"It's all good." I feel like crap for lying to her. If there's one person I try to keep it real with, it's Jenna. She's never judged me for anything. Not that she didn't hold my feet to the fire when I screwed up, but she was always there, no matter what.

Clearly, I can't say that about everyone.

I squeeze my eyes closed, allowing the sound of her soft, melodic voice to comfort me. There are two women who hold importance in my life, and this is one of them. Alyssa is the other. It wasn't until she left the summer of our junior year that I realized how spectacularly I fucked up our relationship.

It's almost as if Jenna can sense the direction of my thoughts. "We really enjoyed meeting Alyssa last week." There's a pause. "Any chance we'll be seeing more of her?"

A smile tugs at the corners of my lips. "I hope so."

"Good. I'll talk to your father, and we'll set something up soon."

"Sounds like a plan." I glance at the digital clock on the dash and realize that it's ten minutes past the appointed time Candace and I agreed to meet up. "I should probably get moving."

"All right. I'm glad you called. Love you."

A thick lump settles in the middle of my throat as I parrot the sentiment back to her, meaning every single word. "Love you, too."

I hit disconnect and pocket the phone before grabbing my keys. It takes everything I have inside to force myself from the safety of the BMW. I grab a few coins from my pocket, adding them to the parking meter before traversing the sidewalk and climbing the thick, cement steps.

As I pull open the door and step inside the shop, air gets wedged in my throat. My gaze coasts over the tables crammed together in the tiny space. There are a few couches and chairs situated around a coffee table. Bright artwork decorates the walls, and alternative rock plays in the background. The atmosphere has a hip vibe to it, which makes sense since most of the patrons look young—early twenties or so. This is definitely an artsy crowd.

It's only when my lungs begin to burn, do I realize that I'm holding my breath. It escapes from my lips in a rush as I decide on a plan of action. No one here looks over the age of thirty.

Even though I'm late, she's later. Or maybe she changed her mind and decided to pull another disappearing act.

How ironic would that be?

Instead of grabbing a drink, I head to a lone table parked in the back and settle on a chair that faces the door. Nerves skitter along my flesh as I slip the phone from my pocket and open the home screen.

I'm giving it another ten minutes, and then I'm out of here. I've already wasted enough of my time on this—*on her*. If Candace failing to show up to a meeting that she requested isn't closure, then I don't know what is.

I drum my fingertips against the scratched wood surface, wishing Alyssa were here with me. She'd offered to make the trip, and I'd turned her down flat. That's a decision I now regret. She's the one person who is able to settle all the chaos raging inside me.

Every time the door opens and the little bell above it chimes, I have a whiplash moment where everything inside freezes, only to realize that it's not her. Tension spirals through me as I shift on my chair before glancing at my phone again.

Twenty-five minutes late.

Why is this even a surprise? I should have expected her to flake.

You know what?

I refuse to sit around and wait for a woman who walked out of my life when I was five-years-old. If I didn't realize it before, I certainly do now—I shouldn't have looked her up or contacted her in the first place. It was an error in judgment. As I make my way to my feet, the door opens, and in breezes a blonde woman with lavender highlights and large sunglasses that cover her face. She's tall and willowy.

Just like I remember. Minus the highlights.

My mouth turns cottony.

Her gaze sweeps over the space until locking on mine. She pauses. Even though I'm unable to catch a glimpse of her eyes hidden behind the dark lenses, I can almost feel the way they slide over me. My breath becomes wedged in my throat as my heartbeat picks up its pace, pounding painfully against my ribcage. She glides through the tiny establishment, skirting around tables until finally arriving in front of me. For the first time in sixteen years, she's close enough to reach out and touch. Resisting the temptation, I tighten my fingers into fists.

There's a moment of hesitation. "Colton?"

That voice.

Deep and comforting. It reminds me of burrowing under a warm blanket on a cold night.

My throat closes up, making speech impossible. I jerk my head into a terse nod. There is so much tension filling the air that it feels like the atmosphere could shatter into a million jagged pieces.

When I remain mute, she advances a tentative step, closing the distance between us. "Would it be all right if I give you a hug?"

The question breaks the strange paralysis that has fallen over me. "Yes." The word is blurted out before I can give it more thought.

Another step brings her close enough to slide her arms around my body. Even though I try to remain aloof, I find myself hugging her tight and burying my nose in the thick strands of her hair. I squeeze my eyes shut and inhale, shocked to realize that she smells exactly the same as she did in my childhood. It's difficult not to tumble backward into the memories of the past.

They're like a wave crashing over me as I'm inundated with images I'd long forgotten about. Time becomes irrelevant. I have no idea how long we stand there and embrace as her warmth seeps into my body.

All I know is that it feels good. Good enough to assuage some of the pain that has been part of me since she walked out of my life.

When we break apart, her fingers trail over my arm before tangling with mine. I stare down at the physical connection—the one she's initiating. Even as we slide onto our chairs, our hands stay linked together.

She pulls off her sunglasses and gazes at me from across the small, round table that separates us as if trying to catalog every minute detail before committing them to memory. "I can't believe how handsome you've become. But then again, you always were an adorable child." She reaches out and traces her fingers along the curve of my cheek before they settle on my chin. I remain mute as she turns my face one way and then carefully the other. It's so tempting to close my eyes and sink into the warmth of her touch, but I'm afraid to do that. I'm afraid if I blink—even for a second—she'll disappear, and this will end up being nothing more than a hazy dream that I'll wake from.

"It's so good to see you again," she says. "I'm glad you reached out."

My head bobs as I frantically search for something to say, but nothing comes to mind. I have no idea where to start. This woman is my mother. My flesh and blood. Her name is on my birth certificate. She cared for me during those first five years. And yet, she's nothing more than a stranger. As much as I wish it didn't, this feels...awkward.

"I've thought about reaching out for a while," she says, breaking the silence. "Thank you for taking that first step."

I shift on my seat. "No problem."

Her fingers tighten around my hand. "I've thought about you so much over the years, but I was afraid to contact you. I didn't want to disrupt your life."

My heart constricts painfully. "You wouldn't have." Maybe if she had reached out, I wouldn't have spent all these years walking around, thinking there was something wrong with me. I wouldn't have felt abandoned. I wouldn't have pushed away the people who only wanted to love me.

She clears her throat and blinks back the wetness that fills her eyes. "Tell me everything. Catch me up."

Once I start talking, I can't stop. It all pours out in a rush of words.

I give her the Spark Notes version of my life. From elementary school through college, along with my plans for the future. Instead of being straight with her about my feelings, I gloss over the hurt and pain she inflicted. Candace sits quietly across from me, squeezing my hand every so often to let me know she's paying attention. The longer I talk, the more my muscles loosen.

"I heard your father remarried some time ago."

"He did," I admit cautiously, "when I was seven."

"And his wife, did she treat you well?"

"Yes." As much as I want to tell her that I couldn't have asked for a better stepmother than Jenna, I'm afraid to say too much. I don't want to ruin the fragile moment unfolding between us. This is going so much better than I expected. I want it to continue. I want to spend more time with her. I want her to share all the details of her life with me. I want to soak up enough to make the sixteen years of silence between us disappear.

Is that even possible?

Her lips tilt at the corners. "I'm glad. It's a relief to know that you were well cared for and loved." Her gaze drops to our clasped hands. "Part of what kept me from reaching out is that I was afraid you wouldn't be able to forgive me for leaving the way I did."

The words tumble out of my mouth before I can stop them. "Of course, I forgive you. I," my tongue darts out to moisten my lips, "I just want to get to know you. I want to make up for lost time."

Instead of answering, she squeezes my fingers before opening up and telling me all about her art and family. I dredge my memory for every little detail, wanting her to know that she was never forgotten even though we weren't in contact all these years.

When I glance at my phone on the table, I'm surprised to realize that two hours have slipped by. As much as I don't want to cut this reunion short, I need to get back for practice, or Coach will have my ass, and I can't afford for that to happen. Not with the way I've been playing.

But I can't walk away from her without having another date firmly set in place. I need to know that we're going to see each other again.

Sooner rather than later. "When will I be able to meet your husband and kids?"

Leif and Surrey. A half brother and sister. It's so weird to think that I have siblings out there. Up until last week, I was an only child. There were times when I was growing up that I desperately wanted siblings. Hell, I would have been content if Jenna and Dad had popped out a few kiddos. They tried for a couple of years and went the fertility drug route, but nothing worked. It would be kind of cool to pick up Candace's kids on a weekend and take them to the movies or amusement park. Maybe Alyssa can come with. We can get to know them together. She can be part of this new phase taking place in my life.

I almost shake my head.

Is this really happening?

It seems almost too good to be true.

"Oh." Candace pins her lower lip with her teeth as her gaze flickers away. "I'm not sure. That might not be possible."

Some of the pretty façade in my head falls away as I crash back to earth with a painful thud. I straighten on my seat. "Why not?"

"My husband, Roger," there's an uncomfortable pause as she shifts on the chair, "he doesn't know that I was previously married."

I blink and attempt to wrap my brain around what she's saying. "*You,*" it takes effort to swallow down the hurt and pain, "*never told him about me?*"

"No," she whispers faintly, "I didn't."

Her tongue darts out to moisten her lips as I retract my hand. "You have to understand what it was like for me."

For her?

I have to understand what it was like for her?

You know that feeling you get when you fall and land flat on your back? The way it knocks the air from your lungs, making it impossible to breathe? You gasp, can't talk, and your eyes sting?

That's exactly how I feel at this moment.

When I remain mute, at a loss, she rushes to fill the void of silence that stretches between us.

"After I left your father, I was in a really dark place. It was my therapist who helped me to realize that I'd been suffering from postpartum depression. The creativity I'd always taken for granted was no longer there, and that was terrifying. It was like having an arm amputated. Who was I without my art? Even though the decision was difficult, I chose to leave." She presses a hand to her chest. "There was no way I could be the mother you needed when part of me was missing." There's an uncomfortable pause. "You understand that, don't you?"

Yeah, I understand perfectly.

When I'm finally able to summon my voice, it's completely devoid of emotion. "You chose your art."

Over me.

Instead of me.

The unspoken words hang painfully in the air between us. The tentative bridge we had been building has now been destroyed.

Her eyes widen. The gathered wetness makes them shiny. "I know that's what it sounds like, but my motives weren't that selfish."

A humorless laugh bubbles up in my throat. Or maybe it's all the emotion I've kept locked away for all these years.

"You might not realize it, but you were better off without me," she whispers.

She just might be right about that. Although, we'll never know.

"It sounds like your father's wife—"

"Jenna," I snap, cutting her off. "Her name is *Jenna*."

"Sorry." She swallows thickly. "It sounds like Jenna treated you well."

For all Candace knows, Jenna could have been pure evil. Thank fuck, she wasn't. I have a couple of friends with stepparents, and they don't get along. I really lucked out in that regard. Jenna is everything that Candace is not and could never be.

Was unwilling to be.

I fold my arms across my chest and press against the back of the chair, needing to put as much space between us as possible. All of a sudden, the walls of the coffee shop are pressing in on me, making it difficult to breathe. I suck air in through my nostrils, filling my lungs, attempting to calm everything racing inside me. The urge to bolt hums beneath my skin, making me twitchy.

"Colton?" She leans forward, stretching her hand out across the table. "Please, talk to me."

It takes effort to fight my way out of the pain that pounds through me before blinking sightlessly at her fingers.

I can't.

I can't bear for her to touch me.

"If you never had any intention of letting me back into your life, why did you bother with this?"

She gulps as if thrown off by the blunt question. "I needed to see with my own eyes that you were okay. That I made the right decision all those years ago."

Ah.

So the point of this little exercise was to assuage her guilt.

Got it.

I clear my throat, unable to sit in her presence any longer. "As you can see for yourself, I'm good. No need to worry or think about me for another sixteen years."

"Colton," her face drains of all color, "I don't want it to end like this."

Yeah, well...it's a little late for that.

Sixteen years too late, to be exact.

This woman could never understand the kind of damage she inflicted. She has no idea the emotional scars I carry around with me or how they've affected every single relationship. Only now do I realize the extent of the destruction.

Silently, I rise from the chair. I think we've said everything that needed to be said.

Her dark eyes widen as she scrambles to do the same. "You're leaving?"

"Yeah." I hear my voice as if from a great distance. "I need to get back to school."

"Please, let me explain it better." Her tongue darts out to moisten her lips as a frantic light enters her eyes. "I didn't do a good job."

"Actually, you did. I appreciate you being upfront and telling me the truth."

She sucks in a shaky breath. "I don't want you to have hurt feelings."

I almost laugh. Is this lady serious? My fucking feelings are already hurt. More like completely annihilated.

"Can we sit and talk for a few more minutes?" She makes one last-ditch effort at damage control.

I shake my head. "No, I don't think so."

"Then let's set up another time to meet. Whatever works for you, that's what we'll do."

I drag a hand over my face before glancing at the exit with longing. I just want to get the hell out of here. Instead of walking away, I mumble, "Do you have any intention of telling your family about me?"

Her shoulders slump as her face falls.

Yeah, that's exactly what I thought. There's nothing more for either of us to say.

I jerk my head into a nod. "Take care, Candace."

On legs that feel shaky, I push my way out of the coffee house and into the crisp fall air. By the time I reach my BMW, I'm sick to my stomach. It takes a couple of attempts to jam the key into the ignition. Relief floods through me when the metal slides home, and I rev the engine. As I pull away from the curb, my gaze flickers to the rearview mirror, only to find Candace standing on the sidewalk, staring after me.

With a heart that feels like it's splintering apart, I realize that's exactly where she belongs.

In the rearview mirror.

Chapter Thirty-Five

ALYSSA

It's two o'clock in the afternoon, and I still haven't heard from Colton. Why hasn't he shot me a text? Or given me a quick call? I'd take anything at this point. I just want to know everything is all right.

That *he's* all right.

As I push through the lobby door of the apartment building and hustle down the cement walkway, I slide my phone from my pocket and peek at the screen for the umpteenth time in the last thirty minutes.

Ugh. Could I feel more like a needy girlfriend?

And we're not even going out.

But still...

After all these years, I finally feel like Colton has cracked open the door, allowing me a glimpse of the person beneath the persona. I now have a better understanding of him. If I'm being completely honest, I'm afraid this meeting with Candace will somehow slam that door closed again, and we'll backslide. There's no way I can deal with him shutting down on me for a second time. If Colton wants to have a relationship, he needs to open up and let me in.

As I reach the edge of the parking lot, a glint of metallic gray catches the corner of my eye, and my footsteps falter as I take a closer look at the vehicle.

Sure enough, Colton's metallic gray BMW is sitting in the lot.

He's back? And he didn't bother to call or text?

A wave of hurt floods through me. It shouldn't. But that doesn't change the fact that it does. As I continue to stare, the door opens, and Colton unfolds himself from inside. One glimpse of his face is all it takes for me to realize that whatever happened with Candace wasn't good. Even from this distance, grief swims around in his eyes. His mouth is a tight slash across his face, and his body vibrates with pent-up energy. Almost as if there is something inside him trying to claw its way out.

My first impulse is to take him into my arms and soothe away all the hurt that has been inflicted, but...

I have no idea if that's what he wants.

Or needs.

Because when it comes down to it, I don't really know Colton.

Those thoughts are slammed home when his gaze flickers in my direction, locking on mine. There's a flash of surprise before it's tucked away behind an expressionless mask. When he stays frozen in place, I tentatively raise my hand in greeting. We stare for a long moment before his legs eat up the distance between us. He stops a couple of feet from where I stand on the sidewalk.

It takes effort to swallow down my disappointment when he doesn't reach out and pull me into his arms. The loss of that intimate connection makes us feel more like acquaintances than anything else. It's disheartening. Up close, his features appear even more haunted. Closed off. It's just as I feared. If he would give me a sign that he wanted me to make the first move, I would do it in a heartbeat.

Instead, I stay rooted in place. "Hi."

"Hey." His mouth never lifts into a smile.

Unsure what to say, I glance at the car. "Did you just return?"

"Yeah." He plows a hand through his hair before muttering, "I should really get moving. I'm already late for practice. I don't need to give Coach any more reason to bench my ass."

With that, he takes a step away, and the question bursts free from my lips before I can rein it in again. "Are you all right?"

He shrugs. "I'm fine." There's a monotone quality to his voice. One that scares me. It's like he's a million miles away, and there's no way for me to reach him.

I bite down on my lower lip before asking, "Do you want me to walk with you to the field?" It's hesitantly that I close the space between us. "We could talk on the way." I don't care if that makes me late for class.

"I appreciate the offer, but I just want to be alone."

"Sure, I get it." My shoulders slump under the weight of the moment. Even though it feels like we've been gradually inching our way into unchartered territory with this relationship, it now feels like we're taking a gigantic step in retreat. And there's nothing I can do to stop it from happening.

Colton shifts impatiently as if he can't wait to get away from me. "We'll talk later, okay?"

One long-legged stride puts an ocean of distance between us. If I were desperate enough, I could leap forward and grab hold of him, but that would do nothing to change the emotional gulf that has developed. Colton is good at closing people off. He's spent his entire life mastering the art of walking away.

A mixture of fear and regret bloom inside me. "Yeah, sure. No problem." As he takes another step, I add pathetically, "Call me."

He jerks his head toward the building. "Gotta go."

Before I even have a chance to lift my hand, he dismisses me, only to disappear inside the lobby without another glance in my direction. A wave of sadness crashes over me, threatening to suck me under. Maybe I was stupid for not anticipating this outcome. Or guarding my heart better against Colton.

Although, I have to wonder if that was ever a possibility.

Somehow, I don't think so.

Chapter Thirty-Six

ALYSSA

Even though I should be plowing my way through this work, I'm staring off into space, lost in the tangle of my own conflicted thoughts. I can't concentrate to save my life which is why I dragged Mia to the library in the first place. I have a test coming up on Friday and a paper that needs to be outlined if I'm going to complete it by the due date. Between fifteen credits, carving out time in the studio, and teaching a couple of classes, I've got a jam-packed schedule and more than enough to keep my brain occupied so that I don't dwell on the Colton situation.

But guess what?

The blond football player continues to dominate all of my thoughts.

I give myself a good mental slap before refocusing my attention on the computer screen. Everything in me deflates as I read over the paragraph for the umpteenth time. I'm irritated that I allowed my advisor to talk me into this upper-level psych course. I thought it would be a blowoff class that would allow me more time to focus on dance.

Ha!

Jokes on me. That hasn't turned out to be the case. Not by a long shot. The professor is a real hard-ass. Now I'm stuck writing a ten-page paper on the measurement of critical thinking.

The measurement of what?

Exactly.

Unfortunately, it's much too late to switch classes and pick up something else. I can't afford to drop it unless I want to take eighteen credits next semester. And, to be clear, I don't. Especially when I'll be busy rehearsing for my final spring showcase.

So, I'm stuck with this class for the duration.

When I huff out a breath, Mia glances up from the laptop she's working at on the other side of the table. "You doing okay?"

Now there's a loaded question. One I'm not entirely sure how to answer.

"Yup." There's a beat of silence. "Why?"

She shrugs and leans back in her chair before stretching. We've been camped out here for a couple of hours. I glance at my screen, dismayed to realize that I've barely accomplished anything.

Ugh. I've blown two hours of prime study time that I'll never get back again.

"You just seem," her brows draw together, "I don't know...*preoccupied?*"

Little does Mia realize that I sped past preoccupied doing ninety on the freeway a while ago.

I drag a hand over my face and try to shake off everything that's been eating away at me. My teeth sink into my lower lip. I have yet to come clean to Mia about my recent involvement with Colton. Then again, is there really anything to tell her about? He's done exactly what I was afraid of and pushed me away.

It's like déjà vu all over again, and it leaves a pit sitting uncomfortably at the bottom of my belly. One that hasn't budged for days.

"So," I hedge, a little nervous about how she'll react, "I haven't exactly been honest with you."

Her brows rise as she pushes her computer to the side. "About what?"

More like who.

"Colton—"

"I knew it!" she crows, pokering up in her chair and stabbing a finger in my direction. "I *knew* something was going on! It's like I could sense a disturbance in the force."

I wince at the accusatory tone that fills her voice. So much for taking this in stride. Although, who can blame her? She was a hundred percent right to be concerned. It was a mistake to get involved with him again. "I'm sorry. I should have been straight with you."

A flicker of hurt flashes across her face as she folds her arms across her chest. "Then why weren't you?"

I shrug and glance away. "After the way my relationship ended with Colton the first time, I felt like an idiot for getting caught up in him again."

"I hate how he hurt you, Lys. You took off for a year because of the guy."

"That's not totally true," I mumble. All right, so maybe there's more truth in the statement than I'm comfortable admitting. I never would have considered the study abroad program sophomore year had Colton not unceremoniously dumped my ass. The only difference is that I now have a better understanding of why he did it. But does that necessarily do me any good?

Nope.

"So what's going on now?" There's a beat of silence followed up by another question. "Are you two a thing?"

"If you'd asked me a week ago, I could have given you more of a definitive answer but now?" I shrug. "I have no idea."

"What happened?"

As tempting as it is to confide in Mia, it's Colton's private business. The last thing I want to do is spread gossip or divulge his secrets. Only now has he started to open up, giving me a glimpse of the demons he struggles with. As much as I hate how he pushed me away, I get it. Every time I think about the pain he carries around with him, it breaks my heart all over again.

The unavoidable conclusion that I've arrived at is that he's going to do it again. Already he's withdrawing from me. Maybe not consciously but that seems to be the pattern of behavior he retreats into.

"He's going through something personal," I finally offer by way of explanation even though it isn't much of one.

She nods as clouds gather in her dark eyes. In a way, Mia can relate to someone not wanting to air their dirty laundry for people to talk about. There's been enough bullshit with her own family—especially now that her parents are separating.

"What are you going to do?"

"I'm not sure. Colton has been really distant this week." And that has everything to do with his mother and what happened when they met for coffee. Even though he's been pretty tight-lipped about the meeting, it's obvious that it didn't go the way he'd hoped. The pain radiating from his eyes when we'd run into each other in the parking lot had been like a knife to my heart. All I'd wanted to do was pull him into my arms.

"You need to talk to him and get it figured out before this goes any further. If Colton can't step up, then it's time to cut your losses and move on. For real this time. I know that sounds harsh, but you deserve better than this."

I swallow down the thick lump of emotion that has become wedged in the middle of my throat. She's not telling me anything I don't already know. As much as I've always had a thing for Colton, I'm unsure if he'll ever be able to open up emotionally and give me the kind of relationship I need. That's not a knock on him. It's just the way it is.

Decision made, I grab my phone from the table and tap on Colton's name before hastily typing out a message and hitting send before I can change my mind.

Are you busy? Can we talk?

My heart pounds a painful staccato against my ribcage as three little bubbles appear.

And then his answer is popping up.

Can't right now.

Any hope I'd been harboring that we could sit down and have an honest conversation crashes back to earth before exploding upon impact. As much as I want to make this relationship work, as much effort as I'm willing to put in, it's not something I can do alone. If Colton isn't willing to meet me halfway...

Then I guess the decision has been taken out of my hands, and I have my answer.

Chapter Thirty-Seven

COLTON

"Good practice, man. Keep playing like that, and you'll be on the field in no time." Beck slaps my back as he saunters past on the way to his locker.

"Thanks." I hate to jinx myself, but it felt like old times out there. Everything Beck threw my way, I caught with ease. There wasn't a fumble in sight. It was nice. Reassuring. As if one piece of the puzzle has finally fallen back into place. With each practice, I've been steadily improving. It's almost like I'm getting my groove back.

All I can hope is that it continues and that Coach has taken notice. So far, he hasn't said mum about it. He's been watching from the sidelines and jotting down notes. It's enough to set my nerves on edge, but I try not to let the pressure get to me.

Which hasn't been easy. Especially with everything that happened with Candace. I was afraid that it would mess with my head even more than before, but strangely enough, it's had the opposite effect. Don't get me wrong, what she said hurts like a mother fucker but...

I can't allow someone who doesn't give a damn about me to totally screw with my life. I've given this person way too much power, and now I'm wrestling it back. It's taken me a couple of days to come to that epiphany, but now that I have, there's peace to be found in the decision to walk away.

Some relationships just aren't viable, no matter how much you wish otherwise. And when it happens to be with your own parent, it's gut-wrenching. Afterall, in a perfect world, these are the people who are supposed to love you no matter what. Who have your back when no one else does. Who you can depend on when life goes sideways. They aren't supposed to be the ones who bring the messed-up shit that turns your life upside-down and inside-out.

But that's the way it goes, right?

No one ever said life was fair.

It only makes me realize how lucky I am to have Dad and Jenna.

Especially Jenna.

I appreciate her now more than ever.

As soon as Coach walks into the locker room, the boisterous voices fall silent. None of these loudmouths want to draw attention to themselves. He grinds to a halt in the middle of the space and snaps out a couple of names. "Reinholtz, Collins, and Montgomery. See me on your way out."

I give him a chin lift in acknowledgment as he stalks into his office, slamming the door behind him with a resounding thud.

Well, fuck me.

I'm not sure if I'm about to get my ass chewed out or not. I'm still a little sore from the last time he lit into me. Coach isn't the kind of guy to pussyfoot around a subject or hold back. If he thinks you're screwing up, you better believe he's going to give it to you straight.

In full, Technicolor detail.

And here I'd been feeling relaxed and good about myself after walking off the turf. Instead of hanging around and shooting the shit with Beck, like I'd normally do, I strip and haul ass to the shower. I want to be the first one in Coach's office and get this over with.

Ten minutes later, with dripping wet hair, I knock on the closed door before peeking cautiously inside. "Hey, Coach, you wanted to see me?"

He pauses the action playing out across the television screen and swivels around to face me before pointing a finger at the chair on the opposite side of the desk. "Park it, Montgomery."

It doesn't matter if this is my fourth and final year playing for this guy, every time I'm called in here, it makes me feel like an errant eight-year-old sent to the principal's office. It's ridiculous. That being said, I do what I'm told and drop my ass on the faux leather chair as the older man scrutinizes his clipboard of notes.

Paper and pencil, if I'm not mistaken.

Coach is old school like that.

"Seems like whatever shit needed to get flushed out of your head has happened."

It's not a question—more of a statement.

I sit up a little straighter. "Yes, sir."

"As long as you continue to play like you are, I'm moving you to first string." He sits back in his chair and gives me a well-honed death stare. I can't help but squirm under the intensity of it. "Kwiatkowski is a talented player, but he doesn't have your intuitiveness out on the field."

"Thank you." This is the closest Coach has ever come to giving me a compliment.

See? It's like I secretly suspected all along. Beneath the hard candy shell lies a soft nougat filling. You just have to take the time to dig deep and find it.

"That being said, you manage to get your head wedged up your ass again, you'll be riding the pine for the season. Are we clear?"

"Crystal."

"Good." He points to the door. "Now get the hell out of here. I've got game film to review."

He doesn't need to tell me twice. I practically jump from the chair and shoot through the door as a wave of relief crashes over me. Most of the guys are still getting dressed. Collins and Reinholtz eye me with speculation, looking a little green around the gills. Can't blame them for that.

As soon as I return to my locker, Beck raises a brow. An answering grin breaks loose across my face.

"Fuck, yeah!" He punches me in the arm. "It's all about controlling the bullshit up here." He taps his temple before shrugging. "Or maybe it has more to do with what you're packing. All I know is that it's one head or the other."

I snort.

The guy isn't wrong.

He grabs his athletic bag and slings it over his shoulder. "You ready to get out of here?"

"Yup."

So damn ready.

I need to celebrate the good news. Or maybe have a little one-on-one party with Alyssa. I really need to fix the situation with her. Unfortunately, old habits die hard, and I pushed her away, needing a little breathing room to get my head straight. I want to explain what happened so we can move forward with this relationship.

Things are starting to look up.

With that thought circling through my head, I push through the heavy locker room door before skidding to a halt when my gaze lands on Alyssa. She's leaning against the far wall with her arms crossed over her chest. For a sliver of a moment, déjà vu crashes over me along with a prickle of unease.

Beck plows into me from behind. "Dude, what the—"

"Oh, hey, Alyssa." His gaze bounces between the pair of us. That's all it takes for him to accurately size up the situation. With one quick movement, he sidesteps me before calling over his shoulder, "Bye, Alyssa." And then he's disappearing down the corridor and around the corner.

Whatever her reason for seeking me out at the athletic center, it's not good.

"Hi." Even though there are only fifteen feet separating us, it might as well be an ocean. There's a palpable disconnect, and deep down, I know it's my fault. I pushed her away instead of opening up and letting her in.

As if to solidify those thoughts, her lips lift into a ghost of a smile as she shoves away from the concrete wall. "You didn't have time to talk the other day, so I thought I'd come here."

I wince and drag a hand through my damp hair. "I'm sorry about that. There's been a lot of shit going on." Shit I needed to work out on my own. "Do you want to grab something to eat, and we can talk?" Maybe then we can get back on the same page.

There's a moment of hesitation. One that has hope rising up within me. But then she shakes her head as regret flickers across her features. "I can't. I'm meeting up with Zoe to work on choreography." She draws in a deep breath before glancing away and forcing out the rest in a burst. "Whatever this is between us, it's not working out."

I can only blink as the words swirl through my head, refusing to compute. "You...*want to break up?*"

"Are we even together, Colton? Wouldn't things be different between us if we were?"

I open my mouth to argue before snapping it shut again. I guess she's right about that. Instead of talking through my feelings, I forced her away, needing to deal with everything on my own.

And now I've screwed up my chance to be with her.

It only reinforces the ugly thoughts lurking at the back of my head that I'll always be a fucked-up mess. No matter how much I try to change, it only takes one little hiccup, and all the shit from my past is flaring back to life, poisoning everything in its path.

And right now, that's my relationship with Alyssa.

"Colton?" Her voice softens as she closes the distance between us, hesitantly placing her fingers on my forearm. "Did you hear what I said?"

Her touch jolts me back to the present. "Yeah." Instead of trying to explain myself any further, everything inside me shuts down. The one girl I've always wanted, the one I was attempting to change for, no longer wants anything to do with me.

Numbness sets in.

I guess that's another painful lesson I needed to learn. Sometimes, as much as you want a relationship to work out, it's just not meant to. It's better to go your separate ways instead of inflicting any more damage.

Maybe she's right.

Maybe that's what we both need at this point.

Chapter Thirty-Eight

COLTON

I pull my BMW into the circular drive and park near the front entrance of my house before cutting the engine, grabbing my duffle bag, and exiting the vehicle. It only takes a moment before I'm up the stairs and punching in the code on the keypad. Once unlocked, I push open the front door and step inside the two-story foyer. As soon as I do, the scent of beef stroganoff hits me full force. I inhale a big breath, doubly glad I decided to get the hell out of Dodge.

Even if it's only for the night.

Jenna pads through the hallway from the kitchen with a dishtowel in her hands. Happiness lights up her dark eyes when she catches sight of me. "I thought I heard the front door." She closes the distance between us before rising on her tiptoes and pressing a kiss against my cheek. I lean down, wanting to make it easier for her. Jenna tops out around five-feet. Sometimes I like to tease her by asking what the weather is like down there. "Why didn't you tell me that you were coming home?"

"It was a spur-of-the-moment decision." When she continues to stare, scouring my face for answers, I admit, "Just needed to get away for a little while."

"Well, I'm glad you decided to stop by for a visit. We're always happy to have you here." She waves me to the back of the house. "Dinner should be ready in about fifteen minutes, so you're just in time."

The closer we get to the kitchen, the more my mouth waters. If there's one thing I've missed while at college, it's Jenna's cooking. She's a culinary whiz in the kitchen. If you asked what my favorite dish was, I wouldn't be able to pick just one. There are way too many to choose from.

I beeline to the mini-fridge and grab an orange Gatorade before twisting off the cap and settling on a stool tucked beneath the massive marble island. After a quick swig, I ask, "Do you need any help?"

It looks like she's got about fifty things going on at once. Jenna shakes her head before grabbing a strainer full of green beans and dumping them into the boiling water. Then she stirs the sauce and peeks in the oven to check the rolls. "Nope. Everything is almost done."

Like I said—total culinary whiz.

I cock my head, listening for other signs of life within the house. "Is Dad home?"

"Not yet." She shoots a glance over her shoulder, her gaze once again touching on mine. "He had a meeting that ran late but should be home soon."

I nod and pick absently at the label on the plastic bottle. As much as I've tried to shut out everything that happened this week, it continues to press in at the edges. If I thought I could escape it by coming home, I was wrong.

Jenna checks the noodles and green beans for a second time. Satisfied that everything is coming along as it should be, she picks up her glass of wine and takes a sip as her gaze roves carefully over my face. "So, are you going to tell me what's going on, or do I have to drag it out of you?"

Fuck.

Although...did I really expect anything less? All the woman has to do is look at me sideways, and she knows there's a problem. If I was trying to run away from it all, this is probably the last place I should have turned up. Unfortunately, it's too late to do anything about it now.

I'm here. And she's staring at me expectantly. I blow out a lengthy breath and try to decide how best to handle the situation. I hate lying.

Especially to Jenna.

"I really don't want to talk about it," I finally mumble.

"If that were true, would you have come here?"

Well, damn.

My gaze jerks to her, and I realize with a flash of insight that she's right. Maybe I told myself it wasn't the reason, but it turns out I was wrong. And my stepmother knows it. Just like she always does. I drag a hand over my face, unsure where to begin. Everything feels like such a mess.

When I remain silent, her voice softens. "Does this have anything to do with Alyssa?"

"Yeah," I pop my shoulder and mumble, "I guess so."

It's a relief when the timer on the microwave beeps, and she swings away. Without her steady gaze focused on me, I no longer feel like a bug under a microscope. Jenna strains both the noodles and green beans before taking the rolls out of the oven and placing them on the counter to cool. Then she pulls out two plates, adds a heaping of both noodles and stroganoff along with the vegetable and a bun before sliding the dish in front of me. After making another one for herself, she settles on a stool at the island.

I dig in, taking a forkful of noodles, meat, and mushrooms before stuffing them in my mouth. The first bite has my eyes drifting shut. Even though Jenna raised me better than to talk with my mouth full, I can't resist saying, "Mmmm, this is so good."

Her lips quirk. "I'm glad you like it."

"More like love it," I add, shoving in another bite.

"I'm sure there'll be plenty of leftovers. I'll package some up for you to take back for Beck."

With a frown, I straighten on the stool. "Screw Beck."

A burst of laughter escapes from her. "No, thank you."

My lips tremble at the corners before I plow my way through my dinner. What is it about a homecooked meal that helps settle everything rioting deep inside? Or maybe it's the company. At this point, I'm none too sure.

"Do you feel any better?" she asks.

I nod. Strangely enough, I do. Although, that doesn't mean everything isn't still a mess.

"Good. Can I get you a second helping?"

I pat my belly. "If I eat another bite, I'll probably explode."

She takes both of our plates before dropping them in the sink. Once she's resettled next to me, I steel myself for what's coming next. "Now tell me what's going on."

The question has everything inside me deflating.

"Come on," Jenna prods, reaching over and taking my hand, "it can't be that bad."

Is she crazy? Of course, it can.

I force out a breath. "I don't know, at the moment, it feels pretty damn bad."

"You know what I've always found to be true?" She doesn't wait for a response. "That when you keep everything bottled up inside, it makes whatever problem you're attempting to tackle feel that much worse." She squeezes my hand. "Share it with me. Let's talk this out. I promise it won't seem quite so dire."

Unable to hold her gaze, mine drops to the white marble countertop before I blurt, "I looked Candace up online." I give Jenna a bit of side-eye to gauge her reaction, but her face remains impassive. As if I haven't dropped a major bomb. When she simply nods, I continue. "She's married with two kids. A boy and a girl."

"I'm aware," she admits quietly. "Your father has kept tabs on her over the years."

That information probably shouldn't take me by surprise. I guess everyone knew about it but me. "Why didn't you guys say something?"

"What would be the point?" Her face scrunches as she tilts her head. "To inflict more pain?"

My shoulders collapse at her astute assessment of the situation.

When I remain silent, lost in my thoughts, she asks, "Are you all right?"

I shrug, wishing that were the worst part of it. "I reached out, and she emailed back, wanting to know if I would be interested in meeting."

Even though Jenna's expression never falters, her hand stills over mine. "And did you?"

"Yeah. We met at a coffee shop."

It's cautiously that she asks, "And how did that go?"

"It was definitely awkward at first, but then we started talking, getting to know one another again, and it was kind of nice."

"I'm glad for you. I think it's important that you spoke with her."

It makes perfect sense that Jenna would feel that way. She's totally selfless. If having a relationship with Candace was something that I wanted or needed in my life, then she would support me.

"We spent about two hours getting reacquainted, and for most of the visit, it felt like reaching out had been a good idea. Like maybe she regretted walking away and wanted to be part of my life." When my voice turns bitter, Jenna's fingers tighten around mine. "Turns out that's not the case."

"Okay." The muscles in her face tense before she encourages, "Tell me what happened."

"I asked when I could meet her family." I jerk my shoulders and shake my head. "Maybe it's stupid, but I couldn't get over the fact that I had halfsiblings out there. Ones I'd never even met."

She lifts her hand to stroke my cheek. "I'm sure you liked that idea."

"Yeah, well, it doesn't really matter if I did or not." A fresh wave of grief crashes over me. "Candace never bothered to tell her husband that she was married or had another child. Since it would be difficult to explain the situation after all these years, she has no intention of telling them or making me part of her life."

"Oh, Colton." With the side of my face cupped in her palm, she closes the distance between us before feathering her lips across my forehead.

"Candace hasn't been a part of my life for a long time," I whisper. "I don't understand why this hurts so much."

"She's your mother, and you still love her. That just doesn't go away. I'm so sorry she did this to you." I don't have to catch a glimpse of her face to know that there are tears shining in her eyes. I hear the thick emotion clogging her voice.

Jenna wraps her arms around me and squeezes tight. It's as if she's trying to extract all of the pain vibrating in my body and take it into her own.

"We won't be seeing each other again," I tell her.

She pulls away enough to search my eyes. "You realize this has *nothing* to do with you, right?"

I shrug.

How could it not have everything to do with me?

This is twice now that I've been rejected by Candace.

Unwilling to have Jenna bear witness to the emotion crashing around inside me, I turn my head, only wanting to lick my wounds in private. Except my stepmother is having none of it. Her fingers settle under my chin before turning my face until I have no other choice but to meet her gaze.

"Don't you dare hide from me. I've been in your life since you were six years old. Bandaging scraped knees, telling you to stop playing video games, and making sure you were home before curfew."

My lips reluctantly quirk at the last example she throws in. Dad was strict about my ass being in the house by an appointed time. Jenna always made sure to send me a fifteen-minute warning. She saved me on more than one occasion when I was having too much fun, and it slipped my mind.

"You've been carrying all this hurt around for your entire life."

"That's not true." When I attempt to shake my head and deny the accusation, her fingers dig into my chin.

"Oh, sweetie," her voice softens, "yes, you have. I remember the first time your father introduced us. We went to a park so you could play on the equipment."

I sift through my childhood memories but am not able to dredge up that particular one. It doesn't matter because she continues, filling in all the blanks.

"After we arrived at the playground, you refused to leave your father's side."

A prickle of unease blooms in the pit of my belly as I still, barely able to inhale.

"Warren kept encouraging you to play with the other kids, but you wouldn't do it. You were so afraid that he was going to walk away and leave you."

Just like Candace.

That tingle in the bottom of my gut turns into full-blown nausea. "It took years before you were willing to take a chance and let me in. Maybe you don't remember that, but I do. And ever since, the people in your life have had to earn your trust."

It takes effort to blink away the turmoil attempting to break loose inside me so that it doesn't have a chance to roll down my cheeks. Only now does it occur to me that I've spent my entire life keeping everyone around me at arm's length. Never wanting to feel too much, never wanting them to get too close. And yeah, running away rather than face my emotions head-on.

"What I've learned in life is that you can't move forward if you're constantly looking back."

She's right about that. I allowed Candace and the past to keep me from people and experiences that could have been amazing.

"Do you know who I feel most sorry for?" When I shake my head, she continues. "Candace. You've grown into such an amazing man. And she missed out on that."

It takes effort to clear the thick lump of emotion wedged in my throat. "If I've turned out well, it has everything to do with you. *You're* the mother that she never could be."

Fresh tears fill her dark eyes before trekking down her cheeks. "You made it easy. And I love you, Colton. I couldn't love you any more if you were my own."

I tug her to me, this time wrapping my arms around her and hugging tight. "I love you, too."

When we finally pull away, there's wetness on both of our cheeks. With my hand secured in hers, she settles next to me on the stool before clearing her throat. "I know you've always been adamant about not wanting to go to therapy, but I really believe it could be beneficial."

I jerk my shoulders. In the past, whenever she's broached the subject, I've shot it down. Even though it's on the tip of my tongue to do it again, I refrain. "Maybe."

The idea of sitting in some stranger's office and pouring my heart out sounds awful. But then again, I'm tired of dealing with all of this on my own. Or maybe, the real issue is that I've never dealt with my emotions, and they've been festering inside me for years.

I suppose it's something to consider.

"Have you spoken to Alyssa about this? Does she know?"

Right. *Alyssa.* That's another problem. One I'm unsure how to solve. Maybe I *do* need professional help.

I plow my hand through my hair. "She broke up with me the other day."

"Let me guess," Jenna says gently, "you shut down and pushed her away after what happened with Candace."

Damn. Sometimes I think my stepmother knows me better than I do. Or maybe I should have done myself a favor and opened up to Jenna a long time ago. She's always been here, ready to listen and help.

"Nailed it," I mutter, feeling defeated all over again.

With a huff of breath, she falls silent.

We both do.

"Can I assume that Alyssa is the girl you were involved with a couple of years ago?"

My eyes narrow. "I'm gonna be honest, sometimes you seriously frighten me."

She snorts out a laugh, and somehow it manages to lighten the mood between us.

"If Alyssa is worth it—*really worth it*—then you need to be honest with her. I know it's scary to be vulnerable with another person. The easiest thing to do is throw up walls and keep everyone out, but in the end, it's a lonely place to be. I think you might realize that now."

My throat closes up as the sound of my beating heart fills my ears, drowning out everything else. "I don't want to be hurt again." Barely am I able to force out the words.

"I know." Jenna's lips lift into a sympathetic smile. "But isn't this girl worth taking a chance on?"

When I remain silent, she says, "Think it over, Colton."

The thing is, I don't have to do that. I already know the answer.

I've always known it.

Chapter Thirty-Nine

ALYSSA

The music stops abruptly as Monsieur Dupre claps his hands together, and we all pause. "We will do it again until it is perfection!"

Ugh. That's so not what I wanted to hear. My muscles are screaming, and I'm out of breath.

For just a moment, my shoulders sag before I straighten and take my position. We've been rehearsing the same piece over and over again. He wasn't kidding when he said that we would keep at it until the movements were flawless. The guy is a real taskmaster. Although, that's what makes him such a sought-out instructor.

When the music resumes, I lift onto the toes of my shoes, stretching my arms over my head and striking the pose before raising one pointed foot in front of me. The music arcs and I continue to hold it until my muscles tremble.

"*Très bien!*" he exclaims.

Instead of dwelling on the discomfort, I force it from my mind and concentrate on the rhythm of the music. Much like the first time, the only thing that soothes the pain of this last heartbreak is dance. I'm able to lose myself in the movement for hours at a time. It helps me to not think about—

Nope. Not going to do it.

Even when he presses in at the edges, I drive myself harder so that my mind is too consumed with the steps and exactness of my performance to give one solitary thought to him.

As one, the class moves through the choreography like a well-oiled machine.

Or, in our case, a well-choreographed routine.

Every so often, Monsieur Dupre will pause the music and critique our positions. Just as I spin on my toes, preparing to leap across the floor in a grand jeté, I catch a glimpse of someone lurking in the doorway. My footwork falters, and I stumble.

Colton.

What's he doing here?

Even though the question sits perched on the tip of my tongue, I can't force it out. Instead, I stare mutely from across the studio, all the while eating him up with my eyes. I hate how tempting it is to close the distance between us. But I can't give in to the urge. Colton has done nothing to show me that he's changed. In fact, he's proven the opposite.

The music is abruptly cut off, and the other dancers turn until everyone is staring at the tall blond football player loitering at the threshold of the spacious room.

"Can I help you?" Monsieur Dupre asks in a clipped tone, aiming a haughty look in Colton's direction.

If there's one thing our instructor detests, it's being disrupted. The world could come crashing down around us, and as long as it didn't interfere with our performance, it would be of no concern.

Remember the band playing on deck while the Titanic sunk?

Yeah, it's like that.

Colton's gaze flickers to him before zeroing in on me again. "Could I have a moment to speak with Alyssa?"

"As you can see," the elegant man waves a hand, "we are in the middle of class. This can wait, yes?"

I expect Colton to nod and slink away. Everyone is staring at him with wide, disbelieving eyes. Instead, he moves uninvited into the sun-drenched room. If I didn't know better, I'd think he had a death wish. "No, it can't. I need to speak with Alyssa now."

All eyes fall on me. I gulp as my heart beats into overdrive. Like everyone else, I can't believe this is actually happening.

"By all means then," Monsieur snaps, "waste more of our time. It's not like we are here, trying to master a complicated sequence of steps."

"Thanks, appreciate it."

I wince. Perhaps Colton doesn't recognize the sarcasm dripping from the Frenchman's words, but I do. Even though I'm one of his favored pupils, there's no doubt in my mind that I'll pay for the untimely interruption at a later date in the form of a punishing rehearsal.

That being said...I don't give a damn.

I want to hear what Colton has to say.

No...I *need* to hear what Colton has to say.

His blue gaze stays pinned to mine as he moves further into the studio. That's all it takes for everyone around us to fall away until it's just the two of us.

"I'm sorry for bursting in here like this, but I had to see you." Another few steps bring him closer. "It couldn't wait another moment."

When I remain silent, at a loss for words, Colton continues, "I'm sorry, Lys. For everything. I never meant to push you away. I needed time to wrap my mind around my feelings. What I now realize is that I should have talked to you about it instead of going at it alone. I let you think that I was shutting down and locking you out."

My throat fills with so much emotion that it feels like it's closing up on me. That's *exactly* what I'd thought. And because of that, I'd pushed him away before he could cut me loose like the first time.

"I did the one thing I promised never to do," he says, voice ringing throughout the room, "I broke your trust and hurt you." His chest rises and falls with every deep inhalation. "I'm sure you've guessed by now that the meeting with Candace didn't go well."

From the pain swimming around in his eyes, that seems more like an understatement. It takes everything I have inside not to pull him into my arms and soothe away the agony that radiates off him in heavy, suffocating waves.

"I've spent my entire life holding everyone around me at a distance so I wouldn't get hurt. It was never a conscious decision, more like a reflex. But I don't want to live like that anymore. I don't want to continually push away the people who matter most. I'll do whatever it takes to make this relationship work." He inches closer. "I love you, Lys. Even when it scared the hell out of me, I still loved you. I never stopped."

Emotion crashes over me, through me, until I'm overwhelmed with the sensation.

Colton clears his throat. "I don't deserve another chance, but I really hope you'll give me one. Let me prove that I can be the guy you not only need but deserve."

Oh, God.

Almost collectively, as if it's a synchronized movement, everyone shifts their gazes to me. Sighs escape from a few of the dancers.

"If you don't want him, girl, I'd be more than happy to take him off your hands," Zoe hollers from across the room.

Her voice snaps me out of the mental fog that has descended. Instead of responding, I run across the floor before hurtling myself against his chest. With a soft grunt, his arms band around me, pulling me close, and squeezing me tight.

"I really do love you, Lys," he whispers against my ear. "You're everything to me. And I hate that I made you feel as if you weren't."

"I love you, too." I always have—even when I didn't want to. Even when I did everything possible to forget about him and move on.

He pulls away enough to meet my gaze. "Now that I have you, I'm not walking out of here without you."

A smile trembles around the edges of my lips before I glance hesitantly at my instructor.

With a shake of his head, Monsieur Dupre rolls his eyes and flicks a hand at me as if he can't be bothered to expend a full movement on my sorry ass. "Leave. You have already taken up enough of my valuable time."

Heat floods my cheeks as a round of applause erupts throughout the room.

"You heard the man," Colton says with a grin, "let's get out of here."

With a quick nod, I untangle myself from him before scampering over to my bag. I shove my shoes into the small duffle and throw on an oversized shirt before hauling up a pair of black leggings. And then I'm dressed and ready to go. Monsieur Dupre will most definitely make me pay for this tomorrow, but I'm not going to focus on that at the moment. How can I when Colton is holding out his hand for me to take?

As I slip my fingers into his, he says, "You know I'm never going to let you go, right?"

Giddiness bursts inside me like an overinflated balloon. For as long as I've known Colton, this is all I've ever wanted. And now, finally, after all these years, I have it.

I have him.

He's mine, and I'm his.

"I'm glad you feel that way," I tell him, "because I have no plans to let you go either."

EPILOGUE

Colton

Three years later...

I roll over and stretch out an arm, only to find the space next to me empty and the sheets already cooling. I crack open a blurry eye and glance around the room. The sun is just peeking over the horizon, painting the vast stretch of sky with pink and purple strokes.

Where the hell did that girl disappear to?

I toss off the covers and pad over to the bathroom.

Empty.

Since it's just the two of us, I don't bother to throw on any clothes. I surprised Alyssa with a weeklong vacation at the beach. One of my father's friends owns a house on Kiawah Island in South Carolina, right on the ocean. We can hear the crash of the waves from our bedroom window. It's the perfect sound to fall asleep to with Alyssa tucked in my arms.

Once I hit the first floor, the scent of fresh-brewed coffee permeates the air. The door to the patio is open. I should have known she was out on the deck. We arrived a few days ago, and she can't get enough of the salty breeze. I push open the screen door and find her sitting at the small, iron table, staring out at the water in the distance. There's something hypnotic about the waves as they roll onto the sandy stretch of shoreline.

"Hey," I greet, stepping onto the wooden planks, "you're up early."

Her eyes flicker to mine before widening when she gets a good look at me. A chuckle escapes as her lips quirk. Her gaze skims down my naked body before settling on my cock. That's all it takes for me to stiffen right up. "Decided to forego clothing, I see."

I arch a brow. "Is that a complaint?"

I'll tell you what, there was nothing but satisfied moans coming from Alyssa when I was buried deep inside her last night.

"Nope." As if to prove her words, she leans forward and presses a kiss against the tip of my erection. "Not at all."

Damn. The feel of her warm breath feathering across my flesh only stirs my arousal.

"Good." My voice drops, turning raspy as I scoop her into my arms and settle on the chair she's been lounging on. "It's not a secret that I love you naked. Speaking of which," I grab the hem of her thin tank top and pull it over her head before tossing it onto the deck, "you're a little overdressed for the occasion." Then I hook my thumbs into her panties and slide them down her hips and thighs before tossing them over my shoulder.

At ease with our nudity, Alyssa settles against my chest, her head resting at the crook of my neck. We fit perfectly together. A sigh of contentment leaves my lips as we watch the sunrise over the water. It's magical.

I almost shake my head at such a strange thought.

Five years ago, I never could have imagined feeling this content with another person. The ghosts from my past were still too fresh. They had a grasp on me that I never realized. All right, so maybe I did, but I never understood how much they were holding me back. How much I was missing out on until I made a conscious effort to face them head-on.

That meant—yup, you guessed it—therapy. Spilling my guts to a dude with glasses and a beard who eventually helped me realize that Candace's decisions had everything to do with her. Not me. Alyssa has been there every step of the way—holding my hand when I needed it, taking a step back, and giving me space when I asked for room.

Without question, she is my person.

And to think I almost lost her.

Thankfully, I pulled my shit together before that could happen.

Every day I make a conscious decision to live in the present and only look back at the past when I think reflection can help. I'm sure that makes me sound all enlightened, but like everyone else, I'm just trying to figure out the baggage I'm stuck with and get through life the best I can. Alyssa likes to joke that I'm now Colton 2.0.

She might be right about that.

A seagull cries overhead as it glides on the early morning breeze, and I brush a kiss against the top of her blond head. "Love you, baby."

She lifts her face until our gazes can lock. "Love you, too. Did I thank you for planning this amazing vacay?"

My lips hitch. "I thought that's what you did last night in the shower. You mean there's more?"

Even as Alyssa rolls her eyes, a twinkling light fills them. That girl can pretend all she wants that she's exasperated with me, but she enjoys our sex life just as much as I do.

"You, my friend, have a one-track mind."

When it comes to Alyssa, you're damn straight, I do.

Always have, always will. That will never change.

We've been going strong for three years. I'm in my final year of business school, and Alyssa is working at a local studio. She also choreographs routines for the Wesley Wildcats dance team. We have an apartment in town that is close to campus but far enough away for us not to feel like we're still living the college lifestyle. If everything goes according to plan, I'll propose once I have my MBA in hand, and we'll return home so I can work with my father. I was supposed to move back after graduation but instead delved straight into business school. It was the right decision for both of us.

"You wouldn't have it any other way," I growl.

Before she can respond, my mouth crashes onto hers. As soon as my lips make contact, she opens. Alyssa is as needy for me as I am for her. She tilts her chin, angling her head in order to give me better access.

There are days when I feel like I could devour her in one tasty gulp. As if I'll never get enough of this sweet girl. Sometimes I can't believe she almost slipped through my fingers. Had that happened, I would have missed out on the amazing life we're creating together.

Her arms tangle around my neck, dragging me closer. With a groan, I reposition her on my lap so that my cock is pressed against her core.

Fuck me, that feels good. But then again, it always feels amazing.

The need to be deep inside her pounds through me, and I thrust my hips until I'm surrounded by her tight sheath. For just a heartbeat, I pause, enjoying the heat of the sun as it strokes over our bare flesh. Is there anything better than this?

Nothing I can think of.

"One of the neighbors could peek outside and see us." Her voice turns breathy. I can't tell if the idea bothers her or turns her on.

My guess is the latter.

"Let them look," I growl. Buried inside her like I am, there is no way I'm going to stop. This is happening. If I have my way, they'll hear her way before they ever catch sight of us.

I thrust my hips, pulling almost all the way out before surging forward again. By the third time, her head is falling back to expose the delicate column of her neck as her eyelids feather shut. A guttural moan escapes from her lips.

Stupid as it sounds, my breath hitches as I watch her. I couldn't rip my gaze away from the gorgeous picture she makes riding my cock. Her cheeks have pinkened, and the long line of her back is arched, thrusting her breasts forward.

She's so fucking beautiful.

And mine.

Five years ago, that thought would have sent a torrent of panic flooding through me. I would have pushed her away, needing to dismiss my feelings for her.

But times have changed.

And I've changed with them.

After all, this is Colton 2.0 we're talking about here.

I'm a new man.
A better man.
For her.

-The End-

Thank you for reading Colton and Alyssa's story! I hope you
enjoyed it!

Want more?
Join my mailing list for an exclusive bonus epilogue that includes both
couples!
https://dl.bookfunnel.com/hccjq2w8po

ABOUT THE AUTHOR

Jennifer Sucevic is a USA Today bestselling author who has published eighteen New Adult and Mature Young Adult novels. Her work has been translated into both German (as well as audiobook format) and Dutch. She has a bachelor's degree in History and a master's degree in Educational Psychology. Both are from the University of Wisconsin-Milwaukee. Jen spent five years working as a high school counselor before relocating with her family. If you would like to receive updates regarding new releases, please contact Jennifer through email, at her website, or on Facebook. sucevicjennifer@gmail.com

Social media links-

www.jennifersucevic.com

https://www.instagram.com/jennifersucevicauthor

https://www.facebook.com/jennifer.sucevic

https://www.tumblr.com/blog/jsucevic

https://www.pinterest.com/jmolitor6/

https://www.wattpad.com/user/jsucevic

Printed in the USA
CPSIA information can be obtained
at www.ICGtesting.com
LVHW040743140824
788116LV00004B/261